THE QUEEN'S BLADE

A BOOK OF THE VIRAGO

S.E. BABIN

OLIVER HEBER BOOKS

LANDS OF
LUNAMOOR
KINGDOM OF ROSES
KINGDOM OF THORNEWOOD
KINGDOM OF LIGHT
KINGDOM OF CRYSTAL
LAKE OF SORROW
KINGDOM OF WOLVES
KINGDOM OF BEASTS
KINGDOM OF WITCHES
LAKE OF MYSTICS
KINGDOM OF SHADOW

CHAPTER ONE

A CELEBRATION

Harlow's eighteenth birthday arrived with revelry and high spirits, though melancholy had possessed her with a tight hold. No matter how she tried, she could barely muster a smile, and nothing seemed to shake her from the mood. She stood outside the ballroom with Evara, mentally preparing herself to step inside with all the well-wishers and court kiss-ups, and felt nothing but exhaustion.

Candles of various colors and sizes floated high above them, kept at bay from melting to a nub by her grandmother's magic. The warm light cast a comforting yet cheerful glow on the guests as they chatted, laughed, and danced in the great ball-room. Every attendee had worn their finest dress for the evening to celebrate Harlow's coming of age and her arrival in the Witch Kingdom, though that had come long ago. Or what felt like long ago.

She'd been here for less than a year now, though her grand-mother had kept her identity secret from everyone until she'd tested Harlow's magic and heritage in a grueling set of trials. At the end, Harlow wanted to crawl back to Nova's kingdom and beg her to cast a forgetting spell. But as Harlow came to realize, magic and its learning was grueling, but not without benefit, and after months of training, she had a firm grasp of what she could and might one day do.

Knowing her potential was daunting, but Harlow had learned to hone that fear into something productive and usable —even though there'd been little to fear in the stronghold of her grandmother's kingdom.

Evara stood at her side, the beautiful guard giving her the side-eye.

"You look like you're marching to your death," Evara remarked.

Harlow dug into the side of her waist. "That's because this corset is killing me."

The guard snorted and gently brushed Harlow's hand away. "Don't let your grandmother see you. You're ruining the beading."

"If I have to wear one more dress that weighs thirty pounds, I swear I'll—"

A cool voice intruded. "You'll what?"

Harlow screwed her face into careful blankness. Evara's head snapped forward, eyes twinkling with amusement. Harlow cleared her throat. "I'll ask you who your tailor is because the embroidery on this dress is *immaculate*."

Evara's lips twitched.

Her grandmother eyed her. "Impudent girl," she said fondly. "Ladies wear corsets, Harlow. Are you not a lady?"

If she had asked her that question six months ago, Harlow might have hesitated. Now, being a lady had been beaten into her with every magic and history lesson.

"Of course I'm a lady," Harlow said. "But ladies can wear trousers," she added hopefully.

"Not to their eighteenth-birthday ball," her grandmother said.

Knowing when she'd been beaten, Harlow inclined her head. "Yes, Grandmother."

The queen chuckled and put a hand on Harlow's arm, gently stopping her. She stepped before Harlow and put her palms on either side of her granddaughter's face. "You, my darling, are kind and beautiful, and *exasperating*."

Evara snorted and tried to cover it with a cough.

"And you must remember that every word you speak, every embroidered bead on your gown, and every strand of hair has its place, and you must know where those are. You will become queen one day, and our people will look to you as the example."

Queen Moira, her grandmother, was still gorgeous. Golden hair was piled on top of her head in an intricate, wrapped braid, and her normally bare face was painted with cosmetics, enhancing Moira's brilliant cornflower-blue eyes—Harlow's eyes—and full lips.

"Yes, Grandmother," Harlow murmured, chastened. Yes, the dress weighed a ton, and yes, her ribs ached every time she inhaled, but there were more important things to worry about. She could wear this stupid gown to please her grandmother for a few hours.

The queen patted her cheek. "Good." She pressed a cool kiss, tingling with magic against Harlow's forehead.

"Any word on Shade?" Harlow asked hopefully. Her mentor and sister's Captain of the Guard had escorted Desminda to the Kingdom of the Beasts months ago, after the kingdom had requested her hand in marriage. Their plan was to visit, seek an alliance, and then travel to the Kingdom of Crystal to peruse Desminda's options for marriage there as well. Even deposed, Desminda's beauty was legendary, and other kingdoms still sought her hand.

They'd heard from Shade upon his arrival to the Beast Kingdom, but not a word since. A growing unease had settled under

Harlow's skin, present for months now, and even her requests to Nova's shadows had gone unheeded. Even the shadows couldn't find him.

He wasn't dead. Nova would know. But something blocked their communication. Powerful magic had to be at play if even her sister couldn't find him.

Her grandmother smiled sadly. "No word yet. If we do not hear from your Shade in the next fortnight, I will send a hunting party out to search."

Harlow smiled gratefully and bowed her head. "Thank you."

"No need to thank me. Anyone who guides and protects my granddaughter like Shade has is worthy of our help."

She stepped back and examined Harlow from head to toe before nodding. "You look so much like your mother." A wistful expression softened her face for a moment before she schooled herself into neutrality. "Now, my dear, go out there and enjoy your birthday. I've had the cook make your favorites, and there are many handsome nobles out there waiting to take you for a spin on the dance floor."

Her guard stiffened almost imperceptibly, but the queen was a shrewd woman. Her lips curved in a hint of a smile, and she leaned forward and spoke so quietly only the two of them could hear her.

"Or a noblewoman, perhaps?" She leaned back and winked at Evara before gliding away, her voluminous skirts swishing against her slim hips.

Evara chuckled. "I like your grandmother." She stepped closer to her side and slid her a glance. "Does it bother you I am not a noblewoman?"

Harlow blinked in surprise. "Why would you ever think that?" Many things had happened over the last several months, one of them being her ... whatever it was she had with Evara.

Friendship, yes, but something deeper. Neither had allowed it to go far, but a hint of a promise lay in the air between them.

Evara looked away, her jaw tightening. "A queen wanted to marry you. I saw the way she looked at you."

Harlow snorted. "Desminda wanted to marry me when she saw a way to use my position to further her own. I wear no blinders when it comes to Thornewood's queen, Evara. She would scratch and claw through stone if there was something on the other side she could use to her advantage."

Evara's face softened. She knew what Desminda was capable of as much as Harlow did. "One day, when this is all over, I will show you far more than a queen ever could."

Harlow's cheeks went hot, and she looked at her feet. Evara's wicked chuckle echoed in the corridor.

"Incorrigible," Harlow murmured.

Evara laughed and held out her elbow. "Allow me to escort you inside the ballroom, Princess Harlow."

The princess winced. "Don't call me that," she hissed. "It's …"

"Fitting?" Evara supplied. "True?"

"Weird," Harlow said with a sigh. She was a princess, but she still felt most at home in leather armor, swinging an axe. Even the magic didn't feel as familiar in her hands as her axe did. Harlow took her elbow, straightened her spine, and allowed Evara to guide her into the brighter light of the ballroom.

A richly dressed herald standing at the top of the stairs spotted her. His spine straightened with an almost audible snap, and he blew on a small horn he'd been holding at his side.

The music abruptly stopped.

Harlow's cheeks heated even more at the scrutiny. Several gasps went up when the guests finally spotted her.

"Announcing Princess Harlow Stonehand, granddaughter

of our most-esteemed Queen Moira, and her loyal guard, Evara."

Harlow barely kept the frown from her face. Guards in many kingdoms lost their surnames when they worked for the royals—something to do with their loyalty now belonging to the king and queen and not their families. She'd always disliked the practice, but Evara didn't seem to mind. Harlow made a mental note to ask Evara about her family. While they talked all the time, both were careful to keep their conversations about the upcoming war or Harlow's training.

There were too many eyes and ears around the castle for Harlow to feel completely comfortable. She trusted her grandmother, but Moira was queen and planned for Harlow to step into her place over the next few years. Of course, that was the normal progression, but Harlow hadn't had an exactly normal upbringing. Plus, there was Miriam to think about, Harlow's aunt, a powerful seer who seemed to have her eye on the throne —who would have taken it had Harlow not shown up looking to ally with the Kingdom of Witches.

While Miriam hadn't come right out and said anything, there was a definite frostiness in her tone when she spoke to Harlow. And even though Miriam was fast becoming lost in her visions for weeks at a time, it didn't mean the woman didn't feel slighted by Harlow's presence.

And judging from the look Miriam was giving her this evening from below, maybe she felt a little more than slighted.

"Come on," Evara whispered. "You look like a stunned deer."

Harlow started and swallowed, her fingers tightening on Evara's arm as the guard led her down the massive staircase. Every step was an exercise in concentration with the stupid dress and shoes she was wearing. If Harlow misstepped, she'd tumble down and break her neck on the hard stone floor below her.

"Easy," Evara murmured. "Your pulse is fluttering like a rabbit."

"How long do I have to stay?" Harlow asked under her breath, even as she plastered a fake smile on her face.

"You can't leave until thirty minutes after your grandmother." Evara guided Harlow to the bottom step and offered her a slight bow before turning and disappearing through the crowd.

Harlow's heart fluttered, a slight panic running through her as Evara became lost among the guests. How she hated courtly manners. Evara couldn't linger around her for fear of rumors of impropriety or insulting her grandmother by implying Harlow's safety was at risk inside the heart of Moira's castle.

Harlow half-curtsied to the people lingering around the floor, something her grandmother told her was expected when she greeted everyone. In return, courtiers swept into a low bow and held it for a few seconds before rising.

Social graces completed, Harlow nodded and made a beeline for the food table, hoping to avoid any other conversation until she could find a dark corner to slip into.

As she thought it, she almost sighed aloud at her behavior. But there was a fact she couldn't refute, and it had become apparent as the weeks passed and Harlow continued to train harder than she'd ever done back in Thornewood: she had no friends in this kingdom. Now that her identity was out, everyone in the castle showed her a hushed deference, and Harlow quickly grew annoyed by it.

Things came to a head when she was training with some of Moira's guards, and Harlow knew they were taking it far easier on her than on their other trainees. Her questioning their methods because of her royal rank had resulted in a full-on brawl with her sparring partner and several more guards, which ended with cuts, bruises, and, fortunately for everyone, quite a bit of laughter.

While she still couldn't call the guards her friends, they were definitely friendlier than everyone else, and had stopped taking it easy on her in training. However, when Moira visited the training grounds, they were a little more careful than usual.

But as far as confidants, all she had was Evara, and even that hadn't gone too far.

The food table was stacked with juicy, dripping meat, several types of potatoes, greens, and an odd salad sprinkled with herbs Harlow couldn't identify. She reached for a plate, but a small, delicate hand reached out and slapped Harlow's hand away.

She jerked her hand back and gasped, searching for the person who'd done it, only finding a short, curvy, dark-haired woman who wore a sparkling green ball gown. "You cannot serve yourself," the woman murmured quietly. "Wait for the attendant."

Harlow swallowed, embarrassment burning on her face. "You—you *struck* me."

The woman kept her eyes steady on me. "A tiny, unnoticed slap on the hand is better than a faux pas that echoes around the kingdom, Princess."

Harlow glanced around, but the woman was right. No one paid any attention to them.

Her fists clenched at her side just as her stomach gave a loud and embarrassing growl. She was starving, and there wasn't a single attendant anywhere around them.

"Excuse me, Princess," a voice said from behind. A servant dressed in the kingdom's colors offered her a bow and reached for a dinner plate. "What will you have this evening?"

The shorter woman stepped out of the way and gestured for

Harlow to go ahead, amusement twinkling in her eyes. "Happy birthday," she said, before slipping away into the crowd.

Harlow shook her head and pointed to the meat first. When the servant placed a dainty portion on her plate, Harlow gestured again. "More please."

The servant looked scandalized but added another small portion. And so it went until her plate practically overflowed. With a murmured thanks, Harlow stayed to the edges of the wall until she slipped through a small exit and ended up in a stone hallway.

Just as the first bite hit her taste buds, a shadow fell over her. Harlow stilled guiltily, just as Evara poked her head into the hidden nook she'd taken refuge in.

"Your grandmother would be appalled," the guard drawled.

Harlow grunted and turned around, exposing her back to Evara. "I'm starving. Can you loosen the laces on my corset?"

"So you can guzzle more meat down?"

"I'll work it off in the yard tomorrow."

Evara chuckled. "Brace yourself." With deft hands, Evara loosened the ties on Harlow's dress until she could access her corset. Once she'd untied the first few laces on the corset and tugged, Harlow groaned loud enough that Evara shushed her.

"People are going to get the wrong idea if you don't quiet down," the guard cautioned.

"I can move again," Harlow whispered. "Thank you."

"Mmm," Evara said as she re-tied the laces. "Hurry up and eat. There's a surprise waiting for you in the kitchen."

"More food?" Harlow asked hopefully, turning around to face Evara.

The guard snorted. "No, you glutton."

Harlow grinned and shoveled down another forkful of potatoes.

CHAPTER TWO

THE REUNION

Once her stomach was full, Harlow left the plate in a nook to later be found by a servant and followed Evara down the stone hall and into the humid and bustling kitchen.

A massive cake rested on the middle table, covered in glittering pink-and-white icing layered in waves. Delicate pearls dotted each layer, perfectly centered on clouds of stiff whipped cream.

Evara cackled at Harlow's horrified expression. While the cake was beautiful and would have delighted most other princesses, this was not exactly the low-key dessert she'd hoped to devour in the privacy of her bedroom.

The head cook spotted her and let out a strangled scream. "No no no! The princess must not see her birthday cake!" She started toward them, her hands held out in front of her, making shooing noises.

Evara took Harlow by the elbow. "Don't worry, Nettie. We're just passing through. She didn't see a thing."

Harlow nodded earnestly and let Evara pull her away.

Evara guided her through the labyrinth of shelves, tables,

and pots and pans, stopping at the back doors leading toward one of the gardens.

Evara stopped, knocked twice on the back door, and pushed it open.

A tall man dressed all in black stood in shadow. Harlow took a step forward, her heartbeat picking up as she tried to make out the figure.

"Hello, Stonehand," the man said.

A choked noise escaped her as she flung herself past Evara and into the darkness, straight into the arms of Shade Montello.

He smelled of horse and dust and her friend. Shade lifted her into the air and swung her around, grunting at the extra weight of her ballgown. She sobbed into his shoulder. His arms tightened around her.

"You look like a proper princess," he said in a choked whisper. "But have you gained weight?"

Harlow barked a laugh and smacked him on the shoulder. "I keep telling everyone—it's this dress! It weighs twenty pounds." She pulled away and studied him. He still held her tightly, their noses almost touching.

Shade was handsome, as always, but a haunted look lurked in his dark eyes. He smiled, white teeth flashing in the dark, and set her down. He scanned her from head to toe before nodding. "Your sister will be pleased to know you look the picture of health."

Harlow took the time to examine him but didn't find her friend the same picture. "Something happened," she said quietly. "Something awful."

Shade's mouth tightened at the edges. "We will speak of it in the morning at the war council. For now, you should try to enjoy the rest of your birthday party."

He chuckled at Harlow's grimace. "Your eighteenth is the talk of the kingdoms. Has the party not been to your liking?"

"It's very peopley," Harlow said.

"Not a word," Evara chastised, amusement warming her voice.

"But true," Harlow countered.

"You should at least go in and do one walk around the ballroom to greet your people." Evara motioned for her arm.

Harlow groaned.

"One round, and I'll take you back to your rooms so you and Shade can catch up."

Harlow visibly brightened. "Just one. Promise?"

Evara made an X motion over her heart. "Cross my heart."

At Harlow's blank expression, Evara snorted. "It's something we say back home. It means I promise. Now come. One round, full of greetings and smiles, and you can leave."

Harlow turned to Shade, who nodded. "I'll wait for you in your wing."

At that word, Harlow grimaced again. She used to share a small room with Nova, then a dorm with several other girls, then a room to herself in Nova's kingdom, until her heritage was revealed. Now, she had an entire wing to mope in, exacerbating her loneliness, and a bedroom larger than the throne room back in Thornewood.

Shade grinned. "There are perks to being a princess."

"One round," Harlow said. "I'll tell the kitchen to send a full meal to you."

A flicker crossed his face, but Harlow couldn't identify the emotion.

"Thank you," he said gruffly. With a slight bow, Shade disappeared into the shadows.

"How does he do that?" Harlow muttered.

"Years of practice," Evara said, taking her elbow and guiding her back through the kitchen. "Now hurry. You need to get out of there before your grandmother figures out your waist is a millimeter larger and flays us both alive."

"You're scared of my grandmother?"

Evara snorted. "I'd be a fool not to be."

They hurried through the stone hall and ducked back into the ballroom with no one the wiser.

"Stand up straight," Evara hissed. "Your grandmother just turned our way."

Harlow's spine snapped straight.

"Now, smile."

She slapped a friendly smile on her face and turned to the small gaggle of women tittering by the drink table.

"You can do it," Evara said encouragingly.

"I know I can," Harlow grumbled. "I just don't want to."

"That's the spirit." Evara gave her a gentle nudge.

Harlow strode over, the smile on her face starting to hurt. When they noticed her presence, their conversation died.

"Hello," Harlow said. "I hope you're enjoying the party."

The first woman, a short, blonde-haired noble, nodded. "Oh, we are. It's delightful."

The other women imitated her nod. "Yes," they said at the same time, sounding like they were in an echo chamber.

"Wonderful. I'm so pleased to hear this. Grandmother will be delighted to know her party is a hit." With a nod, Harlow went over to the next group.

Rinse and repeat. She became the picture of royal elegance, smiling and nodding, and discussing even the smallest of petty annoyances with her grandmother's subjects—Harlow's future subjects.

And then ... then she was done, and Evara waited for her at the same exit they'd used the first time.

They grinned at each other before sneaking out, arms linked together as they hurried through the halls.

Shade lay sprawled on the generously sized couch in Harlow's main room, numerous plates scattered before him on the coffee table. A cask of ale sat half empty on the floor beside him.

Evara kicked off her boots and headed straight for the cask. Harlow grabbed her arm before she got too far and gestured at her back.

With deft hands, Evara loosened her stays on the dress and corset while Shade averted his eyes.

"Back in a few moments," Harlow said, hurrying to her rooms to get out of that godsforsaken dress.

Evara plopped on the couch next to Shade and waved indolently, grinning as Harlow dragged her dress behind her.

When she returned, wearing a pair of linen trousers and a loose blouse, Shade and Evara were talking quietly.

"Any ale left?" Harlow asked.

Evara nudged an already poured glass at her. Harlow reached for it and curled into a chair opposite them.

"Shade and I were discussing Desminda's marriage proposals." Evara's eyes sparkled with mirth.

Harlow snorted. "I take it things didn't go well."

"She's lucky the beasts allowed her to leave in one piece," Shade said dryly. "Their marriage proposal is off the table."

Evara laughed. "And the Crystal Kingdom?"

Shade shrugged. "Desminda refused to allow me to accompany her."

Harlow blinked in surprise. "Surely not."

"The princess has had a marked change in personality these last few months." Shade's eyes darkened. "I am not sure what to think of it."

Evara sat up straight. "How?"

Shade scrubbed a hand over his unshaven cheek. "Her moods are darker. She's quicker to anger." He exhaled heavily.

"There were times she'd disappear for hours at a time. Not a single person in the castle could find her."

Harlow frowned. That didn't sound like her. Desminda had never been one to wallow in misery, though the Thornewood raids had sent her into a deep depression for a while. It didn't take long, though, before Desminda had taken her fate into her own hands and tried to trap Harlow into marriage to secure her own future. That was more the Desminda she knew—manipulative until the end.

"What do you mean by darker?" Harlow asked.

"It's hard to say," Shade said, which was such an unusual thing for him to say that Harlow could only stare.

At her bewildered look, Shade chuckled. "Her moods were occasionally volatile after we entered Nova's kingdom."

"Had to be difficult for a deposed queen to enter enemy territory," Evara murmured.

Shade tilted his head in acknowledgment. "But this was different. She'd started dealing with her plight, as Harlow knows."

Harlow frowned. "In all the wrong ways," she grumbled.

"She was born to be a queen," Shade said. "This is how royals survive."

"By stabbing their friends in the back?" Evara said.

"Royals have no friends." Harlow tipped back her ale.

Shade gave her a startled look, but his face quickly shifted to something akin to sympathy.

"Some royals do." Evara reached over and patted her hand. "Your sister is queen and has many friends inside and outside the kingdom."

Her heart warmed because it was true. Nova was a beloved ruler. Perhaps Harlow could walk in her footsteps one day—if they survived this.

"I caught Desminda muttering to herself several times.

She'd pinch the space between her brows. Here." Shade moved his fingers to touch his face. "And wince in pain. But every time I asked her what was wrong, she'd wave me away and say it was nothing."

Harlow swallowed hard. "Do you think—"

Evara gave her a sharp look, seemingly already knowing where Harlow's thoughts were heading. "You don't think?" She cut herself off.

Shade set his glass down. "Speak," he demanded.

"The Darkness." Harlow whispered the word. "It needs a vessel."

The room fell silent as they all digested the possibility of Desminda being possessed.

"We have bi-weekly council meetings," Evara said, breaking the silence. "There's been no mention of Desminda."

Harlow nodded. "She's right. It's overtaken Thornewood completely. There's been no word of Celestine's fate, but Desminda's queendom ..." Her voice trailed off. There was no way to tell the current state of Thornewood due to the shadows blocking off the kingdom. Nothing could pass through without suffering a dire fate. Two guards from their kingdom had not returned from their scouting missions, their fates known only to the gods who had forsaken them. "It's spread through the Kingdom of Light, but there's still access to the land."

"If The Darkness had Desminda, wouldn't it make more sense for the Kingdom of Beasts to be affected?" Evara asked.

Shade nodded. "But what if she was still fighting it?"

"It's possible she could have suppressed its influence," Shade allowed.

"But if her next destination is the Kingdom of Crystal ..." Harlow's voice trailed off.

"And if she can't fight it any longer, they'll be next," Evara concluded.

"Followed by the Kingdom of Wolves." Shade's expression went grim.

The Darkness threatened them all if it ever moved beyond the boundaries of Thornewood. While it was contained now, it wouldn't stay that way forever. The creature was made of magic and posed a threat to all the kingdoms once it moved against them. She and her father had gone up against it once, and it had *eaten* their power and threatened to consume their lands to settle an ancient grudge. "I think it's safe to conclude its influence is spreading, regardless of whether Desminda is the one possessed." Harlow shook her head. "The creature spoke to me. Maybe it's doing the same to her."

"It could explain her moods and her headaches," Evara said.

"If it hasn't gotten to her, it's trying." Shade let out a heavy breath and refilled his glass. "Do you think it will succeed?"

He so rarely asked their opinion on anything that Harlow was momentarily taken aback. "I—I don't know. She's strong-willed, so it will take a while. Maybe it won't ever succeed. I don't know Desminda like you do, Shade. We had little time together."

"I agree with your assessment. If it's trying to gain access, she will fight for as long as she can. But if it offers her something she can't refuse ..." His voice trailed off.

"Its allure is seductive," Harlow admitted. The creature had gotten inside her head and said everything Harlow ever wanted to hear. It offered her power and freedom if only she submitted to its rule. "It knew my darkest secrets and deepest thoughts and how to manipulate me. Desminda wants security and power. It will offer her both."

"But it's lying," Evara said.

Shade's face grew thoughtful. "And if it's not?"

Harlow sighed. "If it's not, Desminda might accept. She's a powerful healer, Shade. What could something like that creature want with her power? I thought her magic would be anathema to the thing, but if it wants her, I think we need to know why. It could be the key to figuring out how to destroy it."

"What if it doesn't want to use her power?" Evara suggested.

Shade's eyes widened. "It wants to destroy it."

Evara rubbed a hand over her mouth. "We shouldn't have let Desminda go to the Light Kingdom alone."

Shade's face darkened. "She's not alone. Astrid followed her."

Harlow's brows lifted. "Does Desminda know?"

Amusement curled Shade's lips. "Few know when a Bard is following them."

And with that, the talk turned to more positive things, and Harlow relaxed for the first time in a long time. Shade was back with her, and the world felt a little more settled.

CHAPTER THREE

A REUNION

The War Council convened after lunch the next day. Harlow sat next to her grandmother. Miriam sat directly across from her on her grandmother's other side. Her cousin was alert today, for the first time in a while.

Harlow smiled hesitantly, but Miriam didn't respond in kind. Regardless of who rightfully deserved their grandmother's throne, Miriam wasn't pleased Harlow was first in the running.

Although Miriam had never been overly friendly to her from the moment she'd arrived, Harlow hoped as time passed, they'd grow closer. But when her grandmother confirmed her identity, Miriam had withdrawn even further, and eventually, her cousin's visions and magical heritage had overridden her physical body. For the last seven days, Miriam had lain trapped in a vision. Since she was present for the council meeting, that vision had to be pertinent to the upcoming war.

Shade sat at the other end of the table, dressed in his leather finery, his silver sword strapped to his side. He was clean-shaven this morning, but dark circles lurked under his eyes, and his jaw was clenched tight as he surveyed everyone entering the room. Several of Queen Moira's guards entered and dispersed to all corners of the room, silent and watchful. Evara stood behind Harlow's chair, back stiff against the wall.

Separate guards stood behind Moira and Miriam, both well-muscled males with sharp jaws and watchful eyes. A tall, lean woman with calculating green eyes sat beside Harlow—Queen Moira's Magical Advisor. She still hadn't figured out what that meant, but the woman was present at every meeting, so she must be important.

On the advisor's other side sat a rotund man with a jovial laugh and an uncanny way of making people feel comfortable—the queen's Security Advisor. On Miriam's side sat a familiar woman, small, dark, and beautiful. Harlow started when she spotted her, remembering the sharp slap on her hand, but the woman only winked and stayed silent. She'd never seen the woman in any of their council meetings. As far as Harlow knew, the woman didn't hold a place on her grandmother's cabinet, but sometimes things changed fast, or there was important news this stranger had to share.

Two women sat on either side of Shade—her grandmother's closest and most powerful witches. They rarely offered insight during the council meetings, acting as muscle to protect her grandmother from threats, within and without. So far, there'd been nothing to protect any of them from, but as the threat of the Darkness grew ever closer, perhaps they'd have their use one day soon.

The last person entered, taking the last seat at the table, and the doors to the council room boomed shut. But once the locks clicked, and before her grandmother sealed the room from prying eyes and ears, the temperature plunged at least fifteen degrees. Miriam frowned, eyes darting around the room, but her grandmother looked unbothered.

Harlow knew the feeling and embraced it. She smiled as

shadows danced around her, lovingly flitting through her hair and over her skin.

Moments later, those shadows coalesced into a large ball, and her sister, Nova, stepped into the Witch Kingdom. Her sister was always beautiful, but it had been almost a year since Harlow had seen her, and Nova had only become more breathtaking. Her unbound hair curled down her shoulders and sat at her waist, shiny and dark. Nova's eyes were glimmering with magic, the same silvery color as the full moon on a cold winter's night.

Shade sucked in a shocked breath, shaking Harlow to her core. She'd never heard that sound from him. A myriad of expressions played over his face. Shock, relief, grief, and stunned raw emotion. Harlow dropped her eyes, clasping her hands tightly in her lap.

To have someone look at her the way Shade looked at her sister would mean *everything*.

Her grandmother spoke, breaking the tense silence. "Welcome to the Witch Kingdom. We are pleased to welcome you to our home."

Nova offered a shallow bow of respect. "Thank you for your invitation, Queen Moira."

The queen gestured to an open spot at the table. "Please."

Nova caught Harlow's eye and winked before settling in at the table, in between the security advisor and an unfamiliar woman practically brimming with magic. Harlow chanced a look at Shade. He'd schooled his face into careful blankness, though his posture was stiff and straight, and his jaw clenched tight.

It took all of Harlow's willpower not to launch herself from the chair and straight into Nova's arms. She clenched the edge of her seat and steadied her breathing.

There would be time to catch up once the meeting was over.

Her grandmother's eyes lingered on her, warming when Harlow glanced at her. Perhaps this was both an update and a gift to her. Nova was a queen and couldn't randomly pop by to visit her whenever the fancy struck her. Queen Moira had to invite her.

It didn't help that Nova's kingdom was gearing up for war and that it took quite a bit of power for her sister to travel here. She made it look easy, but now that Harlow was discovering the limits to her own power, she was under no illusion that traveling through realms was even close to simple magic.

And it wasn't like Harlow could go and visit her either. Nova was the sister of her heart but not her blood. Their magic wasn't anything alike, and Nova's ability to shadow-walk was limited to people born in her kingdom.

Harlow's power was much less subtle. She could level a building, but magical stealth was far beyond her. Or at least it used to be before Queen Moira's training. Now she could use spell craft to briefly spy, but it wasn't as clever as Nova's shadows.

Her grandmother cleared her throat. "Thank you for being here today. We have quite a bit to get through, so please hold your questions until the end. I will begin, followed by Miriam, then Shade, and finally, Nova."

At everyone's nod, Queen Moira began. "We've received word that The Darkness is spreading out from Thornewood. It has completely consumed the Kingdom of Roses and continues to spread into the Kingdom of Light. At last estimate, only a quarter of their kingdom remains free from its influence."

That wasn't good news, but it probably cleared Desminda from possession.

"Celestine, the heir to the Kingdom of Roses and Thornewood's oppressor, was spotted entering the Light Kingdom two weeks ago." The queen's lips pressed together.

"My spies believe Celestine is possessed by the creature. She no longer answers to her name, and the ground underneath her feet dies when she walks."

A few people gasped, but Harlow was unsurprised. Celestine was as rotten as they came. If the Darkness wormed its way into anyone, it would be her. Perhaps she even welcomed it in.

Queen Moira continued. "At its current rate of speed, we expect the Light Kingdom to be completely consumed in the next seven days."

More gasps. Harlow's stomach twisted, but she held her questions at bay. There would be time later to figure out what this all meant.

Her grandmother nodded to Miriam. Her cousin straightened her shoulders. "My dreams are dark and full of death and destruction," she said quietly. "The Darkness consumes everything in its path. If it is not stopped, I believe all the surrounding kingdoms and queendoms will be swallowed in the next two months."

The room broke into hushed conversations full of disbelief.

"Silence," Queen Moira demanded. When the room had settled, she nodded to Miriam.

"In addition, I believe Celestine is in danger of being consumed. When that happens, the Darkness will seek another host. A stronger one. Anyone with powerful magic might be in danger of possession. But I believe it seeks someone with magic opposite from what it possesses. A mage of light, someone whose power is inherently good."

Shade and Harlow locked eyes. The devastation in them rocked her to her core. If what Miriam said was true, they could only assume the Darkness sought Desminda. Perhaps even now it spoke to her.

She thought back to their journey here and how Desminda

had helped save Harlow and her father. The thing had hurt the healer but maybe ...

Harlow paled.

Maybe it had left something behind.

"There are few powers that can only be used for good," her grandmother remarked. "Can you elaborate?"

Miriam nodded. "I believe he might be searching for a healer."

It took everything she had not to react. Desminda's magic was still a secret to almost everyone. If the deposed Queen of Thornewood was a target, other rulers might try to harm her to prevent her descent into darkness from ever happening, regardless of what it might do to her people.

If they had even survived its influence.

Queen Moira nodded. "Thank you, Miriam. We will send missives to the other kingdoms still unharmed and request they gather up their healers and test them. My most trusted witches have been working day and night to create charms that will prevent possession."

Miriam reached into the silk bag tied at her hips and sat it on the table, untying the loops and unfolding the fabric until a pile of intricate silver medallions was revealed.

"Before you leave today, take one and ensure you always wear it. There was no way for us to test it against what's coming for us, but we believe it will hold the Darkness at bay. At least for a little while."

Miriam passed the bag to the person sitting to her right. Everyone took a medallion and passed it around the room until it came to Harlow. Magic sizzled against her skin as her fingers brushed the silver. She plucked one from the dwindling pile and held it up to the light. A faint sheen of white magic danced against the torch light. The charm was beautiful in a way, etched with ancient symbols and marks. A faint sheen of oil gleamed off the charm. Harlow passed the bag over to her grandmother and discreetly sniffed the charm.

Frankincense and something else she couldn't identify. Holy scents used to communicate with the gods Thornewood had forsaken. Desminda would clutch her pearls if she was here today. The thought brought a smile to her lips as she pulled the charm over her head and tucked it under her shirt. It landed between her breasts, the amulet warm despite its metal content.

Once everyone had put theirs on, Queen Moira gestured to Shade. "Please tell us what you encountered on your travels."

Harlow wondered if he would reveal Desminda's magic—if his loyalty to her had died once he'd found his way to Nova. But when Shade began talking, he never brought her magic up or their thoughts about her potential possession. She didn't know how to feel about it. Was she pleased with his discretion or disappointed he'd left important, potentially earth-shattering news out of his briefing to their allies?

Did he know something the rest of them didn't, or was Shade worried about the information getting into the wrong hands and putting Desminda in danger?

His briefing wasn't anything Harlow hadn't heard last night. They'd encountered no signs of the Darkness on the road, and no, Desminda had not made a match in the Kingdom of Beasts. Her grandmother's eyes flickered with annoyance at that one, but Harlow didn't think anyone was surprised by the news. Desminda had always been headstrong, but before Thornewood was taken away from her, she'd always planned to marry to further her kingdom's power and reach.

Now that Thornewood was out of her grasp, Desminda had gone rogue, refusing to marry for anything—at least according to Shade. Harlow almost laughed during some of Shade's briefing. Desminda had given the beasts a run for their money, so much so they'd almost put her on trial. Wisely, Desminda had decided to leave.

"Perhaps the Kingdom of Crystal will have better luck in securing Desminda as a bride," Shade concluded ruefully.

Queen Moira sighed. "Perhaps a visit is in order."

Harlow's eyes widened. "It's too dangerous," she blurted. "The Darkness has spread through the Rose Kingdom. With the border touching their kingdom, it's only a matter of time before their kingdom goes dark, too."

The queen's lips twitched. "I would not underestimate the power of gems and metals, Harlow. It is a testament to their power that they have not been touched at all by the Darkness's power."

Harlow only knew what Shade had taught her about the Crystal Kingdom, and it wasn't much. She knew how to use crystals in her magic, mostly to focus and hone her power, but using metals was something completely new.

Nova spoke. "I would be happy to visit their kingdom and brief their king and queen on Desminda's upcoming visit."

Shade grimaced but stayed silent.

Queen Moira tilted her head in acknowledgment. "A favor would be greatly appreciated. Your ability to travel so quickly between great distances is wondrous indeed."

Nova bowed her head. "Then it shall be done. I will leave at first light."

Sadness flickered over Shade's expression, there and gone in a heartbeat.

Harlow's heart ached at the thought of only having a few hours with her sister, but she tried not to judge her. Now was not the time for a selfish heart. Though, after some of the things Desminda had done to her, Harlow thought maybe she deserved to deal with the fallout from her actions.

How in the world had Desminda fumbled a proposal from

the beast kingdom unless she'd done it on purpose? Was she holding out for something better from the other kingdom? The Crystal Kingdom was full of mages who handled stone and metals and used them in wondrous ways, but would it complement a healer's magic?

There was no way for her to know without more information on their kingdom, but maybe it didn't matter to Desminda. The Kingdom of Beasts was no stranger to prejudice and discrimination from others due to their shifting magic, and Desminda wouldn't admit she was desperate for a match to save herself from losing her kingdom forever. Was she so prejudiced against them that she turned down a match to avoid the crossing of the bloodlines, or was something else at play?

The former queen had always been ruthless when it came to politics, but even Harlow saw the benefit of aligning with a powerful kingdom. She'd have use of their armies and their magic and could unite both kingdoms if they wrested Thornewood from under the control of the Darkness.

Did the Kingdom of Crystal hold something more advantageous than an army of beasts, or was Desminda biding her time for something else? She shook her head. All this musing was getting her absolutely nowhere but right toward a headache.

"Queen Nova," her grandmother said. "Your request for a visit was urgent. What news do you have of the other kingdoms?"

Nova leaned backward for a moment and looked at Harlow, sympathy swimming in her eyes, before she gently cleared her throat and spoke. "We have reason to believe the Darkness is influencing Desminda."

Shade sucked in a breath. Harlow gaped like a fish. She wouldn't.

"Nova," Shade breathed.

But her sister didn't acknowledge his words. "The former

Thornewood queen is a powerful healer, magic forbidden within her kingdom and kept hidden from all until recently. My shadows have seen something living inside of her. It took me a while to determine what it might be, but I now believe it is a piece of the creature. Somewhere the thing had access to her physical body and left a shard of its magic inside her. We believe she is slowly falling prey to its influence."

The room went dead silent.

Queen Moira sat frozen upon her throne. "How long?" she asked quietly.

Nova shook her head. "There's no way for me to tell exactly, but I believe it's been months. Desminda is still ... herself, but my shadows believe it is only a matter of time before it finds her, and she succumbs to its influence."

Miriam's face paled. "She was in our kingdom," she whispered. "Have we been put under its spell?"

Nova shook her head. "I do not believe so. We think it's a piece of the Darkness's magic, which allows it to speak to Desminda."

"Are you sure?" Queen Moira asked.

Nova hesitated but nodded. "Yes. It is anathema to my magic." She smiled slightly. "Mine belongs to the shadows, but this power is primordial—evil. There is nothing wrong with the dark, but this is more than darkness. It is the essence of villainy." Nova leaned forward. "It is imperative we stop this creature before it possesses Desminda. We don't know why it seeks a healer, but I can only think her magic holds some power against it. The sooner we figure out a way to find the princess, the better."

Queen Moira's face cleared. "I suppose this is the reason you readily volunteered to travel to the Crystal Kingdom?"

A smile flickered over Nova's lips. "Yes, but she knows me. While she doesn't trust me, she knows I mean her no harm."

Harlow wasn't quite sure about that after Nova's big reveal in this meeting, but her sister was in the best place to snatch Desminda from the other kingdom and bring her back here.

"I also propose we try to ally with both the Kingdom of Beasts and the Kingdom of Wolves." Nova glanced at Harlow again. "I believe the Witch Kingdom is friendly with the shifter creatures, and Harlow is beloved by the wolves. If the queen allows it, I would like to take her with me for those meetings. My sister has a way of bringing people around to her thinking."

Harlow's cheeks heated.

Queen Moira sat back and studied Nova for a long moment. "My granddaughter has just been returned to me, and you seek to use her in a dangerous mission."

"Not dangerous," Nova said. "Necessary. We are not enemies with either kingdom, and this threat concerns us all. It is in our best interests to ally while we still can. The Darkness encroaches on the wolves' territory. They will soon have to seek refuge elsewhere. There is no better time to seek an audience and offer our assistance."

Harlow suddenly missed her father so much that her chest ached. Magnus was out on a secret errand for the queen, so secret he'd refused to divulge it to her. Astrid had followed Desminda on to the Light Kingdom with Luci, Harlow's massive mare, as her companion, and hadn't made any contact since she'd left.

Their traveling group was splintering, and Harlow felt as if she stood in the middle of the break. While she felt overjoyed with the thought of spending time with Nova, the thought of her other companions spread out around the dangerous territories sobered her.

"I will travel with Nova and Harlow," Shade said suddenly.

Nova whipped her head toward him. "That isn't necessary," she practically growled.

Queen Moira's eyes narrowed just a hint. Curiosity flared in their blue depths a second before she spoke. "I agree with Shade. He has been a constant protector to my granddaughter. He will stay in that role and include you as well, Queen Nova."

Her sister's jaw clenched so hard, Harlow thought she could hear Nova's teeth grind. Harlow swallowed a smile and studied her clasped hands tucked into her lap.

"As you wish, Queen Moira," Nova said through gritted teeth.

The queen smiled. "Good. Then it's settled. But instead of leaving at first light, I would prefer you spend the next two nights here. Harlow must pack as a princess of the kingdom. There are things she needs to know before she goes. I trust that will accommodate your schedule?"

Nova looked like she'd swallowed a frog. "Of course," she bit out.

Queen Moira rose, sending everyone scrambling to their feet. "There are refreshments at the back wall if you'd like them. I'm afraid I have another meeting and must make haste if I don't want to be late."

Without waiting, the queen sailed out of the room, Miriam right at her heels. Everyone else filed out as well, ignoring the bounty of cookies and cakes. Rare for people to pass on free food, but the news had shaken them all.

Nova sank back into her chair and let out a long sigh.

"Come now," Shade said, his voice a touch too mocking for Harlow's taste. "Surely the company you've been saddled with isn't that bad?"

Nova's silvery eyes narrowed as she looked up at him. "I don't believe you want an answer to that question."

Shade's lips curved into a smile.

Evara breezed into the room a moment later, her eyes scanning the room until they landed on Harlow. Her eyes widened when she spotted Nova, and she stopped and bowed deeply.

"Rise, Evara," Nova said. "Queen Moira didn't include you, but you will accompany Harlow, myself, and Shade to the Beast Kingdom to retrieve our errant Thornewood princess. We will deposit her here for safekeeping and travel immediately to the wolves to seek an alliance."

Evara's eyebrows lifted in curiosity, but she merely nodded.

"We will catch you up during lunch," Nova said, her voice weary.

Now that Harlow could see her sister clearly, she noticed the dark circles under Nova's eyes, and the tight set to her mouth. Clearly, something other than the news she came with had brought that fatigue to her countenance. But now was not the time to ask.

Her sister rose. Harlow followed.

"Come," Nova said, looping her arms through Harlow's. "Let us take lunch in your chambers. I look forward to hearing about your adventures in this kingdom." She leaned down and whispered in Harlow's ear. "And there is more I must tell you."

Harlow nodded and leaned closer to her sister, cherishing her touch and allowing Nova to lead her out.

CHAPTER FOUR

OLD FRIENDS & NEW TRICKS

Nova devoured a full roasted chicken and about three pounds of vegetables. Harlow stared wide-eyed at her sister, wondering where in the world Nova put all the food.

"Using portal magic burns through most of my reserves," she said, amusement glimmering in her eyes. "I require much more sustenance than normal after I attempt it." She glanced down at her plate and chuckled. "Perhaps we can all share the blame for this meal," she said ruefully.

Shade passed the rest of his food over to Nova. Harlow thought Nova might refuse for a moment, but she nodded and slid his plate in front of her, cutting the rest of his chicken before eating that too.

They sat in dumbfounded silence and watched the Shadow Queen eat like a burly warrior. When she was finished, she pushed the plate away and sighed before sinking into the cushions, one hand over her stomach.

"Much better," she said with satisfaction.

Harlow started laughing. "I've never in my life seen you eat that much."

Nova shrugged, a smile tugging her lips up. "When we lived together, there wasn't much food to go around."

Harlow sobered at the reminder.

"And I couldn't access most of my magic, so there was no need for me to eat like a hibernating bear."

Harlow shook her head. "I eat more when I use magic, but never that much. My grandmother might have my hide."

Nova shook her head. "You are in training. Magic burn won't come until you use battle magic or learn more powerful spells." She studied Harlow. "Perhaps we can go to the training fields tomorrow and you can show me what you've learned."

Harlow's cheeks flushed. "If you wish."

Nova laughed. "Of course, I wish to. A queen must know if her bratty sibling has surpassed her own power."

Harlow shoved Nova good-naturedly. "I'm not that good at witch magic," she admitted. "It doesn't come as easily as the other."

"Your father's magic is powerful. Witch magic requires much mental fortitude." She winked at Harlow. "We both know you'd rather run forward and whack something with your axe than strategize about how you want to respond."

Shade laughed.

Nova stiffened, her mouth tightening at the sound, and Harlow wished they'd find their easy rapport once again. She knew they loved each other, but they were lost even though they sat right next to each other.

"Once you master the mental exercises," Nova continued, "you'll master your mother's power. And I know your grandmother has given you some." Her eyebrows rose. "You are practicing those, I hope?"

Harlow winced. "Most of the time."

Nova's eyebrows rose higher.

Harlow sighed. "Sometimes," she grumbled.

"Uh huh," Nova chided. "That's the problem. She didn't give you those to torture you. If you're to master the spells and charms to become even a novice, you must master your mind first."

Harlow slumped against her chair. "But they're so *boring*."

Nova snorted. "Most things worth knowing begin that way. I will practice with you tomorrow."

Harlow studied Nova. "You had to do the same?"

She nodded. "Perhaps not the same way, but the shadows are part of me, and to master them, I had to master myself. So mental exercises are just as beneficial to me as they are to the witches."

"Fine," Harlow said and crossed her arms over her chest.

Nova grinned and straightened, digging for something in her pocket. "Surely eighteen-year-olds do not succumb to pouting," Nova chided.

Harlow rolled her eyes and kept pouting.

"Then I suppose I must keep your birthday present a little longer ..."

Harlow sat up straight and held her hand out.

Nova laughed and placed a small box in her hand.

Harlow's fingers trembled as she opened it. A small silver pendant lay nestled in a tiny bed of silk.

"An axe," Harlow breathed, picking up Nova's gift. A sturdy silver chain slithered out of the box, landing on her lap. She studied the detailed pendant, carved with unfamiliar symbols, pausing when she felt something familiar pulsing from the necklace. Her gaze flew up to Nova's. "It's a charm!"

Nova smiled. "It is." She leaned forward. "These symbols are for protection and fortitude. It will protect you during a fight." She scooted closer. "Would you like me to put it on you?"

Harlow nodded, tears shimmering in her eyes.

Nova pushed Harlow's hair away from her neck and

fastened the necklace before she pulled it forward and tucked it under her shirt. "If you ever have need of me and I am not with you, merely hold the pendant and think my name. It will know if you are in peril and summon me."

Harlow's lower lip wobbled. "Thank you."

Nova drew her into a hug. Harlow sank into her sister. "I'm so glad you're here," Harlow murmured.

"Me too," Nova said quietly. She kissed Harlow on top of her head and pulled away. "Do not take it off until this ... whatever this is with the Darkness is over. Understand?"

Harlow nodded. "I don't think I'll ever take it off."

"Perhaps you may change your mind in the future. But for now, please wear it always."

Shade and Evara had stayed silent almost the entire time, allowing Harlow and Nova to catch up, but Nova pulled away and eyed the loyal guard she'd assigned to Harlow.

"Tell me how Harlow's training is going."

Harlow squawked. "And you were being so nice!"

Evara grinned. "She leaves herself wide open when she swings."

"I do not," Harlow muttered, embarrassment creeping up her cheeks.

"From the blush on your cheeks, we all know you're lying," Evara said.

Harlow clicked her tongue. "I'll pay you back for that."

Shade sighed. "You should go back to a sword for the next few months. Keep your skills sharp."

"I'm better with an axe," Harlow insisted.

Evara shrugged. "It's true, but you're also more vulnerable."

"Plus," Harlow insisted, "I have more control over my magic."

"That's all good and well," Shade said, "but you must remember how easily the creature overpowered you last time."

Anger filled her at the reminder. "It won't happen again."

Shade's eyes softened. "It happens to all of us. I am still prone to making mistakes when I get angry."

"When do you get angry?" Harlow asked. She'd only seen him furious once, and it was at her after that ill-fated dinner in Thornewood when Shade had erupted in a fury unlike anything she'd ever seen. That night was the point in their relationship when she realized Shade cared about her as more than a troop, and their relationship had taken a turn, leading them to this moment.

"It doesn't happen often," Shade said. "But occasionally, someone will push me too far, and I will make a mistake." His gaze flicked to Nova. "That's why mental discipline is good for more than magic. We must always be in charge of ourselves before someone takes advantage of us."

"I know," Harlow said mulishly.

Nova winked at her. "Enough talk of terrible things. Let us speak of the good things we've missed. We do not have much time before we leave, and things get hectic again. There won't be much time to enjoy each other's company."

She looked down at the smattering of empty plates. "But first, do you think the kitchens have dessert?"

Everyone laughed at that, and Evara reached for the bell to call the staff.

AFTER A HEARTY BREAKFAST the next morning, Shade, Evara, Nova, and Harlow headed to the training grounds. Harlow had never shown her sister what she could do after receiving training from both her grandmother in magic and the guards' brutal combat training. She wasn't nervous, exactly, but her stomach was churning.

Harlow wanted her sister to be proud of her. But more

importantly, Harlow wanted to be proud of herself. She'd trained until her fingers bled some days, both with magic and without. While there was always room for improvement in any endeavor, Harlow felt she'd come close to reaching the pinnacle of skill with her axe.

Minus Evara's observations, of course.

Speaking of the dark-haired guard, Evara stood before her, wearing fresh leather armor and smirking, sending Harlow's annoyance skyrocketing. Which, when Harlow thought about it for a moment, seemed to be exactly what Evara wanted to happen. Instead of giving the guard what she wanted, Harlow schooled her face into neutrality and slowed her breathing, concentrating on the exercises her grandmother had shown her in order to prepare her body for magic.

One thing Harlow hadn't been exactly successful at doing, possibly because she was overthinking, was blending her magic and battle skills. She could use battle magic successfully, and she could use her axe with great skill. What she couldn't do, very well at least, was use them together.

And that stuck in Harlow's throat. Being able to do both would change the battlefield. If she could concentrate enough to meld them, Harlow knew she'd be close to unstoppable.

Her grandmother had tried to teach her but had ultimately given up, telling Harlow she'd taught her everything she could. If she wanted to master the skill, she had to let reason go and focus on the result. Easier said than done.

Nova had braided Harlow's hair this morning into two tight braids resting on either side of her head, ensuring she'd tucked the ends back into the plait and secured them with hidden pins. She'd missed Nova's deft fingers. While Harlow could braid, it wasn't easy when she had to do it by herself.

She wore fresh armor, a mix of leather and steel. A western wind blew across the field, bringing with it the rich scent of magic and morning blooming jasmine. Harlow inhaled and exhaled before unsnapping her holster and drawing her axe. With a single nod to Evara, the battle began.

Evara, perhaps sensing Harlow's steady mental state, went immediately on the offensive, launching herself toward her with deadly efficiency and a blur of speed.

Harlow's eyes widened, but she dove out of the way, coming into a roll and back onto her feet in a graceful move. She didn't dare look at Nova or Shade, knowing if she did, Evara would use it against her.

Harlow had rarely been able to get under Evara's guard and was forced to use trickery every time. But today, Harlow was desperate to show Nova what she could do and had spent most of the past evening working on her breath control and focus.

Today, she wanted to show Nova that she was worthy, even if Harlow didn't always feel like it.

Evara grinned at her. "Nice move."

Harlow didn't waste her breath speaking. She'd always known there was something off about Evara—something not quite human, but she'd never had enough courage to ask. But that blur of speed Evara had put on a moment ago had been decidedly inhuman, so Harlow did something she'd never done before.

She opened up her Other sight, a trick her grandmother taught her. It wasn't something other people could see, but it did leave her distracted for a few seconds. Seconds someone could use to their advantage.

A blur went over Harlow's vision before Evara's body lit up like a rainbow. Harlow sucked in a breath at the sight. The guard tilted her head in curiosity, before her eyes narrowed and Evara came for her again.

Evara's aura was a mix of several colors, black being the

primary. There was green and purple and a hint of pink mixed in, along with an angry mass of red.

Her grandmother had told her certain creatures showed certain colors in Other sight. Black was always the magic of the Shadow Kingdom. Green was Earth magic, purple was mental magic, which was almost always mixed with black, pink mostly belonged to the Crystal Kingdom, and red always belonged with shapeshifters and members of the Beast Kingdom.

Evara had never shifted—had never even hinted she could.

But one thing her grandmother had also shown her was how she could combat each of those different types of magic. And one thing beasts hated?

Fire.

Harlow dodged out of the way again, much to Evara's chagrin.

"Are we sparring or running this morning, Harlow?" Evara asked, that same self-satisfied smirk lingering on her face. But there was a hint of uncertainty in it now. Evara knew she'd seen something, but there was no way for the guard to know what it was, and that made her nervous.

Harlow smiled and began whispering the incantation to create fire under her breath.

Evara came at her again, swinging her sword down. Harlow raised her ax to counter and kicked out, striking Evara in the stomach. The guard rolled away, popping back up with a smile.

But this time, Harlow was ready. Fire flickered in her palm.

Evara blinked, then slowly nodded. "Alright, World Breaker. Is that where you'd like to take this?"

Harlow merely pushed more energy into the ball, and it grew to the size of a cantaloupe, then a watermelon.

Evara didn't launch herself at Harlow this time, so Harlow took the initiative. With a battle cry, she sent her axe flying. Not expecting it, Evara cursed and dodged, right into the fireball Harlow had thrown at her.

With a shriek, the guard was enveloped, but Harlow hadn't put any heat into it. It was both fire and not fire and would not harm her.

But it did the trick. Evara went down, rolling and cursing as she tried to put out the blaze.

Nova rose to her feet, her eyes wide with concern, but Harlow raised her hand.

"Wait," she called.

Nova frowned, her eyes on Evara, but she nodded and sat back down.

It took Evara a full thirty seconds to realize she wasn't burning. When she realized, she came to her feet and let out a frustrated shriek before it became laughter.

"Alright, you little firebug, put me out."

Harlow squeezed her fist together, extinguishing the blaze like it had never existed.

Nova stood again and shook her head in bemusement. "Dirty trick," she chided, but she was smiling.

"Very dirty," Evara said, "but clever."

Shade came to his feet and strode over. "You looked like you figured something out about Evara. What was it?"

Nova stiffened. Evara's eyes tightened at the edges. Harlow shook her head. "It was nothing, really. I remembered Evara didn't like fire from one of our training exercises. It came to me just then."

One of Shade's dark eyebrows rose. He didn't believe her, but the look of relief on Nova and Evara's faces made the lie worth it. "Regardless, that was quick-thinking. You disabled your opponent without harming them. In battle, you could use the same thing to give you enough time to reach them and take them out. Good job."

Harlow's face flushed. "Thank you."

Nova studied Harlow for a long moment. "I want to see a few more things. Do you both mind continuing?"

Harlow glanced at Evara, who shrugged. "I'm happy to continue if Harlow is." She grinned. "Though I won't fall for the same trickery again."

Harlow gave Evara a wicked grin. "Good thing I have much more up my sleeve then."

Evara laughed. "I look forward to it. This round is no magic. Weapon only. Let's see what you got, Stonehand."

They headed back out to the middle of the training ring for round two.

And this time, Harlow made the Stonehand name proud.

CHAPTER FIVE

BEASTLY BEHAVIOR

After sleeping like the dead, the next morning dawned bright and cool. Groggy and sore, Harlow packed up the rest of her belongings and met her party in the courtyard.

Her grandmother awaited her with a contingent of guards. Shade, Nova, and Evara already waited a few feet away.

"Grandmother," Harlow greeted. "Thank you for seeing me off."

Queen Moira smiled. "How could I miss sending my granddaughter off to win allies for our kingdom?" She brought Harlow into a tight embrace and murmured in her ear. "Remember your training. Remember what you fight for. Keep practicing, Harlow. I feel the power brimming within you. Embrace it, and come home to us when you are finished."

Tears pricked the back of her eyes, but she nodded. "Of course I will return," she croaked.

"Make us proud," her grandmother whispered, before pressing a kiss to Harlow's cheek and stepping away.

"Is Miriam sleeping?" Harlow asked. They both knew Miriam was usually up and bustling about the castle now, but had taken to using the word sleeping as code for whether her cousin was locked in a vision.

Her grandmother's eyes flickered. "I'm afraid so. She had a long night."

Soon enough, Miriam might not wake up again. Some Seers were so powerful their magic dragged them under. Miriam appeared to belong to that category.

Harlow stepped forward again and whispered in the queen's ear. "I will see if I can find something to help her."

Queen Moira's lips trembled. "I will send a blessed wind at your backs to guide you. Return with Desminda soon, Harlow." She took her face in her hands and smiled at Harlow. "May the goddess watch over you."

Queen Moira stepped away and nodded at Harlow's companions. "May she watch over you all."

Shade and Nova offered her a shallow bow. Evara placed a hand over her heart and bowed deeply. Nova gave her a startled glance but said nothing. When the guard rose again, Queen Moira smiled.

"When you return, I have a gift for you, if Nova allows it."

Nova blinked in surprise but nodded. "Of course. My guards are free to accept gifts in other kingdoms."

Queen Moira nodded. "As long as you know about them."

They smiled at each other before Nova looked away and turned toward the sun. Dark, glittering smoke-like magic poured from her fingers. She waved her hands in a circle, whispering something in an ancient language Harlow had never heard, and pressed her palms toward the sky. Gravel shifted under their feet, and a phantom wind rustled their hair. A moment later, a spinning black circle appeared before them, growing in size until a portal opened, spinning like a vortex.

"I will step through first to announce us. Wait for my signal," she instructed.

Shade nodded, and with a heartbreaking smile, Nova stepped into the darkness.

The wait was agonizing. No one spoke, and the wind from Nova's magic had died, leaving an unsettling silence in the air. Just when Harlow was ready to throw herself into the portal, consequences be damned, several shadows appeared, beckoning them inside—Nova's signal.

With a final wave at her grandmother, Harlow followed Shade and Evara into the unknown.

THE KINGDOM of Beasts appeared surprisingly tame. Harlow chuckled inwardly at her pun-ish thoughts as she looked around. They stood in what appeared to be a bustling town square, surrounded by thick forest. A massive lake with crystal blue water sparkled toward the north, and mountains loomed in the back. Harlow inhaled, the fresh scent of pine and clean air a balm to her soul.

But it wasn't until she looked closer at the town square that she realized why this place was called the Beast Kingdom. Wolves of all shapes and sizes roamed, weaving through gaggles of humans who gave them no mind. A massive bear walking on its hind legs passed right next to them, jolting Harlow.

"Don't gawk," Nova whispered.

"I—Nova! Are you seeing this?" Harlow hissed.

Her sister chuckled. "I've been here before, sister. It's a sight the first time, isn't it?"

Crying birds screamed through the air, and an overly large horned animal that couldn't possibly be a deer passed into the forest, a shopping bag hanging on one of its antlers.

"This is amazing," Harlow said.

Nova looped her arms through Harlow's. "Come. The castle is this way. They're expecting us."

Nova started toward the west. Harlow had been so overwhelmed with the free-roaming animals, she'd completely missed the looming castle.

Shade and Evara seemed much less impressed than Harlow. They'd either been here before or they had no soul. Her fingers itched to scratch every single animal she passed under the chin, and once, Nova had to jerk Harlow's hand away from a particularly beautiful wolf that had stopped to sniff Harlow's boots.

"They are not animals," Nova hissed. "Never pet them without an invitation."

"But they're sooo cute," Harlow breathed.

"They're also deadly," Nova snapped. "Everyone here is a shifter. Be aware. They all have animal forms. While their forms differ, you'd do well to assume everyone you meet is deadly."

"You're making this a lot less fun than it should be," Harlow grumbled before a thought made her stop. "I thought we were going to the Crystal Kingdom first."

"We were," Nova said, "but I received a summons to attend them first."

"A summons?" Shade said. "When?"

"Last night," Nova answered cooly.

"Why was I not informed?" Shade demanded. "Who delivered it to you?"

Nova gave him a veiled look. "This is a kingdom of animals, Shade. There is no way to protect against their dual natures. Assume you are being spied on at all times."

Shade winced as the enormity of that statement registered.

"An osprey came to my window last night," Nova said. "He delivered a message from their king."

"An osprey," Shade said faintly. "Even the wards on the witch kingdom don't keep them out?"

Nova shook her head. "They aren't meant to. The queen has private areas for her council meetings. Those are sealed to prevent prying eyes and ears." She smiled. "I'm sure you noticed some of the windowless rooms?"

Shade frowned which made Nova chuckle.

"A kingdom would be dull indeed without the sound of birds singing and wolves howling. Plus, you don't think the Witch Kingdom is without its own spies, do you?"

Shade exhaled. "I take your point, Nova. No need to keep hammering away at it."

Nova's smile made Harlow duck her head to keep from barking a laugh. Shade had spent so many years away from magic that this was almost breaking his mind.

Now that Harlow thought about it, there were very few animals around Thornewood when she'd been there. The lack of magic had kept the shifters away, and she wondered if there were some who'd been stuck in their animal forms when the magic had gone away.

She hoped they'd made it back here.

The walk to the castle wasn't far and allowed Harlow plenty of time to gawk at the sheer absurdity of the kingdom. Well, absurd to her, but completely normal to the residents. Animals crept and ran and walked and climbed everywhere. It was both amazing and a little overwhelming to Harlow's senses.

She had no idea monkey shifters even existed. Some of the animals she couldn't even identify. There were entirely new worlds out there that Harlow had never known existed. Those books Shade taught by could never do this place justice.

They were greeted at the gates by two swarthy warriors almost twice Harlow's height.

Nova stepped forward. "I am Nova, Queen of Shadows. Your king is expecting us."

The first guard nodded and stepped aside, allowing them entrance. When they passed by, the guards stepped behind them as they walked up to the massive wooden doors.

Before they'd gotten too close, a loud clanking noise, followed by the sound of a rolling chain announced those doors opening. They stopped and waited, and when the doors finally creaked open, a dozen wolves rushed out.

Harlow gasped and took a step back in surprise, but Shade gripped her arm, forcing her to stay still.

A crack of magic came from the wolves and the first one, a large white wolf with glacier-blue eyes, disappeared in a flash of red magic. In its place stood a tall, lean man with the same color eyes. He was gloriously handsome, with shaggy, chestnut-colored hair, high cheekbones, and a tan, weathered face.

He took one look at Nova, and his face broke into a wide, happy smile.

"So, you've returned," he said, his voice deep and raspy. "You are even more beautiful than I remembered."

Shade's grip on Harlow's arm tightened before he remembered he still held her and let go like she was on fire.

"Lief," Nova said, stepping forward. "Likewise. It is good to see you."

Lief gathered Nova into a tight hug, lifting her into the air and twirling her until she laughed.

Shade's breathing wasn't quite normal. Harlow took a step away from him. Evara huffed a quiet laugh. Brave of her in the current circumstances. Harlow chanced a look back and saw death in Shade's eyes. She swallowed hard and turned to face the front.

When Lief set Nova down, his arms lingered around the queen's waist. Nova was breathless with laughter. "I see you are still as incorrigible as you always were."

"I am the king," Lief said. "If I can't be incorrigible, as you say, what's the point?"

Nova shook her head and stepped to Leif's side. "Please meet my friends."

Leif's eyes settled on Harlow, and she resisted shifting with nerves.

"This is my little sister and princess to the Witch Kingdom, Harlow Stonehand."

Leif stiffened. "Stonehand?" he murmured, turning to Nova.

"Yes, the lost princess." Nova smiled. "Lost no more."

Leif tilted his head, his eyes bright with curiosity. "It is a pleasure, Princess Harlow."

Harlow dipped into an awkward slight curtsy. "The honor is all mine," she croaked.

"My honored guard, Evara," Nova continued.

Evara's bow was deeper than Harlow's, her eyes twinkling with mirth as she rose.

"And Shade, former Captain of the Guard to the Thornewood Queen—"

Leif's face visibly darkened, rage flickering in his eyes as he studied Shade.

Nova glanced at the king. "And now he belongs to my court, as my Captain of the Guard."

Leif grunted. "A man with no kingdom is an enemy to all."

Shade's eyes narrowed. He opened his mouth undoubtedly to say something scathing, but Nova shot him a dark look and placed a hand on Leif's arm. "Shade protected Harlow since she was a child and brought her to me when Thornewood fell. He is a consummate warrior and possesses a commendable, loyal heart. To speak ill of him is to speak ill of me."

Leif glanced at Nova, studying her for a long moment. "If you say it is true, then I must believe it so." He placed a hand over his heart. "Welcome to the Kingdom of Beasts. I am King Leif. Please enter my home under guest rules. You will want for nothing as long as you are here." He held his arm out to Nova. "May I escort you inside?"

Harlow made the mistake of looking behind her. Shade looked apoplectic. His fingers strayed traitorously close to his sword. She took a step closer to him, accidentally nudging his arm with her elbow. Shade's fingers unclenched as a slight shudder shook his frame.

Nova nodded and curled her fingers around the Beast King's elbow. "Of course you may."

They turned, making a striking couple, and headed inside. The guards behind them walked around and followed their king.

Shade didn't move for a long moment, waiting until they were several feet ahead before he started after them.

"Easy," Evara murmured to Shade. "You will alienate more than Nova if you persist in this folly."

Shade's attention snapped to her. "I don't know what you're talking about."

Evara snorted softly. "A man like you does not surround himself with fools. Be careful. You will have to swallow your pride and jealousy while you are here. If you do not, this war might be over before it truly begins."

Harlow's heart thumped like a drum inside her chest as she waited to see how Shade would react. He wasn't prone to temper, but today she'd seen a different side of him.

Shade finally exhaled. "Who is he?" he murmured.

"Besides the king?" Evara said, amusement coloring her words. "He used to be Nova's betrothed."

Shade choked.

Harlow winced as Evara shot him an evil grin and walked away. She shoved her hands in her trouser pockets and whistled a jaunty tune as she hurried to catch up to Nova.

She enjoyed that. Harlow shook her head and kept a steady pace with Shade as he started walking.

His face was like a thundercloud. Jaw tight, eyes narrowed, his fingers again strayed to the hilt of his sword.

"Shade," Harlow said quietly.

"This is none of your concern." His voice sent a shiver down her spine. Harlow had never heard him sound like this, harsh and full of rage. Worry filled her.

"We are together in a dangerous kingdom. Nova is my sister and a queen. And I—" Harlow licked her lips. "I know you love her."

His attention snapped to her.

"And I know she loves you too. I see it every time she looks at you. Whatever is happening between you doesn't have to be permanent."

Shade let out a deep exhale. He stopped and squeezed his eyes shut. Like a draining river, the anger slipped away. When he opened his eyes again, his eyes were still haunted, but the rage in them had disappeared. "I'm not talking about this with you."

Harlow opened her mouth to argue, but he raised a hand. "But thank you. I will endeavor to be better."

She watched him for a moment and only saw sincerity on his face. "All right then. Shall we catch up?"

Shade smiled, tired but genuine. "Come, Harlow. We have much to do."

CHAPTER SIX

NOVA

Shade had death in his eyes. Bringing him here was a gamble, and it wasn't her first choice, but she couldn't override Queen Moira's will. Harlow's protection was both of their priorities, but she hadn't expected the queen to add Shade to their party when she should have.

Her thinking hadn't been clear since Shade left months ago. For months, she'd spied on him through her shadows until her conscience had finally gotten the better of her and she'd left him alone. It was common for unmarried queens to get betrothal requests, and uncommon for them to be rejected or unanswered. Nova had opted to reject everything coming to the castle. If she couldn't marry for love, she wouldn't marry at all. If someone tried to wrest her kingdom from her over her decision, Nova would show them exactly how much power she held.

Leif's betrothal came when she was much younger, long before Thornewood became an enemy to their kingdom. Nova never thought much of it until she'd gone to the queendom under a blind fosterage to learn the ways of other cultures, and rescued Harlow from the ashes of a raid.

Suddenly, it didn't matter that she was destined to be a

queen, a wife, or a mother when there was something so small and helpless in front of her. She'd run from the future she'd planned and from Leif, and never thought much about it until she met Shade in the woods and started them both down the path that had brought them here today.

"The dark man seems enamored," Leif observed quietly. "Do you want me to have him killed?"

Nova snorted. "No, you oaf. He is ... dear to me."

Leif slid her a look. "Is he now?" he mused. "Exactly how, dear?"

"I'm quite in love with him, and he is in love with me, but his brain is full of rocks."

"Ah." Leif nodded. "This is the way of men." They turned a corner, Harlow and the rest far behind. "Tell me his story."

"We don't have enough time."

"Tell me the short version."

"I rescued the princess many years ago from the Thornewood raids and loved her like a sister. Shade figured out who she was, and we worked together to ensure she survived."

Leif rubbed a hand over his chin. "I can't believe Stonehand's daughter is alive." He shook his head. "Not knowing where she was must have driven the man mad with grief."

Nova didn't tell him Stonehand knew she was alive. He'd trusted Shade to see to her safety and disappeared for everyone's safety, eventually losing track of where his daughter was.

Nova nodded. "They've since been reunited." She paused and debated whether to tell him the next thing, but she trusted Leif. He'd harbored no ill will over the severing of their betrothal and had asked to remain friends, which she was happy to do. "She inherited his magic."

Leif blinked and swore under his breath.

"And her mother's."

A smile tilted the edges of his lips. "Pray tell me who her

mother is." He frowned. "Wait. You said she was a princess of the Witch Kingdom."

Nova nodded and waited for him to connect the dots. When she saw his eyes widen, she laughed.

Leif swore again. "Marion. Those two must have loved each other, because breeding with those two volatile lines of magic seems risky."

Nova shrugged. "She's doing her best and learning new things every day."

Leif led her into the throne room. "Your party will be here in just a few moments. Is there anything else I need to know before they come in?"

"Shade is a good man. Give him a chance."

Leif's eyes sparkled as he settled onto the throne, affecting a careless pose. "We will see about that." He grinned at Nova's expression. "Anything else?"

"I would like you to train Harlow."

Leif's eyebrows went up. "You wish for a lowly beast to train a princess of the realm?"

Nova rolled her eyes. "You can be so dramatic, Leif."

He grinned. "Please tell me how a beast can serve the Queen of Shadows."

She sighed. "You are dual-natured. Harlow is, too, in a way. Show her how to use both lines of her magic seamlessly. I believe she's close to getting it, but even the witches weren't able to help her."

Leif grimaced. "She is a mage. We are not."

"Mmm. Your people may not be, but you can't lie to me. I know what you are."

Leif gave her a sharp look before exhaling a breath of laughter. "Perhaps you should reconsider our betrothal. We would make a powerful couple. Beautiful, too."

Nova crossed her arms over her chest. "Will you do this

for me?"

Leif's expression became calculating. "What do I get out of it?"

She huffed a laugh. "Considering Harlow has a powerful prophecy surrounding her, I believe she'll end up saving all of us. Is that enough, or do you require a trinket?"

Leif looked momentarily nonplussed before smirking. "I do so love a trinket."

Evara entered the throne room first and paused, looking around before heading toward Nova. Shade and Harlow followed her in, him walking slightly ahead. Normally, the princess would walk ahead of her guard, but Shade was looking for threats. Harlow didn't care one way or another, yet one more thing Nova would need to lecture her about when things got back to normal.

She couldn't quite hide the fond smile curving her lips as Harlow settled beside her. Nova looped an arm over her shoulders.

"Betrothed?" Harlow hissed.

Nova stilled before shooting Evara a dark look.

The guard flushed and dipped her head.

"A long time ago," Nova whispered. "We will speak of it later."

"Plan on it," Shade murmured as he settled on her other side.

It was Nova's turn to flush.

Leif's guards filed in, surrounding the throne and making a wall behind them, preventing anyone from leaving.

Shade stiffened but made no aggressive moves.

"Welcome to our kingdom," Leif said again. "In a moment, I will have one of my servants show you to your quarters, but before I do, I wish to know the reason for your visit."

Nova's eyebrows rose. "You requested my presence."

Leif's brows drew together. He glanced at one of his guards, who slowly shook his head. "Though I am always pleased to see you, Queen Nova, I did no such thing."

Nova stilled. "This isn't a time for jesting. An osprey came to my window in the Witch Kingdom and handed me a missive with your seal."

Leif rose, his face a mask of concern. He leaned over and murmured something to his guard, who abruptly turned and left the room.

"You will be escorted momentarily. I must attend to something." The king swept his fur cape back and quickly left the room, leaving them there still surrounded by guards.

No one said a word. When Harlow opened her mouth to speak, Nova reached over and squeezed her fingers in warning. Wisely, Harlow snapped her mouth shut.

They waited in tense silence until a tall woman with a graying braid entered the room. She smiled and motioned for them to follow.

"My name is Nannette. I will show you to your quarters."

"Thank you." Their party followed the woman out. She led them down a warren of stone hallways until Nova wasn't sure she could find her way out again, before stopping at a dark wooden door. "This one is for your guards," Nan said, pushing open the door and gesturing inside.

"Are there two rooms?" Nova inquired.

Nan blinked. "No, Your Majesty. I was informed—"

Leif. Nova wanted to growl. "I'm sorry, Nannette. You were informed incorrectly. Shade and Evara are not ... together in that way." Nova looked around and noticed the hallway was full of other doors. "Are all of these guest quarters?"

The servant nodded.

"Then Evara will take this one." Nova gestured for her to walk in.

Nannette's lips thinned as Nova opened the second door and stepped inside. The room was large and serviceable. Each had a large window and a separate bathing area. "All the rooms look the same?"

Nannette nodded.

"Good. Then Shade, this one will suit you."

Shade's dark eyes glimmered with amusement. He brushed past her and stepped inside. Nova closed that door and chose the one next to him for Harlow.

As she went to grab the room next to Harlow's, Nannette cleared her throat. "Um, Your Majesty. I have strict orders to escort you to the Royals' wing."

Nova bit down her sharp reply. This overstepping was not Nannette's fault. "That won't be necessary. I am perfectly happy to stay next to my party."

The servant wrung her hands. "Oh, no. That won't do, Your Majesty. The king told me I must—"

Nova interrupted her. "I will handle your king. Please send him to me if he has any issues over where I choose to stay."

Nannette's eyes begged her to follow, but this wasn't up for negotiation. Leif's treading on her personal liberties was one of many reasons Nova had chosen to sever their betrothal. While most of it had to do with the man a few doors down, she'd known their betrothal and resulting marriage would end in unhappiness for both of them.

The last door opened into a room exactly like the others. Nannette's eyes almost bulged out of her head when Nova stepped inside and put her bag on the floor.

"Please—" Nannette began.

Nova held up a hand. "I will stay here, and my word is final. Separating me from my people is not an option."

The servant dropped her eyes. "Yes, Your Majesty." She bobbed her head and turned to hurry down the hall.

As soon as Nova was secured in her room, she kicked off her boots and flopped onto the bed. Closing her eyes, she summoned her shadows.

"Find Leif," she murmured.

The shadows danced in her mind, happy to be called, and disappeared in a wisp of smoke. When she opened her eyes, she stared at the ceiling for a while, mulling over their next steps. She and Leif had a good relationship, but what she planned to ask could strain it beyond repair. But if she didn't ask, and the Darkness swept in to claim them when they could have helped each other, she would never forgive herself.

A tug on her mind told her the shadows had found their target.

Nova wrapped one around Leif's ankle, allowing it to climb up his body until it reached his ear. Leif's surprise made her laugh. It had been a long time since he'd felt her magic.

"Do not punish Nannette," Nova said through her shadows. "It was presumptuous to assume I'd want to stay separate from my people."

His sigh came through their link. "You have never acted like a queen. I'm not sure why I expected that to change."

The sting of his words surprised her. They weren't untrue, but perhaps Nova didn't act in the way he knew royals to act. There wasn't anything wrong with it, but he made it sound like a bad thing.

"I am content to stay in the guest quarters. Nannette tried her best, but I insisted."

"Others will talk about this," Leif warned before sighing.

Nova laughed. "Not if we don't tell them."

"Have you forgotten how much servants gossip?" he said dryly.

"Mine do not," Nova lied.

He chuckled. "Very well. But you will dine with me in my private dining room this evening."

"Leif—"

"I insist. Do not push my goodwill too far, Nova. Besides, there are things I must discuss with you."

She sighed. "Fine. Where will my party eat?"

"There is a separate room for guests. You can dine with them tomorrow."

"Very well, but I'm afraid I brought only travel clothes with me."

"Nannette will return soon with proper dinner wear."

"Overbearing oaf," Nova said fondly.

"Stubborn woman," Leif responded. "Now stop bothering me. I'm trying to spar."

Nova called her shadows back and cut the connection. Shade would not be pleased with this development, but she was more curious about what Leif had to tell her. A yawn stretched her mouth, and she turned to her side. A nap would do them all good.

Almost as soon as she thought it, her eyes drifted closed.

CHAPTER SEVEN

DINING WITH AN OAF

A soft knock on the door came sometime later. Nova jerked awake, momentarily disoriented, before realizing where she was.

"A moment," she called, as she rolled out of bed and smoothed her hair down.

When she opened the door, Nannette breezed in, holding a mass of fabric. Her lips pressed tight against her face, disapproval at Nova's choices still simmering in the depths of her eyes.

Nova greeted her politely as the servant laid the dress on the bed. Nova's eyes widened when she got a good look at it, her heartbeat picking up. This dress looked like it had been made for her. Knowing Leif, it had.

She reached out and smoothed a hand down the skirt's satin. The bodice was made out of shimmering black lace, cut just above the breasts. The long sleeves were made out of the same material, baring the back and shoulders.

It was a dress for a queen and seduction.

"Please do not refuse," Nannette whispered, licking her lips as she studied the floor. "My king is insistent."

Nova sighed. "Very well," she growled.

Nannette didn't move.

"I can dress myself."

The servant blinked. "There are many ties and a corset underneath."

Nova flicked her hand. "My magic will assist me."

Nannette let out a breath and paused before turning to go. Nova almost laughed, knowing she'd alienated yet another person. It wasn't that she didn't like Nannette. She didn't know her well enough for that. It was that Nova was used to doing things on her own. The servants in her own kingdom rarely served her directly. They were paid a handsome wage to keep her estate running. She did not have a personal lady's maid or anything of the sort. The most she kept was a personal chef, again also handsomely paid. Nova tried to take care of her people in such a way that they thought of the Shadow Kingdom as a home, a place of safety, and not a place where they were too scared to leave.

In return, she expected discretion and loyalty and had received it. There were a few times when people had failed her, and they were sent on their way with financial assistance but with strict instructions not to return to the castle. They could live outside the village, but Nova did not tolerate those she could not trust.

Leif's castle was not enemy territory, but someone had lured her here, and that told her she could not trust anyone around her.

The door shut behind her. Nova stared at the dress and shook her head. Before she got dressed, she needed to speak with her people.

. . .

HARLOW ANSWERED THE DOOR IMMEDIATELY, her face filled with relief when she saw it was Nova.

"I was invited to dinner tonight by a nobleman," Harlow began. "Someone named Lord Miner."

A fine distraction for Harlow put into place by Leif, no doubt.

Nova nodded. "He is a nice young lord. Handsome and a good conversationalist." She'd met him a few times during various diplomatic visits. Harlow was much smarter than the poor lord, but then again, she was more intelligent than many people Nova knew.

Harlow did her best not to grimace, but couldn't completely hide it. "Do I have to go?"

"It would be a slight if you did not." Nova inclined her head. "You are allowed to refuse invitations from lower-ranking people, but it is always gracious to accept if you can."

Harlow nodded, though she didn't look happy about it.

Nova threw her a bone. "You will take Evara with you. Perhaps dinner might end early, allowing you to explore some of the village."

Her sister's eyes brightened, and she nodded with excitement. "I'll tell her!"

Lord Miner didn't stand a chance.

They talked for a little while longer before Nova gathered her into a tight hug. "Be careful this evening. Come to my room when you get back."

Harlow squeezed her and stepped back, smiling for the first time since they'd arrived. "Do you have plans this evening?"

Nova kept her expression calm. "Political dinner. It should be over early." It *would* be over early if she had anything to say about it.

Harlow pulled a face, making Nova laugh. "Better you than me."

Nova reached over and tweaked her nose. "You'll be up to your ears in these things soon."

"Don't remind me," Harlow grumbled.

Nova showed herself out and headed to Evara's room. The guard answered on the first knock and held the door open.

"What horrors will befall us today, I wonder?" Evara said.

Nova laughed in surprise. "Let us hope the number is low." She sank into the seat next to the window and pulled her legs to her chest. Evara was one of her oldest friends, though they kept that from most people. She could tell the guard anything, and Evara wouldn't bat an eye.

Evara hopped onto the bed and studied Nova. "What is it?"

"Something doesn't feel right."

"I know." Evara's face turned crafty. "Leif certainly seems friendly enough."

Nova rolled her eyes. "He does it to annoy me. Make no mistake. He is as crafty as they come."

"Who do you think lured you here?"

"I can't say. Perhaps someone close to Leif, but nothing seems wrong where he is concerned. Maybe someone wanted to draw us here for other reasons, but I can't imagine what they would be." Nova put her head on her knees and sighed. "How is Shade?"

Evara said nothing for a long moment. "I believe the man is grieving. But he is difficult to read."

Nova lifted her head. "Over what?"

Evara scoffed. "Really, Nova? For a queen, sometimes you're terribly dense."

Nova's cheeks burned. "Evara!"

"He grieves for *you*, you dolt." Evara rolled onto her stomach and studied Nova. "When will you put the poor bastard out of his misery?"

"I'm not sure I can. He assumes it's my duty to sell myself to the highest bidder and grow heirs in my womb."

Evara grimaced. "I'm sure you've told him otherwise."

Nova nodded. "I have, but he insists if we are to be successful, I must ally myself with another kingdom."

"And what do you think?"

"I think the man is an idiot, and if he can't see reason, do I really want to have children with him if they suffer from the same mental stunting?"

Evara laughed. "Every man is an idiot. Shade's idiocy lies in his poor self-worth."

"How do I change his mind, then? If he can't see how valuable he is to me, how can I make him?"

Evara shrugged. "You show him." She flicked her fingers. "Go seduce the man until he is a sobbing mess."

"Evara," Nova warned. "You are incorrigible."

"Men understand sex and battle. They are not always equipped to understand the heart." She slid a look at Nova. "Have you ever thought of having an heir outside the bonds of marriage?"

Nova's eyebrows rose. "That's quite a scandalous notion outside of our kingdom."

Evara nodded. "Shade would be scandalized, but he would make a great father."

Nova shook her head. "I would never do it. If Shade cannot see how much I need him, I will not trap him. He would stay with me, but it would only be out of honor."

"You underestimate yourself, too. Perhaps this would be a relief. The decision is made for him."

Nova held a hand up. "Enough talk of this madness. A lord has invited Harlow to dinner this evening. I have requested you attend with her."

Evara's face tightened. "Which lord?"

"Miner."

She visibly relaxed. "Easy dinner, then."

"I suggested you two go and explore the town afterward."

Evara's eyes narrowed. "It's not in you to play matchmaker."

Nova's eyes went wide with innocence. "Whyever would I do that?"

The guard snorted and rolled off the bed. "What time is the dinner?"

"Be ready to go an hour before sunset. Dress in your best gear. We are being watched."

Evara nodded and strolled over to the massive armoire. "And what will you be doing?"

"Leif requested my presence this evening."

"Ah. And Shade?"

"He will not be with us." Guilt flooded Nova as she spoke the words aloud. She knew the king sought to drive a wedge between them, but she couldn't figure out why. Was it a game or something more?

Sighing, Nova stood and brushed her skirts down. "Please take care of my sister this evening. I do not expect any issues, but I have not felt at ease since I arrived in this kingdom and won't let down my guard until we return home."

Evara nodded. "You do not have to tell me. I will protect Harlow with my life."

For more reasons than one, Nova did not say.

CHAPTER EIGHT

HARLOW: A MINER ISSUE

Lord Miner was handsome and a good conversationalist, just as her sister said, but he had clammy hands, and that was a serious mark against him. He ate in the way all nobles did, with delicate care and deliberate chewing. Harlow imagined his digestion must be perfect with how long the man took to chew a piece of roasted pork.

The noble was perfectly passionless, his conversation intelligent but lacking zeal. Every bite Harlow took was adequately seasoned, but also dull, in that there was nothing new to experience. Lord Miner's cook scored high on ability but low on imagination.

There was roasted pork and stewed potatoes. Crusty bread and baked vegetables. Nothing Harlow hadn't tasted before. It filled her stomach but bored her soul, and she missed her grandmother's kingdom more than usual. Their cook was a genius in the kitchen, and Harlow had found herself wandering the halls in the middle of the night to raid the fridge in hopes of getting one more bite of some of the delicious concoctions the chef had come up with.

She'd never been overly passionate about food, but as time

passed and Harlow grew comfortable with the changes in her life, she realized it was because she'd never had enough experience with well-imagined meals. When someone was starving, all they sought was something to take the edge off the hunger cramps in their belly. But an expertly cooked meal by someone whose passion lay in the culinary arts could start a revolution.

Unfortunately, Lord Miner's cooking was merely an echo of some of the wonderful meals she'd had recently.

"Princess Harlow?"

Lord Miner's voice intruded into her food reverie. She blinked and started. "Oh. My apologies. Sometimes my thoughts run away from me."

He smiled kindly. "I thought for a moment I must be a dull conversationalist."

Harlow's smile froze for a brief second before she laughed brightly. "No, never!" she breathed, lying through her teeth. "You possess a vast knowledge of animal husbandry."

From behind her, Evara let out a soft cough.

Lord Miner's expression brightened. "Our family is known for our spectacular dairy products," he said proudly.

"Right," Harlow said. "A mark of familial pride." She prodded at the potatoes swimming in a sea of bland gravy.

"Exactly!" Lord Miner said, his handsome face pleased with Harlow's understanding of dairy product pride.

She was bored out of her mind and itching to leave, but one thing her grandmother had drilled into her head was propriety. Harlow might be a princess, but rudeness was always unacceptable. Lord Miner hadn't done anything wrong but bore her, so she squared her shoulders, smiled politely, and waited for the next course to come.

An hour later, and with Harlow about to faceplant into her flan, Lord Miner made his move.

"Has your grandmother spoken to you about marriage plans?" he asked politely.

Harlow choked on the gelatinous, unflavored mush. Evara stepped forward and moved her water closer, nudging Harlow's shoulder with her hip.

When she finally caught her breath, Harlow shook her head. "No, she has not."

Lord Miner nodded. "A pity. I must tell you I've thrown my hat into the circle of willing suitors."

Harlow stared. Willing. As if marrying her was something where eligible men had to be rounded up and *surveyed* before being sorted into willing and unwilling categories. "I see."

"I would make an advantageous match," Lord Miner droned on. "Especially with my unparalleled animal husbandry abilities …"

Harlow tuned him out when he started waxing poetic about the wondrous healing powers of raw milk and the rare goats he kept toward the back of his lands.

When he finished, he reached for her hand. It took everything in her power not to grimace at his cold and clammy touch. "I would be so pleased if you put in a good word with your grandmother. The chemistry you and I have is simply marvelous, and I look forward to a glorious future together.'

"Of goats," Harlow said faintly.

Evara coughed again.

"Er. Excuse me?" Lord Miner said.

"With your goats. And the milk. And husbandry," Harlow murmured. She reached for her napkin and wiped her mouth before carefully folding it and standing. "Dinner was such a pleasure. Thank you so much for welcoming me into your home, Lord Miner."

A wrinkle appeared between his pale brow before he

lurched to standing. "Of course." He offered a small bow. "Are you feeling okay?"

"I must confess, I feel a headache coming on. My sincerest apologies. The air is different in this kingdom, and I'm feeling a touch faint."

Evara's strong fingers wrapped around her elbow, holding poor, frail Harlow aloft. "I will escort her home, Lord Miner."

"Surely she can't walk all the way," he protested.

"We do not plan to walk." Evara steered Harlow from the room and out of the lord's vast mansion. It wasn't until they exited the gates of his property that Harlow drew in a gasping breath of fresh air.

"Please kill me," Harlow groaned.

Evara laughed. "Is animal husbandry not to your liking? You haven't met his goats yet, princess. I'm sure you'll change your mind once you meet everyone."

"Stop," Harlow muttered, pinching the space between her brows.

She started to pause, but Evara's fingers tightened. "We can't stop yet. If Lord Miner spots us out here and realizes we didn't take a carriage home, he might make us go back in."

Harlow stiffened and kept walking.

"Good girl."

Harlow let Evara lead her on, her head clearing with every step she took. When the town square came into view, Harlow let out a long breath.

"Better?" Evara asked.

"You don't truly think my grandmother will force me to marry him, do you?"

Evara's amusement faded. "I do not know your grandmother well. Royal lines are funny things. If your grandmother sees more advantages than disadvantages ..." Evara trailed off.

"It is possible, then."

Evara tilted her head in acknowledgment.

"I do not think I would like goats."

The guard snorted. "They are angry, loud things, but I once had a cheese made from their milk and have never forgotten it. Perhaps this match—"

Harlow shot her an aghast look. "Do not finish that sentence."

Evara grinned and led them into the throng of shoppers.

They spent two hours visiting the various booths and indulging in foreign sweets. Harlow took a bag of some type of delicious nuts with her to bring back to her sister and picked up a pair of the softest gloves she'd ever felt.

Thankfully the vendor only told her after she'd paid and packed the gloves away that the material came from a local lord's herd of rare goats.

Evara purchased a few hand-carved daggers and a multi-colored scarf that brought out the different hues in her eyes.

For Shade, Harlow purchased a puzzle box that even she couldn't figure out. The man had very few possessions, but it was small enough to travel with relative ease and made out of a beautiful wood she'd never seen before.

The night had proven cool and clear with a gentle wind stirring Harlow's braid and rustling the leaves in the trees above. Evara asked if she wanted a carriage, but Harlow declined. It wasn't too far back to the castle, and she could use the exercise, especially with her training regimen out the window during this visit.

Also, it gave her the chance to clear her mind and try to erase the lingering dread over the dinner with Lord Miner. She'd never thought too much about marriage, because it wasn't in the cards for her. Before her journey to the Thornewood castle, she was an impoverished orphan with barely a few coins to her name.

But now she was a princess, and for some reason, she hadn't fully thought about the duties and responsibilities that came with the title.

"I do not wish to marry," Harlow said quietly.

Evara's face tightened. "Ever?"

Harlow lifted a shoulder in a shrug. "I do not know. But Lord Miner would never be on that list."

"Some kingdoms are more lenient with marriage," Evara said.

"Like Nova's?"

Evara nodded. "Marriage has advantages, and they are used to strengthen a power base, but the queen has more power than most kingdoms combined."

"And therefore, does not need a husband," Harlow concluded.

"But what about you?" the guard asked.

"I'm split between two worlds with magic that don't exactly fit together. I am only advantageous in that my blood is royal."

Evara gave her a long look before shaking her head. "You truly believe so little of yourself?"

Harlow's lips thinned. "If I cannot master my power, how am I to help stop what is coming?"

"You are still new to this world and a fledgling mage. There is plenty of time to learn how your powers work and how to wield them." Evara's sympathetic look cracked something in Harlow's heart.

Feeling sorry for herself got her nowhere. She wished her father were here. He'd been gone for months now, and Harlow's training had suffered for it. No one else possessed their familial magic, so no one else could train her in the way she needed. Powerful magic rose in her when her emotions were high, making her mental exercises even more important, but it had saved her life more than once. If she could figure out how to wield such magic on command, other kingdoms would tremble.

The thought buoyed her, lightening her steps for the first time in weeks. She smiled at Evara. "Thank you for getting me out of that house."

The guard chuckled. "Fainting at a lord's house is a poor look for a future queen."

Harlow clicked her tongue and playfully shoved Evara. "Hurry up, you brute. I want to see if King Leif has any better desserts stashed in the kitchen."

CHAPTER NINE

NOVA: THE BARE NECESSITIES

As dinners went, hers proved mostly uneventful. Leif proved a charming and witty companion, as she expected, but the discussion he insisted on never materialized. When Nova asked about it, he appeared confused and asked if she was sure he'd requested it.

Not wanting to agitate him, Nova dropped the subject, but the incident bothered her for the rest of the evening. Was Leif under the influence of magic? Shifters were resistant to many spells, but not all. Had he eaten or drunk something that affected his cognition?

She started back to her bedroom, hesitating at the door. She hadn't seen Shade since yesterday when he'd stared at Leif like he wanted to kill him in cold blood. Nova exhaled and turned, making the short walk to his bedroom. Tapping twice on the door, she pulled her shawl closer to ward off the draft in the stone hallway and waited.

Just when she thought he wasn't going to answer, and she'd turned to return to her bedroom, the door cracked open. Shade's hair was mussed, and he had a five o'clock shadow—both unusual enough for concern to twist in her stomach.

"Shade?" She started forward.

He shook his head. "What do you want?"

Nova opened her mouth and snapped it closed just as fast. She stared at him and suddenly felt foolish. They were *both* foolish. Why couldn't they just be who they were and embrace what they wanted?

Shade watched her warily and stepped back to shut the door.

"Open the door, or I will force my way inside." Her voice was soft and deadly.

Shade lifted his chin. "Is that how you want to play this? Overpower me and tell me how weak I am?"

Nova snorted. "Is your self-confidence so low that you assume you are weak? Do you think I would love someone with a fickle, weak heart?"

Shade blinked. His eyes narrowed.

"Let me in. I will not ask again."

A ghost of a smile lit his lips, and he stepped aside, sweeping the door open. "As my queen commands."

She rolled her eyes and swept past him. Her gaze trailed over the room, taking in the military cleanliness and the small bag he'd taken with him. Nova settled into a chair by the small balcony, adjusting her voluminous skirts. She wished she'd changed before coming, but it couldn't be helped now.

His dark gaze trailed over her attire and stilled on her face. "You dined with the king tonight."

It wasn't a question.

Nova tilted her head in acknowledgment. "I did, and that's part of why I'm here."

Shade scoffed. "To tell me you are once again betrothed, I'm sure."

Nova's nostrils flared. "You are trying my patience. It is not like you to be so ..." She took a deep breath. "Shade. Please. Sit down. There is something we must discuss."

Anger flashed over his face before he took a chair on the opposite side of the room. She barely held back vicious words at his choice.

She sent her shadows out to every corner of the room, sealing them in a cone of silence.

Shade did not speak, merely watching her with those dark, fathomless, unreadable eyes.

"Something is wrong with the king," Nova began.

Shade didn't interrupt or ask any questions while she spoke. When she finished, she crossed her hands on top of her lap and waited.

"What is it you wish me to do, my liege?"

A strangled scream erupted from her lips. "I wish you to stop being a dolt!" she snapped.

Shade laid a hand across his heart. "My apologies. I never wish to displease you."

"You are being deliberately obtuse." Nova stood, cursing her ridiculous skirt. "I wish to know your thoughts."

When he stayed silent, she sighed. "What happened to us? You used to trust me."

Shade frowned. "I still trust you."

"Then why are you sitting there like a bump on a log and not offering anything to this discussion?"

"It is not my place to offer advice about another kingdom's liege, especially when he is betrothed to my queen."

Nova pinched the space between her brows. "He is not my betrothed," she said through gritted teeth. "And this jealousy is unbecoming of my Captain of the Guard."

Shade exhaled. "Am I?"

"Are you what?" she snapped.

"Your Captain of the Guard."

Nova wanted to wrap her hands around the man's throat and throttle him. Twice.

"We have never spoken about your position or lack thereof since you left the kingdom. Why would I replace you?"

"Your be—"

"If you say betrothed one more time ..." she snarled. Nova exhaled. "Shade. I'm going to say something, and you might think it is cruel, but I think it needs to be said."

Shade crossed an ankle over his knee and leaned forward. "Speak your mind, my queen."

Nova strode over, tall enough to look down at his face as he sat before her. She tilted his chin up with her index finger. "You are being a massive idiot," she breathed. "I am a queen and can marry whom I please. You are driving my patience to the brink. If you wish it, I will drag us to the throne room this second and force Leif to wed us. Think very hard about this and know that I can force your hand. But I want you to come to me willingly. Stop throwing yourself on every sword you find. Be mine because you want to. Don't discard us because your sense of duty and lack of self-worth tell you I deserve an advantageous match or someone better."

She stared down at his unreadable face, though something was flickering in his eyes, some emotion she couldn't read. "There is no one better. There is no match more advantageous to my heart than you. I don't care about money or power, for my kingdom has enough to survive for hundreds of years. You are the one I want." She bent over so close their noses almost touched. "So stop punishing me for wanting to make this permanent."

Nova closed her eyes and continued. "Marry me, Shade. Be my husband and my partner in life. Do not continue to make me suffer by your preconceived notions of how royalty behaves. If I were like the others, I would not have saved a child at the poten-

tial cost of my life. I never would have stayed with her and sacri-
ficed my duty, nor would I have fallen in love with you. You are
my home. My heart. The only one standing in the way of this is
you."

His trembling hands wrapped around her waist. "I do not
deserve you." Shade's voice broke.

"After tonight, I'm not sure you do," she said dryly.

Tears shimmered in his eyes. "You truly wish for me to be
your husband?"

"You still doubt me after that romantic speech I gave?"
Nova's voice trembled. "Let us go tonight. Into the village. We
will keep it from Leif. From everyone until we return home."

She held her breath and watched an array of emotions wash
over his face. Uncertainty, awe, sadness, relief, and finally, resolution. "Tonight?" he croaked.

Nova nodded. "Tonight," she breathed against his lips.

His eyes shut as he pulled her against him, inhaling her
scent. "Yes," he said quietly.

Nova stilled. "Yes?"

He nodded against her chest.

The shell around her heart cracked and shattered for the
last time. "I hope when you are my husband, you are not this
difficult again."

Shade's crack of laughter made her smile. His hands untied
the belt at her waist. Nova shivered as deft fingers made quick
work of the loops and stays until he gently pushed her away and
stood, sliding the dress down her body.

His face went feral as she stood before him in only a corset
and stockings.

"Keep the sound barrier up," he growled as his fingers
worked to loosen her corset.

Nova nodded breathlessly. Shade bent to claim her lips in a

brutal kiss. She melted into him, her fingers gripping his leather vest so tightly they ached.

And when the corset fell to the floor, and he scooped her into his arms and gently laid her on top of his bed, Nova was glad the room was soundproofed.

A FEW HOURS LATER, a man and a woman wearing nondescript clothing breezed into town, knocked on the door of the local priest's home, and whispered their request.

While taken aback by the request and the identities of the two who stood outside his home, the bear shifter had always had a soft heart for the sweeter things in life and ushered them inside, ordering them to wait a few minutes.

He hurried into the cool night and gathered two of his most trusted friends, quietly telling them what had happened and what he needed them to do.

When they all gathered inside and the couple stood before the bear's fireplace, the room awash in a golden glow, the priest quietly said the words of binding, forgoing his usual sermon in favor of speaking from the heart.

And when the dark queen married a commoner and their lives were joined legally and spiritually, the bear shifter felt some piece of the world click into place, and he wondered if, after all the darkness they'd all suffered, these two might bring a little light back into everyone's lives.

CHAPTER TEN

CLARITY

Their hopes for an alliance were dashed the next morning after Leif had forgotten they were his guests and seemed surprised by their presence at breakfast.

Harlow had watched the entire thing with curious, concerned eyes and only spoke when they had all gathered in Nova's rooms.

"Something is wrong with him," she whispered.

Nova nodded. "He's being influenced by something."

"The Darkness?" Harlow asked.

Evara leaned against the wall on the other side of the room. "It has to be, but who can we trust to ask?"

Shade ran a hand through his hair, the wedding band normally worn on one's left hand hidden on a long silver chain tucked under his clothing.

"We trust no one," he said. "Not until we figure out what's going on."

"My grandmother will be upset," Harlow said. "These kingdoms border each other, and they've always been friendly. The king's lack of cooperation suggests he plans to turn against her."

"We can't jump to conclusions yet," Shade cautioned. "It's a setback but not dire. Yet."

"It would be different if it was anyone but the king. I can't use my magic to probe without his permission. Doing so would be an act of war."

Shade nodded. "Is there any other way to find out?"

"If Desminda were here, I would think so," Harlow murmured. "She senses dark magic better than anyone else I know."

Nova winced. "I do not think she is welcome to return."

"Spurning a wedding invitation to wed the king's son will do that," Shade said dryly. His brow furrowed. "Speaking of whom, where is the prince?"

Nova blinked. She hadn't even thought about the boy since she arrived. Wasn't that strange? "I'm not sure. He kept the prince close after his first wife died, but no one has even mentioned him since we arrived."

"Can we sneak Desminda in once we retrieve her from the Kingdom of Light?" Harlow suggested.

Evara laughed.

"No," Nova said, a smile curling her lips. "I don't know if Leif formally banned her, but he may do so if she returns. That would complicate relations if she ever regains her kingdom."

"I will try one final time to speak to Leif before we leave."

Nova pretended not to notice Shade's dark look when she mentioned the king's name. No matter if he'd shaken himself out of his jealous slump, he still didn't care for the king's influence in Nova's life. Even if it was many years ago.

"I should go with you," he said.

"So you can glower at him the entire time?" Nova said, amusement coloring her words.

Evara snickered.

"No," Shade drawled. "If he is under a dark influence, someone should be with you in case he attacks."

Nova shook her head. "I am quite capable of defending myself."

Evara pushed away from the wall. "Shade is right. We all know you're capable, but it never hurts to have someone else with you in case he's planning an ambush or something equally unsavory."

"Fine," Nova relented. "It should be you, though."

Shade sucked in a breath. "What?"

Nova held up a hand. "Leif purposely antagonizes you, and you let him. Evara is neutral."

The guard nodded and adjusted her sword. "I am ready when you are."

"Let's pack up first. Then we will request an audience."

Everyone but Shade left the room. When the door shut, he turned his annoyed look onto her.

"I'm right," Nova began.

Shade barked a laugh. "You think I cannot be neutral?"

Her eyebrows lifted. "It was already difficult before. Now that you are my husband, I dare say it will be impossible."

His nostrils flared. "Come here, wife."

Nova grinned. "Why should I?"

Shade stalked toward her. She let out a tiny shriek and escaped to the bathroom, but there was nowhere to hide.

Perhaps that was what she wanted ...

THE KING LOUNGED CARELESSLY on his throne, crown askew atop his head. Two guards stood on either side, watching Nova and Evara with expressionless faces.

"King Leif, are these your most trusted guards?" Nova asked.

Leif glanced up at them and flicked his hand. "Oh, yes. They are."

Well, that seemed convincing. "What I must say should only be heard by your most seasoned and trusted confidantes."

Leif gave her a sullen glance, which was completely unlike him. "I told you they are fine."

With a soft curse, Nova sent her shadows out. Time froze around them. Leif blinked in surprise and started to stand, but she lashed him to his seat.

"How dare you!"

Nova stalked to the throne. "I am doing this because I am your friend."

His teeth pulled away from his lips. "You are a traitor!" A frisson of darkness rolled through his irises.

Ah. There you are. She gently probed his body with her magic, searching for the magical influence and found it sitting very close to his heart. It was small enough for her to yank out, but risky to try. If Desminda were here, the healer might find it easy, but Nova was more used to working with shadow rather than light, and for her, it was a much more delicate operation.

Nova turned to her guard. "Evara," she said quietly. "Can you retrieve a magic safe container?"

The guard blinked in surprise and nodded. "I may have to steal it."

Nova snorted. "Do whatever needs to be done so we can save his life."

Evara hurried from the throne room, and Nova turned back to the king. "How long have you been in there?" she asked.

His eyes turned to black, completely rolling over the whites of his eyes. "Clever queen," the voice that was not Leif said. "You cannot escape my influence. No one can."

"Perhaps," Nova agreed. "But this is a tiny piece of you which tells me you are still not whole, are you?"

The Darkness inside him seethed. Anger rolled over Leif's features.

Nova tucked her hand into her pocket, wrapping her fingers around one of the amulets from the Witch Kingdom. Her party hadn't taken them off since Moira had given them to everyone, and she only had two extras. Giving the king one seemed like a worthy way to gain his trust and secure their alliance in this war. But first, she had to wrest the dark force's influence from the king.

The guards stood stock still, seeing a clever illusion of Nova fruitlessly bargaining with Leif, but the real battle was before her.

Evara returned a few moments later, holding a small black bottle pulsing with deadening magic. Nova grimaced when Evara pressed it into her hands discreetly.

The king's eyes snapped to it, but he couldn't see what it was.

"What did she give you?" he demanded.

"Nothing," Nova said.

He struggled to rise again.

"Leave this kingdom," Nova said, "and I will allow this piece of you to survive."

The Darkness laughed, a sound that grated against Nova's heart. "As if you could control any part of me."

Nova smiled. "You know nothing about me." By now, her shadows probed Leif's entire being, slowly surrounding the thing living inside of him. If it were allowed to keep growing, the king would eventually lose every piece of himself, the thing like a parasite, dependent on his magic to exist.

She could not allow that to happen. With a whispered prayer that she wasn't about to commit accidental regicide, Nova pulled.

Leif's scream of agony shattered her heart because it was the king and not the Darkness, but his pain was soon overshadowed by the thing inside killing him slowly shrieking with outrage.

She methodically extracted the piece until a small piece of black smoke peeked from Leif's mouth. Nova hurried with the container, uncorking the small bottle, and coaxing her shadows to carefully deposit the dark magic.

It took an agonizingly long time, and Nova was sweating by the time it was finished, but eventually, every single piece of it was gone, and Leif slumped against the throne, unconscious.

Evara finally spoke. "What will you say when you drop the illusion, and they see their king half dead?"

Nova grimaced. "I haven't thought that far."

"How long can you keep the illusion going?" she asked.

"As long as I need to."

Evara nodded and stalked to the throne, heaving the king up and over her shoulder. "Let's go."

Nova blinked, then decided not to overthink this and followed Evara out of the throne room.

They managed to get the king to Nova's room without incident, but when Shade opened the door and saw what Evara held, he swore viciously.

"Of all the foolhardy—"

"Can it, Shade," Evara barked, sending the captain into stunned silence. "This was the only option we really had if we were to walk out of the throne room without causing a diplomatic incident."

"Kidnapping was your best option?" Shade finally asked.

"Yes," Nova said.

Evara dumped the boneless king onto the bed before adjusting him to a semi-seated position by piling pillows behind him.

"How long until he wakes up?" Shade asked.

"I've never performed magical surgery before, so I can't rightly say," Nova said quietly.

Shade looked over at her with wide eyes before he exhaled and rubbed his face. "Right. I'm not sure why I asked."

Nova smiled innocently. "It's the Darkness." She started as she realized she was still holding the amulet. "Here," she said and tossed it to Evara. "Put this around his neck."

"Is he dead?" Shade asked.

Nova gave him a withering look. "If I murdered the Beast King, we'd be leagues away from this place by now."

"Just checking," Shade said, giving Leif a dubious look. "Do I need to stand guard at the door?"

Evara shook her head. "Nova is maintaining an illusion. Once the king wakes up and we explain to him what happened, we will take him back."

"And what exactly happened?" Shade asked.

This was the closest to panic Nova had ever seen him. She quickly gave him the run-down on what happened. By the time she finished, Shade's expression had grown dark. "Where is the expelled magic?"

Nova slipped a hand into her skirt and pulled out the bottle.

Shade swore and took a step back, making Evara laugh.

"I bet he wishes he was back in Thornewood right about now," she murmured. "It has to be calmer than this."

Shade snorted. "It was calm until Harlow came along."

Harlow, who was sitting quietly in the corner, blurted, "Hey!"

Nova grinned and gently shook Leif. "Wake up," she said quietly.

Leif didn't stir. She slapped him on both cheeks, not hard, but enough to sting.

Shade sucked in a breath.

"Relax," Nova said. "We were betrothed once."

Harlow snickered.

"Leif," Nova urged. "You must wake up."

When Leif still didn't move, Nova sighed and gestured toward Evara. "Fetch me a pitcher of water, please."

"Nova," Shade warned.

"It's only water. If anything rouses him, it might be that." When Evara returned, Nova shook him one more time, but when he stayed motionless, she tipped the pitcher and poured the entire contents onto the king's face.

Leif sucked in a gasping breath, choked, then rolled onto his side.

"There we go!" Nova said cheerfully as she waited for the king to rouse himself fully.

When Leif's coughing fit concluded, he rolled onto his back and blinked up at Nova, who loomed over him. His eyes narrowed. "As pleased as I am to have a beautiful woman atop me in bed, I have to admit I don't remember how we got here."

Shade bared his teeth. At Nova's quelling look, he smoothed his expression, but his hand still loomed too close to his sword.

Nova patted Leif's cheek and moved from the bed. She held out the bottle of magic and shook it at him. "Have you been feeling off lately?"

The king visibly recoiled when he saw what Nova held. "What is that?"

"A piece of a creature responsible for possessing you."

Leif sat all the way up. He pressed his palm against his forehead and winced. "How long?"

Nova shook her head. "No idea. I expect at least a month or two with how quickly your behavior changed. Do you remember anything?"

Leif's brow furrowed. "Much of it is foggy. It was interested in how many soldiers I had ..." His voice trailed off, and he swore a second later.

"It's seeking intel," Shade supplied. "And it appears it got what it needed."

Leif swung his legs over the side of the bed. "I can't begin to thank you for what you've done."

The amulet swung against his neck. Leif's fingers caught it and held it up to the light. "What is this? Magic pulses from it."

"Anti-possession charm," Evara supplied. "I wouldn't take it off."

Leif's face paled. "You think it will try again?"

"Not this piece," Nova said, "but we can't rule anything out."

"How did it get in?" Leif wondered aloud.

"That's something we can't answer." Nova held her hand out and helped the king from the bed. "We have bigger issues. If we don't get you back to the throne room, your guards might come in and drag us out soon."

Nova could hold the illusion for long periods of time, but she couldn't prevent someone from walking in on it and seeing something amiss. Once an illusion had too much scrutiny, it would fall. For now, the illusion still held, but it was only a matter of time before someone went looking for Leif.

"Of course." Leif swayed when he took a step forward.

Shade stepped over and wrapped a firm hand around the king's elbow. "I have you," he said gruffly.

Leif glanced at Shade. "You do me a great service despite the grief I caused you."

Shade's lips tightened. "I serve at the will of my queen."

A faint smile appeared on the king's face. "As do many," he agreed.

Shade walked the king to the door, only letting go when Leif appeared to walk under his own control. Nova and Evara followed him out.

"Is there a place we can speak in private?" Nova asked.

"Let us go to the throne room first and relieve the guards," Leif said. "Then I'll take you to my private quarters." Some of his color came back as they walked, and when he re-entered the throne room and Nova dropped her illusion, the guards blinked in surprise at seeing Leif all the way across the room instead of on his throne but said nothing.

Most loyal indeed, Nova thought.

Leif relieved one of the guards. The other one escorted them back through the halls and into another wing. "Wait outside," Leif instructed.

The guard's eyes flicked to Shade first, then Nova, before stepping aside and waiting outside the king's quarters. "You know how to alert me," was all he said.

Leif nodded and opened the door.

Now the real negotiations would begin.

CHAPTER ELEVEN

BACK HOME

They were back in the Witch Kingdom later that afternoon, with no one the wiser about what had happened to King Leif or Shade's brand-new role in Nova's kingdom. Nova dropped her sister off in her quarters and left her with Evara, motioning for Shade to follow her.

"We will stay together," Nova announced at the door to her room.

Shade paled. "We will not," he said hotly. "No one knows about us. Me staying here is the height of impropriety."

Nova grinned. "That's why you're going to put your things down, and we're going straight to Queen Moira."

He stilled. "You're going to tell her?"

Nova tilted her head and studied him. "Why wouldn't I? You are my husband and now, the rightful King of Shadows."

Shade blinked in surprise as if he had simply not thought about his new title. "King," he murmured, then grimaced, making Nova laugh.

"Yes. King." She reached for the door. "Now, put your things down, and let's find the queen."

Queen Moira was having tea and happily invited them in

when Nova requested an audience. Her eyes widened slightly when she saw them before a knowing smile tipped her lips up.

"I expect I know what you're about to tell me," she said.

So Miriam's gifts were not unique to her father's line then. Queen Moira appeared to have a touch of the Seeing ability as well.

Nova bowed her head. "I have taken Shade Montello as my husband," she said without preamble.

"I wondered if this would come to fruition." She smiled at Nova before her gaze lingered on Shade. "I'm glad your heart finally pounded your pride into submission."

Shade's cheeks colored slightly. He cleared his throat. "I am ruled by many things, Your Majesty. This is the first time my heart has won."

Queen Moira must have liked that answer because she invited them to sit down and share tea. Once a serving girl had poured everyone a cup, the queen pushed a tray of cookies over and said, "Now tell me about your visit with Leif."

Nova left out Leif's possession. Queen Moira might be an ally, but she was a crafty bird, and Nova could see her using the information against him at a later time. It was better they approach an alliance on equal terms if they hoped to be the victor in the end.

"They've agreed to lend their armies?" Queen Moira asked.

"They have, with the caveat that any servants under your command who belong to their kingdom are allowed to abandon their positions if they so desire." Nova had no idea there were shifters inside the Witch Kingdom. She'd never sensed anyone, but Leif was adamant they were here.

Queen Moira's face darkened for a brief moment, so fast Nova almost missed it, but the queen nodded. "I will have to travel to them and let them know."

"Travel?" Shade inquired.

"They do not work in the castle," was all the queen would say.

Shade's hand gripped Nova's under the table, and Nova squeezed back. The queen's words were both curious and disturbing, and it would pay to know why some of Leif's people were working for Queen Moira and why Leif wanted them released before he would send aid.

"When do you leave for the Crystal Kingdom?" Queen Moira asked.

"Tomorrow morning," Shade quickly said.

Nova shot him a look but didn't contradict him. She would have liked a day of rest and respite, but if Shade thought it best to move quickly, she wouldn't begrudge him.

"Good," the queen said. "Once Desminda is returned, we can approach the Darkness on our terms before it is too late."

The conversation turned to other things, and when their tea was finished, Nova and Shade quietly excused themselves. They didn't speak until they were back in Nova's room.

To her surprise, Evara and Harlow awaited them.

"Did you tell my grandmother about the lord?" Harlow asked, her words a little too breathless to be casual.

Nova bit down her smile. "No. If the lord wants to request your hand, there are proper protocols to be followed. You have some time before a message will arrive." Nova winked at Shade. "And who knows? We will be in the Crystal Kingdom tomorrow, and somewhere else soon. Perhaps any messages would be … delayed."

Hope shone like a beacon in Harlow's eyes, and Nova pretended not to notice Evara's rapt attention. While Queen Moira was less rigid than other rulers, even Nova didn't know if she would approve of their relationship—if it moved past the initial stages.

Evara would make a good leader, but the secret living under

her skin might be too volatile for Queen Moira to approve their union—if that was what Harlow even wanted. Desminda had burned her sister deeply, scoring her tender heart in such a way that Nova knew it would take a long time to heal. And Evara ... she was much too conscious of the beast inside her to believe someone could truly see her and still love her.

Nova turned her thoughts to more important things. She rarely dallied in matters of the heart. They would either solve it or they wouldn't, and Harlow was now an adult. She could handle her own affairs.

And now for the news she hadn't yet shared with them. Evara might be delighted, but she still wasn't sure how Harlow would react. "Please come a little closer. I have ... news," Nova said.

Shade stilled, one of his dark eyebrows rising as if to ask, *Are you sure?*

She winked. One thing she'd always been sure about was Shade Montello.

Harlow gave her a wary look but came over and sat on the edge of the bed. Nova reached for Shade and drew him closer. Evara's eyes narrowed as she settled next to Harlow, a little too close for propriety, but Evara had never been one to stand on ceremony when she wasn't in public.

Nova drew a deep breath to tell them the news when Harlow suddenly gasped.

"You got married!" she blurted.

Shade barked a laugh. Nova felt the wind go out of her sails. "Harlow!"

Her sister's eyes darted back and forth between them. "I'm right?" she asked in a small voice.

Nova nodded.

Harlow lifted her hands and covered her face. She took a deep breath, but when she let it out, it sounded like a sob.

"Oh," Nova breathed. She nudged Evara aside and sank next to her sister, bringing Harlow in for a tight hug.

Harlow buried her head in Nova's neck and cried. Shade shot Nova a helpless look, but Nova shook her head. Until she knew why Harlow was crying, she wouldn't assume. Nova could only hope they were relieved and happy tears, but few people were qualified to guess what an eighteen-year-old girl was thinking at any given time, and Nova wasn't one of them.

Evara rose and stood by Shade, staring at Harlow with an odd expression. "Is she okay?" she murmured quietly.

Harlow's head abruptly jerked up. "You're a king," she whispered, her eyes wide o's.

Amusement curved his lips. "It's strange."

Harlow nodded. "Very." She giggled before standing up and hurtling herself into Shade's chest. He grunted in surprise before wrapping his arms around her.

"You're my brother now," she muttered against his leather vest.

A soft expression stole over his face. "I suppose I am." He held her for a few seconds. "But this does not mean I will not still kick your ass in training."

Harlow snorted and pulled away. "I should have known you wouldn't allow much time for emotion."

She patted his chest and stepped away before turning to Nova. "I'm so happy for you."

Nova smiled and held her arms out. Harlow tackled her onto the bed in a flurry of silk and lace. "Why did you keep this a secret from me?" she demanded, pinning Nova's arms to the bed.

Nova laughed. "We decided on a whim."

"He must really love you to become a king."

Nova's face softened. "I know." Shade never looked for

power. He was content to enforce rule, not one to seek it for himself.

Harlow let go of Nova's arms and flattened herself on top of her sister. She was much smaller than Nova, but her weight, with the addition of Harlow's immense dress, made breathing hard. She tolerated it for a moment, allowing Harlow to come to terms with the new pecking order, before she tilted her sister to the side. All that silk didn't stand a chance, and Harlow slid off the side of the bed.

"You are a terrible queen," Harlow squawked from the ground.

Nova peered over the side and stuck her tongue out. "Just to you."

They grinned at each other before Shade cleared his throat. "There is much to do before we leave tomorrow."

Harlow groaned and picked herself up. "Is this the way it is to be? Now that you're a king, you're going to order us all around all the time?"

Shade grinned. "It is quite handy, isn't it?"

Harlow rolled her eyes. "Don't forget that one day I might be a queen."

Shade's expression sobered. "How could I ever forget?"

Harlow looked down and sighed. "Everything is changing."

Nova straightened her skirts and rose. "Yes, but we have the opportunity to unite our kingdoms, and that is something few people can say."

Harlow and Evara opened the door. "But at what cost?" Harlow asked before she stepped into the hallway.

CHAPTER TWELVE

ALMOST A QUEEN AGAIN

The Kingdom of Crystal was vastly different from the Beast Kingdom. Harlow felt like she'd just stepped into a world of magic the second she entered the portal.

Thornewood possessed the vast majority of Luna stones, the gem responsible for their kingdom's magic supply, but this kingdom seemed like it was built of one massive gemstone. While they stood on the grass, every stone glittered in many colors, and four giant spires loomed high above the clouds, each made of a different type of stone.

Two guards stood before them. Nova stepped out of the portal, looking every inch a Queen of Shadows, and stopped a few feet away.

"I believe your king expects me," she said imperiously.

The guards nodded and turned, slamming their staffs on the ground once.

Shade stayed one step behind Nova. He had not been officially crowned as king yet, so he technically was only her consort. He still held considerable power, but he could not walk beside Nova as her equal yet.

Harlow stayed behind Shade, her position not technically

correct since she was a princess, but Nova didn't insist on proper protocol with Harlow even though she should, and she always felt comfortable being away from the center of attention, so there she stayed. Evara walked a few steps behind her.

The guards led them over a crystalline bridge and into one of the larger spirals. Harlow breathed in fresh, cool air and wondered where all the trees were.

Her stomach was tied in knots. Desminda was here, somewhere, or at least she had been up until a few days ago. They hadn't parted on the best of terms, and now that Desminda might be fully possessed, Harlow had no idea how their first meeting in almost a year might go.

Evara had said little, only whispering that Harlow was not to go anywhere alone with Desminda "no matter what the little minx said." It had made Harlow laugh, and she'd assured Evara she wouldn't let that happen again.

A strange music sounded in the air above, the tone created with an instrument she'd never heard before. High, crystalline, and soothing, the music soared through the clouds and over the kingdom.

She itched to ask what the sound was, but hesitated to speak when Nova was quietly following their escort.

They stopped at a set of carved reddish doors that opened when one of the guards tapped his spear against the surface.

Without a word, the guards entered the castle.

As castles went, this was the quietest place Harlow had ever been in. They saw no nobles, no servants, and no children as they walked through sparkling gemstone hallways. No one spoke, and after a while, the silence turned eerie.

The back of Harlow's neck tingled as they walked. Someone or something watched as they were escorted to the throne room. Mahogany doors opened without any prompting, and the guards sailed through, with Harlow's party behind them.

Two occupied iridescent thrones sat in the center of the room. One held a lean, pale man. The other a younger, almost identical version of the first. Beside the throne stood a familiar dark-haired woman.

Harlow almost stumbled. Desminda stood beside the second throne, her face a mask of indifference, but her eyes burned molten gold.

She was not happy to see them.

The man rose from his throne and stepped off the dais, his pale purple robes matching his strange eyes.

The guards stopped a few feet away and turned, each heading in opposite directions until they stood on the sidelines by the raised seating area.

"Queen Nova," the man spoke, his voice far deeper than Harlow expected. "What a pleasure to have you visiting my kingdom."

Nova offered a shallow bow. "Your home is beautiful, King Adama." She made brief introductions, keeping Shade's new royal status secret.

"It's a pleasure to meet everyone," King Adama said, his eyes lingering on Harlow before turning to the second figure sitting on the smaller throne. "This is my son, Prince Naiam."

Nova nodded in greeting. The prince dipped his head a fraction but did not smile.

"And you know the lovely woman standing beside him."

Nova smiled. "Indeed, I do. Princess Desminda, how lovely to see you again."

Desminda's eyes flashed just once, but she bowed her head. "Queen Nova. What a lovely surprise."

Harlow almost laughed at her borderline insolent tone.

Nova's smile sharpened. "I'm happy to see this visit is working out. Our visit to the Beast Kingdom uncovered many interesting events after King Leif hosted you."

Desminda's eyes widened a fraction. King Adama turned to Nova. "Oh?"

Nova nodded. "Desminda is a memorable figure," was all she said.

The prince's eyes flashed in anger.

"We are close to announcing a betrothal—"

"Father!" the prince hissed.

"Relax, Naiam. They are royalty. Your secret is still safe. Since they are the ones who encouraged Desminda's visit, you owe them some gratitude."

From the look on Naiam's face, he'd rather chew on rusty nails.

"There are still some contractual obligations to work out, but we look forward to joining our kingdom to hers."

Harlow noticed her sister did not bring up the fact that Desminda had no kingdom, but she watched as Nova's eyebrows lifted in surprise before her face settled into mild curiosity. "Oh?" Nova said. "How delightful. Weddings are always such wonderful reprieves in times of uncertainty."

Desminda looked like she'd swallowed something sour.

"I agree!" King Adama said. "And it is far past time that my son married and settled down." He smiled genially at them. "I am close to passing my crown to my son and would like to enjoy my grandchildren while I'm still at least a little spry."

Nova's grin sharpened into something almost feral. "How delightful! From what I know of Desminda, she would make a *wonderful* mother."

Harlow pressed her lips tight to keep from laughing.

The absolute last thing Desminda wanted was children tugging at her skirts, demanding her time. Imagining Desminda with spit-up in her hair was so far beyond anything she could imagine, Harlow had to look at her feet to keep the princess from seeing the amusement glittering in her eyes.

How far Harlow had come from being the girl who so ferociously defended her future queen to this person almost delighting in Desminda's annoyance. But she wasn't the same naive girl who deceived her way into the Virago. Harlow was a princess now, maybe soon a queen.

When she looked up, Harlow noticed Desminda's gaze resting on Shade, who carefully did not look at her. There was such a raw vulnerability in the look she gave him that it dried Harlow's amusement up and made her heart ache. While Harlow would never be as power hungry as Desminda, someone could not help the way they were raised. Desminda grew up knowing she would become the ruler of a powerful kingdom. That was her destiny.

Until, in the space of a few terrible moments, that destiny was unceremoniously ripped away from her, forcing Desminda to flee or die. Harlow had thought she'd lost everything too, until the moment she stepped into the Witch Kingdom, when her world opened into something larger than her, something borderline fantastical.

King Adama and Nova spoke for a while, but Harlow tuned them out, all her focus on gawking at the castle's lovely architecture and strange lines. Although they stood in a tower, it didn't feel like it, and that took great skill to attain.

"Please, allow Desminda to escort you to your chambers."

Harlow blinked in surprise and watched as the king gestured for Desminda to step off the dais. There was no way King Adama knew of their history unless Desminda had told him. He probably knew of Shade, as he was quite infamous as Desminda's protector and the former Thornewood queen's most loyal guard. But whether he knew of Nova's influence and their flight to the Shadow Kingdom when everything had gone so wrong was unknown.

Desminda brushed past them and headed toward the door, looking back only once to ensure they were following.

Nova slowed down until Harlow walked beside her. "Be careful," she murmured in an almost inaudible tone. "Something is amiss."

Harlow nodded. Nova discreetly squeezed her fingers and caught up to Shade. No one said a word until they reached the first room.

"Queen Nova," Desminda said, gesturing at the door. "These are your quarters."

Nova nodded gracefully and opened her door. Shade stepped inside, quickly scanned the room, and set her bag down beside the bed before stepping back out. "I will follow you to the other rooms, so I know where everyone is staying."

"We've placed you together," Desminda said. She gestured at two more doors, all next to each other.

"Then this is perfect," Nova said, her voice kinder than it was before. For the King to force Desminda to show them to their guest rooms like a common servant ... Harlow couldn't fathom why. His behavior was a slap in the face.

"Would you like to come inside?" Shade asked.

Desminda hesitated. Her eyes darted back and forth down the hall before she gave a hurried nod. Shade quickly opened the second door and ushered her inside.

The rest followed, Evara locking the door behind them.

Desminda hurried toward the window and pulled the curtains until the room plunged into gray dimness. "Light a lamp," she urged.

Evara quickly struck the flint until a flame appeared, tilting the oil lamp until the wick caught. When Desminda came into view again, her face was drawn with worry.

Harlow took an involuntary step toward her, reaching out before she caught herself.

"Sit down," Shade demanded, "and tell us what has transpired."

Desminda sank into one of the plush chairs and sighed, not bothering to straighten her skirts. Her head tilted back, exposing her golden throat. "There is something wrong here," she said hoarsely.

Nova gave Shade a meaningful look. Due to the volatility of Harlow's magic, she kept it tightly leashed most of the time. Her grandmother told her when she gained more control, she could loosen the reins, but until then, she had to be conscious of it at all times. It took a lot of Harlow's energy at first, but now it felt like second nature.

Curious, Harlow loosened her hold and sent a tendril of power out. Darkness slammed into her, flooding her magic, spiraling through all her senses.

Harlow gasped and froze, eyes forced open through no will of her own, willing her to see what had taken hold of the Crystal Kingdom.

"Harlow?" The voice was muffled and sounded like it was coming through a corridor.

A gentle shake on her shoulder, but Harlow couldn't move. Darkness suffocated her, its malevolence everywhere.

"She's not breathing," someone snapped.

A loud crack of sound and a stinging pain snapped her out of it. Harlow coughed and dragged in a ragged breath.

Nova was on her knees before her, hands wrapped around Harlow's hips. "Can you hear me?"

Evara's hand was still raised.

"Darkness," Harlow croaked.

Nova nodded grimly. "You seem unnaturally attuned.'

Harlow sank to the floor. Nova helped her down and dragged Harlow against her side. "Are you okay?"

"This place ..." Harlow shook her head. "It won't last much longer."

Desminda sighed. "I felt it as soon as I passed over the border, but I couldn't escape." The aggravation in her voice almost made Harlow laugh.

"You're trapped here?" Shade asked.

"And betrothed apparently," Desminda said dryly.

"You sense the magic, too?" Nova asked.

Desminda absentmindedly rubbed her chest, right in the spot the Darkness had once struck her. "I, too, am unnaturally attuned." She grimaced. "The Darkness has sought me out for months. I've been able to fend it off, but every moment I spend here weakens my ability to keep it away."

This was both good and bad news. Desminda wasn't possessed. The only dark magic Harlow sensed on her was that tiny spot in her chest, and she suspected Desminda might be able to heal herself. Harlow wasn't the only one who came into her magic untrained. While Desminda had always known about the powers she possessed, she grew up in a kingdom where magic was considered abhorrent and had never learned how to utilize her powers in the proper way.

But Nova was here now, and maybe she could help Desminda. Her grandmother wasn't the deposed queen's biggest fan, but if Desminda was one of the keys to destroy the Darkness, Queen Moira wouldn't hesitate to guide her.

"If we take you back with us, King Adama may see it as a declaration of war," Nova said.

Desminda nodded wearily. "His son is not unkind and suspects something is wrong with his father, but he is too loyal to question his behavior."

"This kingdom is too close to Thornewood to not be affected," Shade mused. "Have you heard news of your queendom?"

Desminda's jaw tightened. "Covered in true darkness. No

one who goes in comes out again." A tear slipped down her tanned face. "I fear my birthright is no more."

"And the Rose Kingdom?" Nova asked.

Desminda swallowed. "Celestine slipped through the border. Rumor is she is ... not herself. The Rose Kingdom is also shrouded in the same darkness." She ran a trembling hand over her face. "The Light Kingdom still stands."

Nova's shoulders slumped in relief. They were working with the same intel, then.

"That leaves the wolves." Shade's expression was grim. "Almost half the kingdoms of Lunamoor are covered."

"The Darkness doesn't like my magic," Desminda croaked. "It has never said so, but it recoils every time I use my healing power." Her lips curved in a feral smile. "I think its influence lessens, but King Adama has banned me from using my power."

Evara frowned. "Why?"

"He said it frightens people."

Nova snorted. "If that isn't an indicator he's been influenced, I don't know what is."

She rose from her spot on the floor and offered Harlow a hand up. "We will meet them for dinner this evening and discuss an alliance."

At Desminda's alarmed look, Nova smiled. "We must pretend to know nothing. But it doesn't mean we have to tell King Adama the truth about anything." She gave Desminda a curious look. "Do you care about the prince?"

Desminda's cheeks colored. "As a friend. He does not deserve to come to harm over his father's decisions."

Evara dug in her pocket and tossed Desminda one of the charms. "Then put this around his neck and warn him to never take it off."

Desminda studied the charm, frowning, before tucking it into her pocket. "Do you have another?"

Evara nodded. "Yes, but they appear to favor low-cut dresses in this kingdom, and you do not want to draw the king's attention to it. If you can break away in a few hours, return to our quarters. I'll affix the charm to a strip of leather for you to wear on your ankle until we can return to the Witch Kingdom."

Desminda grimaced. "I don't think Queen Moira will welcome me back." An apology lingered in her eyes.

Harlow's heart thawed some more when she noticed the look. "She's the one who suggested we bring you back."

Desminda's eyes widened in surprise. "Truly?"

Nova nodded. "You must leave now. You've been inside for too long, and the servants are bound to gossip if you continue to dally."

Desminda paled and rose to her feet, hurrying toward the door.

"And we demand new bed linens!" Nova shouted, wincing in apology. "And hot water for baths!"

"Yes, Queen Nova," Desminda said meekly, a dimple in her cheek appearing as she struggled not to smile. "I'll fetch it at once." She wiped her expression and fled the room.

Harlow sank onto the bed. "Everything is a mess," she groaned.

Nova laughed. "The kingdom is not lost to darkness, so all hope is not lost." She flopped next to Harlow. "But we must watch every word we speak when we are outside of these walls."

Everyone nodded in understanding. "How soon can we return to the Witch Kingdom?" Evara asked.

"I'm hoping by tomorrow. The king will most likely not agree to an alliance unless he's trying to betray us. Once we work those details out, we can go through the portal. In the meantime, we need to figure out how to break Desminda's betrothal." Nova let out a sigh. "I wonder if the prince will be devastated."

Shade snorted. "Men usually are when Desminda spurns them."

Harlow laughed. "She seems ... better."

"Being chased across kingdoms by an entity hellbent on your destruction and then getting forced into an unwanted marriage is enough to humble even the most arrogant," Evara murmured.

Everyone fell silent at her words.

"True," Harlow said after a long moment, making everyone laugh.

A rapid knock on the door silenced their conversation. Nova rose.

"Your Majesty," a young voice said from the other side, "King Adama wishes to let you and your party know dinner will be served promptly at six. I will be here to escort you, then."

"Thank you," Nova said. "We will be ready."

Her footsteps faded away.

"Tonight, we must be vigilant and vague. No, we have not heard any news. No, we do not know Magnus's whereabouts. No, we do not know any more than anyone else. Are we clear?"

Nods all around.

Nova's smile this time was faint. "Good. And if anyone asks for Shade, do not tell him he is staying in my quarters."

Shade grinned and shooed them all out. Harlow clucked her tongue in dismay but couldn't stop her grin from shining through.

Her sister was finally happy, and that made Harlow happy, too.

It was about time.

CHAPTER THIRTEEN

NOT UNDER THE INFLUENCE. JUST A JERK

Looking at King Adama gave no hint that he was under the influence of anything nefarious. Not like the Beast King.

It wasn't too big of a leap to assume the king was working with the creature voluntarily, a fact that made Harlow sick to her stomach. Knowing what she knew, she wondered, not for the first time, how someone could agree to give the creature anything. Her sister would say what she always said, "Power corrupts."

Harlow wasn't dumb, but she still had trouble wondering why. If someone was a king, they weren't dumb either. King Adama had to know this thing's only goal was to destroy everything. Did he somehow naively assume the Darkness would spare his people?

Could he truly be that stupid?

Shade would say absolutely. But if King Adama was, how in the world had he been crowned?

Harlow sighed. The world's problems were not hers to solve, especially not at the world's tensest dinner party.

She sat on Nova's left. Evara stood behind them, her posture rigid and her eyes straight ahead. Harlow didn't doubt for a moment that nothing escaped her notice. Shade stood directly behind Nova, a fact that had bothered Harlow to no end. Shade was the current Shadow King. He should be sitting at her side. Earlier, Nova had opened her mouth to defend her position, but Shade had interrupted, saying simply, "I serve my queen no matter what position I hold. Wherever she tells me to go, I will go. Whatever she tells me to do, I will do."

Harlow barely held down her annoyance, but his statement was so romantic it made her want to gag. It had served to shut her up, though, which was what Nova and Shade both wanted.

The King sat at the head of the table and to Nova's right. Prince Naiam sat to the king's right, Desminda next to him.

She looked resplendent, dressed in the jewel tones the Crystal Kingdom favored, the lavender gown almost glowing against her dark skin. Her black hair was piled atop her head in numerous elaborate braids, the tresses decorated with crystals that flashed blue under the warm candlelight.

Harlow had barely held her gasp in when she first beheld Desminda. *Luna* stones. The former Thornewood princess's entire head was dotted with Luna stones. What a shameful display of power, considering other kingdoms still could not access their magic. Their eyes met across the table, Desminda's heavy with regret and Harlow's no doubt flashing with fury.

Nova's fingers reached for Harlow's under the table, and she gave them a soft warning squeeze, informing Harlow her face was showing too many of her emotions.

Harlow ducked her head and steadied her breathing before she looked up again. King Adama, like most royalty, was oblivious to Harlow's inner turmoil, focusing instead on the banal conversation he was currently having with his son about stalled trade from the Rose Kingdom.

Harlow almost scoffed. *Trade was stalled because everyone was probably dead,* she wanted to scream. She took heart in

Prince Naima's slightly befuddled expression as he spoke to his father, as if he thought the same thing but was too scared to address the elephant in the room.

It wasn't long before the king turned his attention to Nova.

"I assume you're here for an alliance," the king said matter-of-factly.

Even Harlow knew this was an egregious breach of protocol. There should be at *least* half an hour of polite banalities before someone broached the actual topic of conversation, followed by another twenty minutes of hemming and hawing and attempts to politely change the subject before veering back onto topic and *finally* hashing things out, or at least delaying a resolution until a committee was formed to further beat the subject to death.

For King Adama to jump right to the heart of the matter was both concerning and a little refreshing. Harlow wasn't sure how to feel about the situation they were in, and part of her wanted to applaud the fact that they might escape dinner in less than three excruciating hours, while a larger part of her wondered if this approach was about to go awry for everyone very quickly.

Nova's polite smile faltered, and Harlow knew she was wondering the same thing. "Yes, but I am here as a representative of both my kingdom and the Witch Kingdom, appointed by Queen Moira herself."

His eyebrows went up in polite but feigned surprise at the revelation. King Adama had known about their visit before they arrived, showing he, too, had his fair share of spies within Queen Moira's kingdom. Harlow would ask her grandmother about that once this was all over. Were spies to be tolerated or obliterated? It seemed, perhaps, a little of both.

"And what assurances does the Witch Kingdom bring to the table to secure our aid?" King Adama sipped on his third glass of ale and offered Nova a bland smile.

Her sister's fingers tightened around Harlow's.

"We bring powerful magic users," Nova said, her voice an octave lower than normal. She bristled with internal rage, though Nova's face remained perfectly impassive. "Can your kingdom say the same?"

King Adama's smile froze. "We have no need to brag about our mage's power when our kingdom holds a large portion of the Luna stones."

Nova grinned, showing a few too many teeth. "Witch magic has no need for the stones."

Harlow blinked in surprise. Was that true? Harlow had been in training for well over a year now, but it felt like there was still so much she didn't know. Her grandmother had never once mentioned those stones, so perhaps it was. Yet one more thing she'd need to ask later.

King Adama's eyes flickered. He hadn't known either. Interesting.

"With our power and your stones, I believe we have a good chance of creating a formidable force to fend off the approaching Darkness, don't you, King Adama?"

Prince Naima's face paled. Desminda's eyes narrowed as she watched the queen.

The king steepled his fingers and leaned forward. "Have you thought about allying with the creature?" King Adama said.

Nova sucked in a breath, but the king raised a pale hand.

"Hear me out. The creature seeks the source of magic, does he not?"

"I wouldn't know what it seeks," Nova said cooly. "All I see is what it destroys."

"We've taken something from it, and the creature only wants it back."

Nova tilted her head like a cat about to pounce. "My question is, how would you know what it wants?"

Prince Naima looked positively ill. His mouth gaped like a fish as he watched his father. For the first time, the prince seemed to notice what they all knew. The king was already in over his head and didn't care whom he took down with him as long as he gained what he was promised.

The pale king smiled, an unnerving expression that sent a chill down Harlow's spine. How could she ever be queen when she would have to deal with people like this? People who only cared for their own wants and needs, even when they ruled an entire kingdom of people.

Her sister smiled back, even as Harlow felt the tension in Nova's body. She was the kind of queen Harlow wished she could be, but how did one learn to face monsters without blinking?

"Do you believe in evil, Queen Nova?"

Her sister scoffed. "Of course I do. I've seen it many times during my life."

King Adama toyed with his wine glass. "I do not. Everyone wants something. Who am I to begrudge someone what they seek?"

"Even if what they seek will make countless people suffer?"

"The Darkness seeks magic, Nova. It wants its power back, power stolen by the golden-eyed heirs."

Desminda's brow furrowed.

Harlow's breath caught. She knew only one golden-eyed woman in her entire life, and that woman sat directly across from her.

Prince Naima stilled, his expression morphing from dismay to outright horror. "Father—"

The king raised his hand again. "Thornewood stole the creature's body and forced its magic—its life force—into the stones hidden underneath their mountain."

Desminda's eyes went wide as she realized what the king

spoke of. The Luna stones—Thornewood's magic source—possibly contained the creature's stolen magic.

Nova stiffened. "This cannot be true. The stones have always held Thornewood's magic. It is the source of much of the magic in all the lands of Lunamoor."

King Adama nodded. "Stolen from the creature prowling our nightmares."

Harlow could see Nova's mind working. "The Darkness already possesses the stones, does it not?" she asked. "It controls Thornewood, so it already has what it desires. You have no bargaining chip."

Most of the stones were inside the kingdom the Darkness currently ruled, so Nova's point was both valid and *interesting*. If the creature had already gained what it sought, why was it still so intent on seeking the golden-eyed heir?

The king's face darkened. "It seeks revenge on those who stole its promise."

"You sound like the creature's tool," Nova said.

Behind them, Shade shifted. Harlow didn't dare look, but she knew the man well enough to know his hand had drifted closer to his weapon as he prepared for the worst.

"If you were kept imprisoned for thousands of years, stolen from, and defiled, wouldn't you want revenge upon those who subjected you to such treatment?" King Adama snapped.

"I am not immortal, nor am I evil," Nova remarked. "Thornewood is a loss, its people either dead or beyond our help."

Desminda jerked at the revelation. Harlow sent her a warning look and shook her head once.

"If the creature agrees to stay within the confines of Thornewood, we will not attack."

Harlow jerked her attention to her sister. What was she doing?

King Adama laughed. "It will not agree to such a one-sided bargain."

"One-sided?" Nova tilted her head. "How so? It regains its power and the territory it claims was taken from it. You are welcome to give the Darkness the stones your kingdom possesses."

"You've forgotten about the heir."

Prince Naima stood. "Father, you are speaking of my betrothed!"

King Adama flicked his hand at his son. "Do you honestly think I'd allow someone who could not maintain control of their own kingdom to sully our bloodline?"

Prince Naima paled.

"She is here while we wait for the Darkness to collect her."

Desminda rose, clasping her trembling hands before her. "I'm a prisoner," she said quietly. "This was your intent the entire time."

Desminda had unwittingly delivered herself like a gift to the Kingdom of Crystal. She sent a pleading look to Nova, who did not look at her.

For the first time, Harlow wondered if her sister was so hard-hearted as to leave Desminda to her own devices and defy the Witch Queen. Her face was so ... impassive, so uncaring.

Harlow shook herself from those maudlin thoughts. No. Nova knew what was at stake. They needed Desminda. Even if the Darkness only planned to kill her for what her family had done long before she was ever born, the point remained that it wanted her.

Even if she turned out to be only a chess piece in this terrible game, any advantage they could obtain, Nova would take.

Before the queen could speak again, a massive boom shook the castle. Glass shattered around them. Shade swore and dove for Nova, ripping the queen from her seat, covering her body with his.

Harlow's arm almost jerked from the socket as Evara did the same, clutching Harlow to her chest as she rolled the princess underneath her.

"Shh," Evara snapped when Harlow opened her mouth to scream. They'd never been pressed this close together. Evara's fingers dug into Harlow's upper arms, and her braid lay against her neck, the dark hair soft and silky. Harlow swallowed hard and lay perfectly still, breathing in Evara's deep, exotic scent.

The metallic hiss of a sword being drawn from its scabbard caught her attention.

"It's Shade," Evara whispered. The guard's eyes darted around as the room continued to rumble. King Adama yelled something, but the sound was drowned out by a ferocious roar.

Above her, Evara stiffened. She leaned down and whispered in Harlow's ear. "Can you get Desminda?"

Harlow jerked her head in a nod. She wasn't sure she could, but she'd try her best.

"Good. Take her even if she fights you. Meet us back in Nova's quarters."

How they'd all get there, Harlow had no idea, but Evara wouldn't tell her to do something if she didn't have a plan. "Okay," she whispered.

Evara rolled off and pressed a dagger into Harlow's palm. "It's not an axe, but it will serve you well." Their eyes met in the shadows. "Be careful."

Harlow nodded and came to her knees, eyes darting around as she studied the damage.

A scream shattered through the room. Desminda.

"Let go of me!"

Harlow lurched to her feet, cursing the stupid dress tangling around her ankles. What she wouldn't give to be in pants again.

She picked her way around the rubble and ruined dinner that had slid off the table, ducking to stay level with the table and avoid the king's notice.

"Father! She is a royal. You cannot simply—"

A crack of fist against flesh. A horrified gasp.

"I AM KING!" Adama screamed.

Harlow stopped at the corner edge of the table. Once she stepped around, they would notice her. But she needed to get Desminda and get out of this room.

She stepped forward just as Darkness poured in through the broken windows and vents.

CHAPTER FOURTEEN

THE DARKNESS ARRIVES

The king noticed the presence first, completely ignoring Harlow's presence as she hurried toward Desminda.

"My lord," he breathed, falling to his knees as shadows coiled around them.

Shade loomed behind him, dust in his dark hair, a sword gripped tight in both hands. Harlow saw the indecision on his face, the knowledge that if he raised the blade and harmed the king, he would commit regicide, a crime punishable by death.

"No," Nova croaked. "Shade." The queen was on her feet, blood dripping down one side of her head.

Harlow's fingers wrapped around Desminda's arm. "Come with me," she whispered.

Desminda stepped closer to Harlow.

"No," Prince Naima begged.

The Darkness touched Harlow's arms and cheeks, oily and malevolent. Screams sounded outside the doors of the dining room.

"You may come with us, prince," Nova said hoarsely. "But if you do, you will fall under my reign. Your father is corrupted. Know you may never see this kingdom again."

The prince's stricken face turned toward Nova. He swallowed once, looked at Desminda, then at his father.

Darkness swirled around the king, some soaking into his skin, darkening the pale blue veins into a pulsing ebony.

"Your will be done," the king whispered, his head still bowed.

Prince Naima nodded once, grief shining in his eyes. Harlow tucked the dagger into her belt, grabbed both of their arms, and started running.

She'd worry about the propriety of manhandling royalty later.

"Shade!" Nova called.

Harlow didn't look behind her. "The king won't be distracted for long. Don't stop."

They burst through the doors, jerking to a stop at the destruction of the hall. Parts of the ceiling had fallen, littering the stone floor with massive chunks of plaster and wood. Priceless tapestries lay destroyed on the floor, and expensive paintings lay cracked and ruined.

Prince Naima made a sound of distress.

"Material wealth won't save your life," Harlow barked. "Follow me."

She took off at a brisk jog, careful to avoid sharp rock edges and nails, hissing as her skirts snagged on everything. The sound of footsteps behind her spurred her on.

"It's the rest of your party," Desminda said quietly, her breathing ragged as she tried to keep pace with Harlow yet failing.

"Thank the gods," Harlow muttered.

What should have taken less than a minute felt like it dragged on forever, but they finally reached their quarters. Harlow finally looked and spotted Evara picking her way through the rubble, followed by Shade and Nova, the guard holding the queen by the elbow as she, too, struggled with her blasted skirts.

Nova lifted her hand and made a series of complicated gestures.

Recognizing the magic, Harlow pulled Naima and Desminda behind her. The beginnings of a portal glittered before them.

"STOP!" A voice roared.

"Definitely don't stop," Harlow breathed, watching as her sister's mouth moved, chanting the ancient words to open the travel portal.

Shade grunted and swept Nova into his arms before taking off at a full hurtle. Evara reached them first. Her vest was torn in several places, and blood dripped from a wound on her arm. She offered Harlow a feral grin, but her smile dimmed when she saw Prince Naima. "You picked up a stray."

Naima snorted, the first sign of humor he'd shown since this entire thing had started.

"If my choices are to live or die, I hope you will not judge me for choosing to live," he said, bowing his head to Evara.

The guard's eyes narrowed. Her response was a tired grunt. Desminda stood quietly, watching the portal form. Her golden eyes were tired, and her posture slumped.

Shade reached them a few seconds later, carefully setting Nova down.

"Is the king still alive?" Evara asked.

A chilling, sibilant voice hissed through the ruined hall. *"There you are, golden-eyed queen."*

Desminda froze. The hair on the back of Harlow's neck rose. She'd recognize that voice anywhere.

"Don't look," Nova warned, but Prince Naima's eyes

widened at seeing his father's face. Black veins pulsed in King Adama's cheeks, flowing down to his neck, and the whites of his eyes had disappeared into complete darkness.

"Father?" Prince Naima shouted.

"*A worthy servant you will be, prince,*" the thing occupying his father said. "*Hand over the false queen, and I shall allow you to live.*"

Nova's mouth worked as she struggled to open the portal. Harlow's heart pounded in her chest, her throat clicking with fear. Her fingers tightened on Desminda's arm.

"Let me go," Desminda whispered. "If I am the only thing it wants, you're better off doing as he asks."

"No," Shade snapped.

"*Your father will return to you when I am finished with him,*" it continued. "*And perhaps, you should also like to serve me, princeling.*"

Prince Naima took an involuntary step back.

"Your father will never return," Evara whispered urgently. "Not like he was before. He serves the Darkness. You heard him at dinner. It will not stop until it devours everything." Her eyes shot to Nova, who'd broken out into a cold sweat as her fingers moved in that strange, repetitive pattern.

The portal finally coalesced into a hole of glittering darkness, different from anything that creature had created. This was cold, dark magic, but never evil. It was the magic of creation, for everything starts in darkness and ends the same way.

"Go," Nova croaked.

Harlow didn't hesitate. She let go of Desminda and shoved her hard, straight into the portal. Desminda screeched and toppled over, the portal sucking her straight into wherever Nova had directed it to go. Prince Naima's jaw dropped, but Harlow didn't give him a chance to react either. She shoved the prince harder than she had Desminda before Evara reached to do the same thing to her.

Shade also reached for her, but Harlow was already running. As his fingers grabbed for her arm, Harlow twisted and poured all her strength in shoving him away. Shade swore, stumbled, and fell into the portal.

But Harlow's intention was not to follow. She ran, not toward the portal, but to her sister. Magic rumbled in her veins. Not the cool, steady witch magic, but the destructive, world-rattling power of her father's.

Nova's eyes went wide. "Harlow. No!" But she couldn't do a thing. If she broke her concentration, the portal would close, trapping them in the Crystal Kingdom.

But Harlow was past listening and staying quiet. A scream tore from her throat as magic ripped from her body, straight toward the king. Underneath her feet, the ground fractured, splitting open as she focused every bit of it on the possessed king.

King Adama's eyes cleared for a brief second, widening in alarm, as the castle above cracked. Massive hunks of stone fell from the ceiling, smashing to the ground, sending deadly shards of shrapnel in all directions. Her sister hissed, throwing up a shield around them, but Harlow shoved Nova's power away.

She controlled the earth. It would not harm her.

From above, an enormous piece of one of the castle turrets plunged toward the ground. Harlow caught it with a flick of her finger and sent it sailing straight toward the king. Even through the noise of the world tearing apart, Harlow heard his grunt and the cracking of bone. Blood sprayed in all directions as King Adama died.

Nova sucked in a sharp breath. "Oh Harlow," she breathed.

Shadows brushed against Harlow's skin, not those of the creature, but Nova's gentle guardians. They lifted her from the ground and carried her toward the portal, gently pushing her inside.

Seconds later, Harlow was tumbling through infinite darkness.

CHAPTER FIFTEEN

SECRETS

Nova came seconds behind her, reaching for Harlow the moment she tried to stand.

"Wait," she urged.

Shade stalked toward them as Nova closed the portal. He stopped, jaw tight, and scanned them from head to toe. Nova helped Harlow up and pulled Shade close, whispering what Harlow had done.

His eyebrow lifted, but he said little about it, only, "We cannot tell Prince Naima. He deserves to know of his father's death, but not that it came at Harlow's hands."

"Agreed," Nova said quietly. Her sister studied her, and Harlow squirmed under her perusal. "Why?"

There were a million ways she could have answered the question, but none of them were as true as what she finally said. "He was corrupt and weak, and he would not have stopped until we were dead."

Shade let out a heavy breath. "While all that may be true, you are extremely fortunate you were the only ones in that hall. Committing regicide is a crime punishable by death. It doesn't matter if he is weak or corrupt. One person cannot decide some-one's future based on their feelings."

Harlow wanted to feel sorry for what she'd done, but she couldn't. This thing had taken and taken from her and from the people she loved, and thousands of people suffered under its influence. One could not bargain with evil. Bargaining implied a negotiation between two parties. The Darkness had no inten-tion of keeping its promises. All it wanted was destruction.

Harlow nodded. She had no energy to argue, but she wouldn't apologize. Shade huffed a sad laugh and put his hand on her shoulder, squeezing gently.

"For what it's worth, I never wanted any of this for you."

Harlow blinked away sudden tears. Her childhood might have been poor, but it had love, and even though she hadn't been with her real family, it never mattered. Love was not an inconvenience, and it didn't matter whether blood was shared. She loved Nova and Shade with everything she had, and she'd loved her foster mother and father.

I never wanted this for you ... Shade's words whispered through Harlow's mind, regret shining in his eyes.

"I never would have met you if it hadn't," Harlow said hoarsely.

Shade blinked in surprise and did something he rarely had before. He pulled her in for a tight hug, pressing his cheek to the top of her head. "You are so much like your mother," he whis-pered against her hair.

A tear slipped down her cheek. "I very much would have loved to have known her."

Nova ruffled Harlow's hair. "Come. We don't have much time before your grandmother discovers we've returned." She frowned at their surroundings. "I meant to get a little closer to the castle, but sometimes the magic doesn't cooperate when I'm under pressure." She looped her arm through Harlow's.

"Remember, say nothing about your role in King Adam's death."

"Do I tell my grandmother?"

Nova visibly winced. Shade gave her a sympathetic look and shrugged. When Nova spoke next, her words were slow and halting. "I would never tell you to lie to your grandmother or your queen."

Shade chuckled.

"But," Nova drawled, "if your role in his death is revealed, it could cause great ... complications for Queen Moira." She exhaled. "There was no one else in the room and no one spying on us. Everyone was otherwise occupied with saving their own skin, so no one knows about this except for us three." Nova paused for a moment. "I will allow you to decide whether you wish to keep it that way."

Harlow rolled her eyes. "All you had to do was say yes. I'm not an idiot."

Shade burst out laughing. Nova shot him a dark look and sighed. "I know you aren't, but politics can be exhausting."

"Tell me about it," Harlow muttered.

Desminda, Naima, and Evara all sat against a massive tree, their faces drawn with exhaustion. Evara stood as they approached, favoring one leg.

Nova's face sharpened. "You're injured?"

Evara waved her concern away. "I landed funny on the trip back. No reason to worry."

Prince Naima rose, holding out a hand to help Desminda up. The princess accepted, her cheeks coloring prettily. She ducked her head, only to frown as she fruitlessly tried to wipe the dirt from her skirts. Harlow's heart lurched at their easy manner with each other. Desminda might insist she didn't have feelings for him, but many happy and fruitful marriages in Lunamoor had begun with friendship.

Harlow looked down at herself and winced. They'd all arrived home dusty and filthy, and none of their clothes were salvageable. Her grandmother wasn't one to react emotionally to much of anything, but she had this look she'd give when she was disappointed. This was one of Harlow's good dresses, and she knew she'd be getting one of those looks as soon as the queen spotted them.

"Prince Naima," Nova said.

The prince's pale skin was smudged with soot and dirt, but he still looked regal as he straightened and inclined his head.

"I'm so sorry to tell you this …"

His eyes closed briefly. "My father is dead."

Nova nodded. "The castle lies in ruins. Your father was struck by falling debris."

Prince Naima accepted this at face value, though Harlow felt Desminda's curious stare. His jaw tightened, and he lowered his eyes. "Despite what you saw today, he was once a great man."

Nova's expression softened. She reached and took his hands. "He was your father, prince. There is no need for you to justify his heart to us."

Prince Naima nodded. "I saw this coming. Little things at first. Odd things he'd say, but I never thought he would allow that thing in."

"Evil whispers seductively," Nova said. "Let us head for the castle. The world might look different once we've cleaned up and had the chance to warm our bones."

QUEEN MOIRA GAVE Harlow the look when she spotted their bedraggled party trying to sneak through the kitchen to avoid her eagle eyes. Unfortunately for them, the queen was going over next week's dinner menu with the head cook when they stumbled inside.

"It appears you have quite the story to tell," Queen Moira said, her eyes resting on Prince Naima.

The prince bowed. "I must apologize for my abrupt arrival. Things within my kingdom are not ... well."

One of her pale eyebrows rose. "From the look of you lot, I can only assume it's much worse than not well."

A faint smile appeared on the prince's lips.

Queen Moira leaned to whisper something in the cook's ear.

"At once," the woman murmured, hurrying away.

"Please," Queen Moira gestured, "sit for a brief spell. Hot tea and cookies will be served shortly. While you eat, I'll have the servants run fresh bathwater for each of you."

"Thank you," Nova said, making a beeline for one of the long tables. "We have much to tell you this evening."

"I'll ensure my schedule is clear. We will take our supper in my chambers this evening."

Harlow started. That was unusual. Her grandmother was usually all about the formality of a good, six-course meal, no matter what day it was.

At her look, Queen Moira smiled. "Unusual, yes, but I'm afraid I have news of my own. News I wish to keep from curious ears."

A servant arrived just then, holding a tray of cups with a small teaspoon of herbs inside each and a pot of hot water. Steam rose above each cup as she poured hot water inside, and Harlow inhaled deeply, hoping it was her grandmother's special blend of black tea and bergamot she loved so much.

As the herbs bloomed in the water, the sweet scent of bergamot rose. Harlow smiled and held the cup to her nose, inhaling deeply.

Her grandmother chuckled. "It's Harlow's favorite. If you can't tell," she added dryly.

Prince Naima sniffed curiously. "It smells wonderful. What is it?"

As Moira spoke to the prince about the tea, Desminda shifted in her seat. She hadn't said much since they arrived. Harlow watched her and realized Desminda was uncomfortable. A year ago, Harlow might not have noticed, but part of her training both as a royal and as a mage was paying attention, looking for body language to determine how someone was feeling.

A stab of empathy went through her as she realized. Desminda had nothing, even less than she had before. Now, all her marriage prospects were gone, though Harlow didn't think that was exactly the case—not with how close Prince Naima was sitting next to her—and the Darkness was hellbent on finding her.

The ruler of the Crystal Kingdom was dead, and Prince Naima had left with them. Harlow winced. Perhaps she hadn't thought things all the way through before she'd shoved him into the portal after Desminda. He could always return home, but there was no way to tell if his kingdom was still under the Darkness's control after his father's death.

Conversation moved to mundane things as they drank tea and ate the cookies another servant had brought them. But as time stretched, Harlow wanted nothing more than to sink into a hot tub, scrub her skin pink, and take a long nap.

At last, Queen Moira rose. "Sherissa will escort you to your rooms where a bath will be waiting for each of you." She nodded to Prince Naima. "I've taken the liberty of procuring clothing for you while we try to clean the ones you're wearing." They all pretended not to notice her wince when she scanned her eyes over the state of everyone's clothing.

Sherissa appeared as if out of nowhere and gestured for them to follow.

Finally, Harlow thought. She couldn't wait to take that nap.

CHAPTER SIXTEEN

RELENTING

Harlow never got the chance to lie down and rest. As she soaked in the tub, lost in thoughts about everything going on, a half-baked idea formed. She hurriedly scrubbed her skin raw and dressed, her hastily twisted braid slapping against her cotton tunic as she rushed to find Nova.

When she pushed through the doors to her sister's chamber, her mouth open to blurt her idea, she spotted Desminda, Shade, Nova, and Magnus, her father, gathered in the sitting area.

Harlow's mouth snapped shut when Magnus rose, and her heart squeezed.

"Father."

Magnus smiled and held open his arms—a good thing since Harlow was already hurtling toward him. He scooped her up and swung her around. "Harlow."

She'd never felt safer in her life than when she was in her father's arms. Magnus was a mountain of a man, looming over even Shade. His blond hair was longer than usual, and he smelled of the road and horse. Familiar magic pressed against her skin as she squeezed him.

He set her down and gently pushed her away from him,

keeping his massive hands on her shoulders as he peered down at her with bright blue eyes. They weren't Harlow's eyes. Close, but not the perfect cornflower blue of Marion's, like Harlow's were. Whatever he found on her face made him frown. "You've expended a lot of magic recently."

Harlow's cheeks colored. "Maybe we can speak of this later?" Desminda was pretending not to pay much attention, but her posture was far too alert. After everything, Harlow didn't trust Desminda as much as she once had. They might be on the same side for now, but it didn't mean they played for the same team.

Desminda had always looked out for herself, no matter how it might affect everyone else.

Magnus' brows furrowed before giving her a short nod. "After dinner?"

Harlow nodded. "I've missed you."

He brought her in for another hug. "I've missed you as well. Astrid is not far behind me. I expect she'll be here tomorrow."

"With Luci?" Harlow asked hopefully.

He chuckled. "With that angry beast."

She snorted. "He's only angry with certain people."

Magnus shook his head and took his seat again. Harlow perched on the edge of the couch next to him.

"Now tell us why you came running in here looking very un-princess-like," Nova demanded, amusement glittering in her eyes.

Seeing Magnus had made all her thoughts fall right out of her head. "Oh! I think we should go into Thornewood to investigate how far the Darkness's influence has reached. If we can get any citizens out, we should try."

A beat of dead silence before everyone except Nova started shouting over each other.

"That's insanity!"

"Do you want to get yourself killed?"

"Of all the insane ideas you've had, this one tops them all."

Nova locked eyes with Harlow and waited for the furor to die down. "I don't think it's a terrible idea," Nova began, only for the shouting to start up once again.

Nova let it go on for a little while before raising a hand and shouting. "Enough!"

When everyone fell silent, Nova sighed. "Our intelligence grows poorer every day, and some of our agents are presumed lost or dead. We are blind right now. Although we assume everyone in Thornewood is a loss, what if it's not true? If we could save them, shouldn't we try?"

Magnus rubbed a hand over his unshaven jaw, his expression troubled. "I don't like it. I'm amenable to traveling close to the border to see if we can gather any intel, but actually going inside?" He shook his head. "If we do go ahead with it, Harlow should not be the one to go. She's the only viable heir in Queen Moira's line."

Harlow bristled. "I think I should be the one to decide that."

Nova and Magnus laughed. Shade covered his mouth to hide his smile.

She slumped against the back of the couch. "Life was much easier when I wasn't a princess," she grumbled.

"But you are," Nova said. "You no longer control all of your decisions, as much as you may want to."

"Desminda, Shade, and I know Thornewood best," Harlow insisted. "We're the most qualified to go in."

Desminda shook her head frantically. "I do not wish to return there while that thing wrecks my castle."

Anger filled Harlow. "Thornewood is your land," she spat. "Do you not feel any guilt over someone else dying to save your kingdom?"

Desminda went scarlet. Silence fell in the room, but not

even Prince Naima defended her. Instead, the prince turned his head to watch her, a thoughtful look crossing his face.

"I—" Desminda swallowed. "I am afraid," she said, and sighed.

"We would all be fools if we felt no fear," Magnus said. "But inaction combined with fear makes a weak leader."

Desminda flinched at his words. She swallowed hard. "I do not wish to see my kingdom in ruin," she confessed. "It is hard enough lying awake at nights with only my imagination to tell me what is happening there."

"We will bring this to Queen Moira this evening," Nova decided. Her gaze landed on Harlow. "I think you and I should go. Magnus if he is not too tired from his journey. Shade, as well, and perhaps Astrid."

"Not me?" Desminda said.

"Not you," she confirmed. "Queen Moira has other plans for you. Ones we are not yet privy to."

Desminda ducked her head, but not before Harlow saw the relief in her eyes. Disgust filled Harlow's belly. How could she have ever wanted more from Desminda? The thought of how things might have gone had Harlow not discovered who Desminda really was sent a curl of anger through her.

And suddenly, after all this time, the thought of losing Thornewood didn't bother her as much as it once had. She'd left nothing behind there. No friends, no loved ones. Thornewood might have been her home for a time, but almost everyone she cared about was here in this castle. The others were not too far away, either inside of Nova's kingdom or on the way to them.

Knowing this did not cool her desire to see Thornewood freed, however. Every citizen in the lands of Lunamoor deserved freedom from a tyrant, and none of the other kingdoms were communicating with each other. Or at least not that she could tell. Three of those kingdoms were slowly being overtaken by darkness. The Kingdom of Beasts and the Crystal Kingdom were already touched by it. While they'd been able to free the Beast King, the Light Kingdom was still an unknown.

"Have you spoken with Lucien?" my father asked.

Nova smiled. "I have. He has not heard from Celestine since his defection to my kingdom, though he believes she was already under the creature's influence before he fled."

Magnus nodded. "She's either dead or completely overtaken."

Harlow winced. Celestine was a terrible person and had made their lives miserable, but no one deserved to die in such a horrible way.

"One less obstacle in Desminda's way," Evara remarked, a sharp smile on her face.

Her dark humor made Shade chuckle, even as Nova sent her a quelling look. Evara's lack of shame more than the comment made Harlow laugh.

"We have dinner in an hour," Nova announced, standing to shoo everyone out. "I'll see you in the dining room. No one is to bring up this idea to the queen. I'll be the one to broach it." Her eyes lingered on Harlow, who rolled her eyes and stood.

"Fine," Harlow groaned. "But it's a good idea. You all know it."

Nova snorted. "Go!" She frowned at Harlow's appearance. "And for the love of the gods, do something with that hair."

Harlow stuck her tongue out at her sister and scurried from the room.

A DEADLY SILENCE fell over the table later that evening when Nova broached the topic of infiltrating Thornewood to Queen Moira. Their entire party, including Harlow, bowed their heads, suddenly finding their roasted potatoes *very* interesting.

"You wish to send my granddaughter into certain death?" Queen Moira asked, though everyone sitting there knew it was not a question.

"I will be with her," Nova answered, her voice not betraying an ounce of fear. Harlow wished she had that ability because underneath the table, her knees were quaking.

"Ah." Queen Moira clicked her tongue. "So, you would drive one princess into certain death while following her inside to leave your own kingdom rulerless?"

"My kingdom would be taken care of," Nova said. "I've spent years making contingency plans, as every good ruler does." The last part of that sentence made Harlow bite her lip. An intentional barb at her grandmother, perhaps one she deserved.

Queen Moira snorted. "Harlow is not my only heir. While she might be the best one, if something were to happen to her, I have other people who will step up to rule."

"There is no need to justify anything to me," Nova said. "I will leave a king behind." An edged smile curled her lips. "But Harlow and I make a formidable pair. If there is anyone who could make it out, it would be the two of us."

"Just you two?"

"Evara, Shade, Magnus, and possibly Astrid who is due in soon."

Queen Moira's lips thinned. "Why must you take Harlow?"

"Grandmother," Harlow began.

Nova shook her head once, a sharp gesture that made Harlow close her mouth.

"My granddaughter can speak when she wants to," Queen Moira snapped.

This was going swimmingly. Harlow sent an apologetic

glance to Nova. "I am more familiar with Thornewood than anyone here."

"Except Shade," the queen said.

"Shade has no magic to speak of. Evara has never stepped foot in Thornewood. My father left the kingdom years before." She was the best one to go in. Harlow's magic was dangerous and powerful, and she'd stood against the Darkness once before. She could do it again.

"And Desminda?" the queen asked.

Desminda kept her mouth shut.

"You wished for her to be returned to your kingdom because the creature seeks her. We should not risk taking her inside." Harlow watched her grandmother's expression go from anger to annoyance and finally to resignation.

She would allow it, but Harlow knew she would pay for this when she returned.

If she returned.

CHAPTER SEVENTEEN

INTO THE HEART OF DARKNESS

Queen Moira relented, but warned them they would be under surveillance by the kingdom's most talented witches. No one argued the point. Harlow thought they were lucky they got as far as they did and was still surprised her grandmother had agreed.

Knowing Queen Moira, her decision was based on the benefits far outweighing the risk. If they knew what they were up against, they could attack it from within. So far, the creature had been insidious, slowly corrupting Lunamoor's most powerful in order to turn the kingdoms into chaos.

This raiding party had one major goal. Find Celestine and destroy her, leaving the creature without a body. It would weaken it temporarily, but it would give them time to regroup and find a way to destroy it permanently. During their absence, Queen Moira and the other trainers would examine Desminda's powers and attempt to determine if she really was the key to end this entire thing.

Magnus's presence was for another reason entirely. Magic in Thornewood and the surrounding kingdoms was still not free. According to Lucien, the Luna stones were slowly being corrupted, and he thought the reason might be the presence of the Darkness.

They filed back to Nova's chambers without anyone talking about it beforehand. Everyone knew there were many things to speak about, and if they were going into Thornewood, there was much work to be done before the trip.

"Cake?" Nova said, before the doors had even shut.

A chorus of agreement rang out, making Nova laugh. Queen Moira was a good queen, but she rarely had dessert at the dinner table. Nova released her shadows, her magic a cool breeze against Harlow's skin. "Find us someone who's amenable to fetching us dessert."

Her shadows bobbed and swept underneath the door.

Shade watched his new wife, an amused tilt to his lips.

She grinned back and kicked her slippers off before sinking onto the couch with a groan. Harlow did the same, scooting closer to her sister and leaning her head on Nova's shoulder.

Evara stayed by the door, one ankle crossed over the other, keeping a watchful eye on any comings and goings. Shade settled across from Nova. Magnus sat in the chair next to Shade, and Desminda took the smaller couch, curling her feet underneath her skirts.

Prince Naima had elected to eat dinner in his quarters this evening, giving Desminda a brisk farewell before disappearing to his rooms.

No one said a word about it, but from the way Desminda's face fell, his brisk dismissal stung.

"Maybe they'll bring honey cake," Harlow said, glancing at Desminda from under her lashes. It was Desminda's favorite and was popular in Thornewood.

A dimple peeked from Desminda's cheek. "That would be most welcome."

They smiled at each other, and Harlow's heart lightened.

She couldn't keep holding Desminda's upbringing against her. Someone who'd never experienced strife or heartache dealt with things differently than those who had. But Harlow's patience was beginning to run thin. Her intuition told her they were running out of time to join their kingdoms together to form an alliance to fight The Darkness, and they couldn't continue to wait for Desminda to conquer her fear over her power.

She hoped spending time with her grandmother would mold Desminda into the queen she might one day be. Harlow was not the same person she was when she arrived. While Moira might be family, it didn't mean she'd taken it easy on her granddaughter. The opposite was true.

These last few days were the most relaxing ones she'd had in months, and she'd almost died.

A slight knock sounded. Evara straightened, peered through the peephole, and opened the door, revealing a young woman with light brown hair. Nova's shadows danced around her hair. "Hello," she said with a deep bow before rising. She was a pretty thing, petite and fair. "Your ... friends bade me come."

Nova lifted a hand, and the shadows swept back into her skin. "Thank you." She leaned forward and, with a conspiratorial grin, said, "Is there any extra cake?"

The woman's eyes sparkled. "I'm sure I can find something in the kitchen."

"Thank you." Nova smiled. "Whatever you can spare would be greatly appreciated."

The woman nodded and swept back out the door in a hurry. In less than ten minutes, two other servants came in holding large silver trays. With a flourish, they lifted the lids, set them aside, and hurried out of the room without a word.

Harlow gasped when she saw the array of treats.

The woman from before came back in, dipped her head, and smiled. "I hope this will suffice."

"You are my *favorite*," Harlow breathed.

She laughed, but quickly covered her mouth. Nova raised a hand. "Please don't. You are free to express yourself in my chambers."

The woman blinked in surprise and dipped her head in acknowledgment. "Th-thank you."

"Tell us what you've brought. I recognize some of these, but there are a few unfamiliar treats."

She stepped forward and gave a quick description of each. Honey cake was one of the items on the tray. Desminda's eyes brightened when she spotted it.

"Thank you, very much. I'm sorry, I didn't catch your name."

"Terra."

"Terra. Wonderful. We appreciate this and will hide the trays if you need us to."

Terra smiled again. "That won't be necessary. I'll return in ... would an hour and a half suffice?"

Harlow snorted. "More like thirty minutes. The only thing left on this tray will be crumbs."

Nova shook her head in exasperation. "That will be perfect, Terra."

She curtsied and left as quietly as she'd arrived.

The door hadn't even clicked before everyone started reaching for the treats.

Nova barked a laugh when Shade and Harlow got into an elbowing match over the last chocolate cookie. When they'd finally settled down, Harlow was right. Nothing but crumbs rested on both trays.

"Gluttons," Nova said fondly.

"Sustenance before plotting how to save the world is a must," Evara said.

Nova rolled her eyes. "You all just had dinner." She daintily bit into her crunchy shortbread and chewed for a moment. "Let's talk about entering Thornewood first."

TWO HOURS LATER, and just as the sugar high was wearing off, everyone knew their roles for their entry into Thornewood. Desminda had slipped out an hour prior, pleading a headache.

But as they readied themselves to head back to their rooms, Queen Moira entered. Everyone but Nova jumped up from their seats and bowed when she entered.

Harlow's heart beat like a drum against her chest.

"Please sit down," the queen said.

Evara shut the doors as the queen walked over. To everyone's surprise, she kicked off her slippers and sank into the chair closest to the fireplace. Even at her age, she was still a beautiful woman, but tonight, as the firelight flickered over her face, faint wrinkles appeared at the edges of her eyes and lips. Exhaustion was evident in the bluish half-moons under her eyes.

"What did you decide?" she asked.

Nova went over our plans. The queen listened intently, nodding in the appropriate places. "Do you think you will find anything?" she asked.

"There's no way to tell," Magnus said. "Unfortunately, I do not have a Seer in my pocket."

Queen Moira's eyes tightened at the edges. "And mine has fallen into another deep sleep."

Harlow walked over to stand beside her grandmother, offering her support in the hand she laid on her shoulder. Her grandmother reached up and covered Harlow's hand with her own. She'd sworn to try to help her cousin, but so many things had happened, Harlow hadn't given it a second thought. Guilt speared her. Maybe they'd find something in Thornewood to help her, though it seemed unlikely.

"Please return my granddaughter home to me safely," Moira said desperately. "She is all that I have."

Nova reached over and touched Queen Moira's hand. "I swear to you, Harlow will be safe."

The queen nodded, stress lines bracketing the edges of her mouth. "Thank you." She rummaged through one of the pockets of her skirt and pulled out a small silver talisman. "I noticed your weariness when you use your travel spell."

Nova stilled, but Moira raised her hand. "Peace, Nova. No one else said anything about it." She reached over and dropped the talisman into Nova's hand. "It is good for a one-time trip back here for a party of up to five." Moira smiled faintly. "I believe the odds of a needed hasty exit are much higher this time. Since your shadows can't go near the borders, this is everyone's best option of getting away in a hurry."

Nova stared down at the talisman before nodding. "This is quite a gift. Thank you."

"I am the only one who worked on the spell. No one else knows it or knows what I've created. And no one will ever know." Moira lay a hand over her heart. "A gift from one queen to another who saved the most precious thing in her life."

Harlow squeezed her grandmother's shoulder gently.

Nova's voice was thick the next time she spoke. "It is not necessary, but thank you. Harlow is also precious to me."

Moira rose and smoothed her skirts before reaching for Harlow to draw her into an herb-scented hug. "Be careful, my darling. Remember who you are."

Harlow kissed her grandmother's cheek and stepped away. "I will see you soon."

"Be sure you do," Moira said, and slipped out of the room.

"I like her," Magnus said.

"I hope so," Nova said dryly. "Your daughter may one day rule in her stead."

Magnus didn't look so thrilled about that prospect, but he stayed quiet.

"When should we leave?" Shade asked.

"Three days should be enough time to prepare. I can't open the portal too close to Thornewood, or they may sense our presence."

"How do we know where is too close?" Harlow asked.

"I'll send my shadows out to gauge," Nova said.

Magnus's attention snapped to her. "What intelligence have you gathered by doing so?"

Nova shook her head. "I don't dare send them into the darkness, so I haven't sent them back since Thornewood plunged into shadow. I'm afraid I'm at the mercy of intel scouts."

"Who are not returning," Shade said grimly.

The room fell silent before Evara spoke. "I'll ensure everyone's weapons are sharpened and maintained before we leave."

"And I will take care of the horses," Shade added.

The doors thumped open, revealing a bedraggled and weary bard. She offered them a tired smile, swayed on her feet, and fainted dead at the threshold.

CHAPTER EIGHTEEN

BUSTED

"We aren't leaving tomorrow, are we?" Evara asked as they all stood around the bed, staring down at the bard. Astrid's red hair spilled like blood against the white pillow case, and her face was almost bone white. Whatever she'd gone through must have been bad because faint bruises dotted her face, collarbone, and arms, faded enough to tell everyone they'd been glorious when they first appeared.

Astrid had risked much to fight on their side. The bards went into hiding many years ago, hunted not only for their unique magic, but their unnatural ability to create music. Astrid was the only bard Harlow had ever met, but cryptic clues from Astrid led her to believe there were many more out there watching and waiting for their time to reenter the world.

"Grandmother is sending her best healer in," Harlow said quietly, her heart pounding against her chest. Astrid did not look well and hadn't moved an inch since Magnus had carried her inside the guest room, gently laying her underneath a thick quilt. Harlow didn't miss the tender way her father had brushed Astrid's hair away from her face as he settled her in, but she tucked her emotions away. Her mother was long dead, and it was none of her business. It didn't matter anyway. They'd all be dead if they couldn't figure this out, so Magnus should grab whatever joy he could find in life while he still could.

Shade glanced at Nova. "Do you know what happened?"

Her sister, still shaken, slowly shook her head. "The last time my shadows found her, she seemed fine. Whatever hurt her found her a few days ago. Perhaps longer."

A soft knock on the door revealed a petite blonde healer carrying a large basket that clinked when she walked. She hurried over to the side of the bed, carefully setting it on the table by Astrid's pillow. Several glass bottles filled with different color liquids were inside, and small wooden bowls spilled over with herbs. Harlow smelled lavender and vetiver, but there were a few things she didn't recognize. Healing wasn't one of her abilities, or at least not one of her main ones. Every witch could heal, but Harlow was much better at breaking things than fixing them.

Healing was Desminda's specialty. The princess stood beside Magnus, her brow furrowed and eyes glowing as she studied the bard through whatever way her abilities allowed. The healer glanced up at Desminda and watched the inspection before the princess exhaled and sucked in a ragged breath.

"Broken ribs," Desminda said, bending down to brush her fingers over Astrid's rib cage on the left side. "At least two." Her hands moved down. "Dislocated knee. Multiple contusions. She has a broken toe on her right foot." Tears shimmered in her eyes. "Broken finger, last one on her left hand, though it's healing better than the others. I don't think that injury happened at the same time as the rest." Her golden gaze swept upward, over Astrid's stomach and chest. "She's ... sick."

The healer blinked, her expression morphing from concern to urgency. "In what way?"

Desminda leaned closer to Astrid, peering at her chest. "Something in her lungs. Some kind of fluid."

The healer swore and rose to her feet before hurrying away.

Nova watched the door she'd disappeared from.

"Will she be back?" Shade asked quietly.

Desminda nodded. "Infections of the chest and lungs require … more. The healer probably thought her injuries were only physical, caused by trauma. She's probably fetching different herbs."

Magnus got on his knees beside the bed, carefully taking Astrid's hand in his own. Harlow swallowed hard and looked away, embarrassed by the twisting feeling in her gut. Nova's lips thinned when she realized what was happening, and she stepped closer to Harlow, twining her fingers in her own.

"Is there anything else wrong with her?" Harlow asked.

Desminda nodded. "Dislocated shoulder and a broken cheekbone." She sighed and straightened. "I do not know how she was able to walk in here."

"Bards possess unique magic and train for battle when they are children," Magnus said. "She wasn't safe until she arrived here, so she persevered."

The healer came back in, this time carrying three additional bottles. She pressed the back of her hand against Astrid's forehead and frowned. "Everyone should leave," she announced. "The healer princess may stay."

No one moved.

A flash of annoyance sparked in the healer's eyes. "We cannot be distracted. Everyone out." She made a shooing motion.

"I'm not leaving," Magnus rumbled.

The healer blinked, opened her mouth to say something, and shut it when Magnus's expression grew dark.

"Fine," she breathed. "But everyone else, out."

Nova finally nodded, and they moved as one. No one went back to their own chambers, instead filing back into Nova's.

"She'll be okay, won't she?" Harlow asked, curling on the couch and pulling her knees against her chest.

Nova settled close beside her. "She'll be fine. Two of the kingdom's best healers are with her."

"And my father." Harlow's voice sounded small.

A smile played over Nova's lips. "And Magnus," she agreed. Nova slung an arm over Harlow's shoulders and pulled her close. Shade and Evara stayed standing, dark guardians watching over them.

Hours must have passed before a knock came on the door. Harlow jerked awake first, but Shade had already opened the door, revealing an exhausted Desminda. Shade reached a hand out to steady her when she swayed on her feet, and she melted into his side. He swore and scooped her up.

"Is Astrid okay?" Harlow blurted, concern for the bard overriding her concern for Desminda's current state.

"She will be fine," Desminda whispered before her eyes fluttered shut.

Shade swore and opened the door, grumbling about the women in his life not knowing their limits.

Nova grinned and hooked her fingers into the crook of Harlow's arm. "I think it's time for everyone to rest. We will see Astrid tomorrow."

So tired she could barely stand up, all Harlow could do was nod and let her sister lead her back to her chambers.

Her dreams were full of dark things, shadows and whispers, and fire. She battled and battled until she couldn't lift her arm, and still darkness came for her, for everyone, for all the things she couldn't help but love.

When she woke before the sun the next morning, her eyes were full of grit, and her heart felt empty. How could she let others walk into certain death when all this started with Desminda's bloodline? She pressed her face into the palms of her hands and exhaled before rising from the bed.

Harlow dressed quickly, strapping her axes to each side of her body, and her sword to her back. She tucked the dagger her father gave her into her left boot and shrugged a warm jacket on before slipping from her room like a wraith.

The kitchens were cold and empty, the fire long extinguished. Harlow worked quickly, swiping a satchel from the hook and filling it with sausage and cheese and a loaf of yesterday's bread, before she hurried to the stables.

Luci wasn't hard to spot, the beast towering over the other mares. She snorted and stomped softly when she saw Harlow.

"Luci," Harlow breathed, reaching up to touch the mare's cheek. "Astrid is going to be okay. Thank you for escorting her."

The horse stilled, as if relieved. Knowing Luci, the horse understood every word Harlow said.

"I need to go to Thornewood. Are you up for it?"

Luci jerked her head once and stilled. Harlow patted her before reaching for the saddle. She made quick work of readying the horse and was about to climb on when the sound of a male's throat clearing made her freeze.

"I should be disappointed, but you are so very predictable," her father said from outside the stall.

Harlow's shoulders slumped as she opened the door, allowing him in. Magnus took one look at her and sighed. He offered her a hand. She stared at it, frowning.

"Take it and I'll help you up."

Harlow stared at it like it was a snake, making Magnus laugh. "I plan to accompany you."

She finally accepted the hand up and settled into the saddle. Luci shifted underneath her, but Magnus murmured something to the horse, and she settled immediately.

"Wait here," he said.

A few minutes later, Magnus appeared in front of Luci's stall, seated on another horse.

"Come. If we wish to leave without notice, we must go now."

Harlow gently nudged Luci forward.

Moments later, hooves thundered out of the Witch Kingdom toward Thornewood's darkness.

CHAPTER NINETEEN

GUARDIAN OF HER HEART

Nova's shadows wrapped around her ankles an hour later. Her sister's voice whispered in her mind.

Do not tell me you've gone off on a fool's errand.

Harlow winced. She'd rarely heard her sister's voice so sharp. *Father is with me.*

Nova said nothing for a moment. *At least he recognized your foolishness before you'd gone off and gotten yourself killed!*

Harlow didn't respond to that. *How is Astrid?*

She will live. Unlike my reckless sister.

Harlow sighed. *Father and I will be back as soon as we can.*

I am sending Shade after you.

He won't catch up.

You better hope he doesn't, Nova said ominously, her shadows slipping away into the soft morning light.

Magnus's chuckle brought her back to earth. "Nova caught up?"

"Yes," Harlow grumbled. "She's sending Shade."

Her father winced. "We better speed up then."

A begrudging smile tipped her lips. "That's the same thing Nova implied."

Magnus grinned and nudged his horse forward. "Come on, Shadow. Run like the wind."

Luci whinnied and shot forward like a shooting star without Harlow's urging.

Her hair blew away from her face like a golden streamer, and the first genuine smile she'd had in weeks stretched her lips. Riding on Luci was true freedom. With the wind in her face and the great beast underneath her flying over the earth, even the Darkness couldn't squelch her joy.

She wasn't sure how long they rode, but Magnus's horse tired out before Luci did. Her father held up a hand. "We will stop in a few minutes and rest. There's a town maybe ten minutes away where our mounts can get water."

Harlow followed behind him, and soon enough, civilization came into view a short time later. Relief filled her. It had been a while since she'd ridden such a long time on horseback, and her thighs and hips burned from muscle disuse.

People parted around Magnus like a break in a river as he rode through town, Harlow close behind him. He stopped at a small, two-story inn and tied their horses up, glaring at anyone who stopped to give Luci anything more than a quick look.

"Will she be okay out here?" Harlow asked.

Magnus chuckled. "She'll only be out here for a few minutes. Once we get our room, we'll move both horses to the stables." He patted her on the neck. "But even if she did have to be out here for any length of time, I suspect Luci could take care of herself."

Luci nudged Harlow's shoulder and nibbled at a stray curl. Harlow laughed and stroked Luci's face before following her father inside.

The place smelled of cut wood and fresh stew. She inhaled deeply, her shoulders dropping in relief.

The innkeeper was a burly man with a kind face who greeted them with a smile.

"One room," Magnus said, pushing a silver coin over.

The man's eyes narrowed as they settled on Harlow, disapproval pursing his lips.

Magnus grinned. "Relax, friend. She's my daughter."

The innkeeper didn't seem to take this at face value until he studied them closely. Then, seeing the remarkable similarities between them, he finally grunted. "Apologies. Sometimes, unsavory people come into my inn. I meant no offense."

Magnus lay a hand over his chest. "And no offense is taken. Thank you for looking out for my daughter."

The man nodded and pushed change over the desk. "Dinner is served promptly at six. Simple fare. Bread and rabbit stew tonight. Ale and wine. My wife, Martha, is the cook, and if you're kind to her, she might give you seconds on the house." He winked at Harlow and handed Magnus a key. "Stables are around the back. Check-out is nine in the morning, sharp."

"We will leave far before nine," Magnus said, taking both the key and his change. "Thank you."

He smiled and pointed upstairs. "You and your lovely daughter will be at the end of the hall. There's a bell for a bath. Service stops at eight."

Magnus lifted the key in acknowledgment. "Let's take care of the horses first."

They left Luci and the other mount happily munching on fresh hay and ventured upstairs carrying their meager belongings. Their room was clean and supplied with fresh linens and a sliver of soap and drying towels. A small window let weak light seep in, casting the room in odd shadows. Someone with a feminine touch had placed an ewer of fresh water on the dresser, two chipped glasses, and a large bowl with a small towel for hand washing.

"Nice place," Harlow remarked, reaching down to test the softness of the bed.

Magnus set his small bag down. "Nicer than usual." He chuckled. "I can recall some interesting places I've stayed during my travels. I slept with my axe under my pillow and a glass by the edge of the door to alert me to bandits."

Harlow glanced at him with alarm.

"Do not worry, daughter. I suspect our friendly innkeeper runs a tight ship."

She let out a breath of relief. "Good. We have enough to worry about without getting mugged."

"I agree." He motioned at her bags. "Get settled in and we'll get some more provisions. I took a small bag of clothing, but I didn't get the chance to raid the kitchens before I left."

Harlow chewed on the side of her lip. "Sorry," she murmured.

"Like I said before, I am not surprised. Putting friends and loved ones in danger is something your mother loathed, too."

"I would hope everyone loathes it," Harlow muttered.

Magnus lifted a powerful shoulder in a shrug. "You'd be surprised." When he didn't elaborate, Harlow set her things close to the edge of the bed by the window, washed off the worst of the dust with the ewer water, and re-braided her hair into some semblance of order.

MAGNUS SPOKE while they walked through town, pointing out certain things Harlow didn't notice. "This town is about halfway to Thornewood and close to the border of the Wolf Kingdom."

"We're still in grandmother's kingdom?"

Magnus nodded. "She will know where we are until we cross the border. Once we are in the Wolf Kingdom ..." he paused. "I believe we will be welcomed, but many things have changed over the years, and I can no longer be certain."

"Do you think they will recognize me?" Harlow asked.

Magnus smiled, sadness tinging the edges. "I do. The wolves are not like us. While they hold human forms, they are more in touch with their animal instincts than their human ones. They'll recognize you by scent. Do not be afraid if one approaches you."

"Easy for you to say. I've never seen a real wolf." She'd seen her fair share of coyotes, which she thought were wolves until Shade had laughed and educated her otherwise.

Magnus stopped at a colorful stall selling an assortment of cheese. The woman's eyes lit up when she spotted him, an appraising look appearing on her face when he bent to study the labels. Harlow was used to that look on women's faces when her father walked into a room, and she barely refrained from rolling her eyes when the woman approached him.

"Good evening. I offer free samples if there's anything you'd like to taste."

Magnus glanced up. "Not necessary. We're travelers, so we aren't purchasing for enjoyment. Only sustenance."

The woman's face fell. "You are not staying in town."

"We leave at first light."

Seeing her chance to get to know Magnus a little better fading away, the woman pointed to a crumbly cheese toward the middle of her display. "This will last the longest, then. It has a sharper taste and is a little drier than my other cheese. But it will travel well, if that's what you're looking for."

Magnus nodded. "Then we will take two."

The woman packaged everything up, adding a protective covering to the cheese and including a small wooden knife before she wrapped everything in butcher paper and handed it over. When Magnus reached for it, she moved the package away from his grip. "It's a shame you won't be here a little longer. I plan to close my stall down in half an hour."

Harlow didn't refrain this time. She let out a huff of laughter and moved one stall over, still within earshot.

"I am here with my daughter and do not plan to dally," Magnus said, not returning even a hint of the woman's attention. "I'm sure you understand." He dropped a coin into the woman's hand, retrieved the package, and came to stand beside me.

"I don't mind going back to the inn if you want to stay," Harlow said under her breath.

Magnus stiffened. "Absolutely not. First, I would not abandon you—"

"I'm eighteen."

Magnus huffed a laugh. "I still won't abandon you." He bent and murmured in her ear. "I have no interest in bed sport."

Harlow cringed. "Father," she groaned in embarrassment.

Magnus laughed. "Come. We need more bread and a few other provisions before dinner."

HARLOW AWOKE to a heavy weight on her chest and cold steel against her cheek.

"Scream and I will slit your throat," a soft feminine voice whispered in her ear when Harlow opened her mouth to do exactly that.

Harlow froze, her mind spinning with things she could do to save herself. Where was her father?

But as she mentally discarded every spell she'd ever learned, she realized the voice sounded familiar.

"Evara?" she hissed.

A wicked chuckle sounded before the weight lifted itself from her chest, and Harlow stared up at her leather-clad guard.

Harlow let out a disgusted sound. "I almost pissed myself!"

"It would serve you right," Evara said as she crawled over Harlow to sit on the edge of the bed. "What were you thinking?"

Harlow tugged the covers higher and glared at her. "I was thinking I don't want anyone to die."

Evara snorted. "Which is why we were all going together. So we could keep that very thing from happening!"

"How did you find us?"

Evara tossed the knife in the air, catching it deftly by the handle every time. "I have secrets of my own, you know."

Harlow glared at her. The only light in the room came from moonlight streaming in through the gauzy curtains. "Where's my father?"

"Downstairs. He's playing cards with some shady-looking fellows."

"So you decided to leave him to his own devices and come harass me?"

"Magnus has no need of a guard, Harlow. He could wipe those men out with a single look. But you were supposed to have more than feathers inside your head. Your father rode with you to keep you from getting killed. He wouldn't have abandoned us to go on his own quest."

"I would have found my way back."

Evara rolled her eyes. "Maybe. But what if you hadn't? Would you let Nova's shadows discover your demise and break your sister's heart?"

"I'm not sorry for it," Harlow snapped.

Evara paused the knife tossing and studied her. "Why do you think your life is worth less than mine?"

"It's not," she said sullenly, knowing Evara would taste the lie in the air.

"No, it's not," she agreed, "but you seem to think it is." Evara stood and began untying the stays on her leather vest.

Harlow froze. "What are you doing?"

"I need a place to sleep since someone forced me out of a perfectly warm bed in a palace to come find her." Evara arched an eyebrow at Harlow, let her vest drop from her shoulders, and kicked off her boots and pants until she stood in a long white tunic. With deft fingers, she unbraided her hair and shook her dark hair out until it was a wild mess around her face.

Harlow's mouth went dry. "We only have one bed."

Evara stared. "I'm well aware. Now shove over."

Harlow didn't move for a beat until one of Evara's dark eyebrows rose. She scooted over to make room for the guard who then sank into the soft mattress with a deep groan. "Your father should be back up in an hour or so. Get some rest." With that, she turned her back to Harlow and went still.

But Harlow's mind wouldn't shut down. She'd shared countless beds with Nova, but this felt different somehow. Her fingers itched to run through Evara's silky tresses. She longed to touch Evara's skin to feel if it was as soft as it looked—to know how the guard's calloused fingertips would feel against her own skin.

"I can almost hear you thinking," Evara said softly. She turned over to face Harlow, and all Harlow could do was thank the gods the room was dark so Evara wouldn't see the furious burning of her cheeks.

"Sorry. I'm having trouble sleeping."

Evara lifted her hand and cupped Harlow's cheek. Her breath caught, heart fluttering against her chest like a trapped butterfly. When she rubbed a thumb across her cheekbone, Harlow's eyes closed. Evara's touch was innocent, but Harlow's thoughts were anything but.

And when Evara moved closer and pressed her lips against

Harlow's, all thoughts flew right out of her head. Strong fingers worked through Harlow's braid until her curls were loose and fell down her shoulders.

"Your hair is a golden river," Evara said softly when she'd pulled away.

Harlow swallowed.

"You can touch me if you'd like." The guard smiled at Harlow's hesitation, but it wasn't a judging smile. Evara's look was open. Welcoming.

Harlow's fingers stroked Evara's jaw, her thumb stopping on her full lips. Evara's hand covered Harlow's, and she leaned forward to kiss her again. Harlow's hands moved to Evara's hair, thick and wild, silken tresses sliding over her arms like a waterfall.

When they finally broke apart, Evara gathered Harlow close. "It is not the right time."

Harlow stiffened, embarrassment raging through her veins.

Evara shook her head. "No," she said vehemently. "Do not do that. Your father is due soon, and we are walking into a battle we might not survive." She took Harlow's chin firmly, Evara's hazel eyes burning into hers. "When we do this, this war will be over. You and I will be alone. And I will not stop until you are screaming my name. Do you understand?"

Harlow blinked, every nerve on fire. "Um." She nodded. "Yes."

Evara smiled and pressed a last soft kiss against her lips. "Try to sleep. Dawn will come early. You are safe."

And even though Harlow's mind spun with scenarios and what ifs, Evara was warm and soft, and Harlow's eyes soon drifted closed.

CHAPTER TWENTY

A WATCHER

Morning came far too soon. Evara's warmth was gone when Harlow opened her eyes, a chill brushing against her skin from the poor insulation in the room. Her father had lit a candle that flickered in the room, highlighting his massive form as he quickly packed his bags.

He sensed her rousing and nodded to her when she sat up. "The horses are saddled and ready."

"Evara?"

Magnus fell silent a beat too long, and color rushed to Harlow's cheeks. Curse her pale skin. "She's in the stables awaiting us."

Harlow nodded and slid out of bed, quickly washing her face and neck before getting dressed. Her father stepped out of the room. "Meet me downstairs when you're ready."

She nodded and finished lacing her boots before re-braiding her hair into a tight plait. It took her less than a minute to gather her things, and when she was ready, she blew out the candle and followed Magnus.

When she spotted Evara in the stables, Harlow said nothing. Her tongue was tied, and nothing she thought she could say sounded right in her head. But Evara, as usual, was cool and level-headed.

She tossed Harlow a water skin. "Extra for today," she said quietly. "We don't know what we're getting into, so make sure you take it with you when we breach the shadows." Their fingers brushed as Harlow reached for it, making her breath catch. Evara winked before turning to mount her horse.

Harlow tied the water skin to Luci's saddle bag, and murmured greetings to the mare before she climbed on. The morning air held a humid chill, and Harlow shivered before reaching down to unpack her cloak. As the heavy cloth settled around her, she sighed and nudged Luci from the stable.

No one talked for a long time. The town still slumbered, and the only noise was their mounts' hooves as they rode away. A fog had settled all around them, casting an unearthly pall over the small village. Clouds of mist left fingers of dew clinging to Harlow's skin and hair, and she shivered as she nudged Luci to go faster.

"Don't ride too far," Magnus said. "If we lose sight of each other, we may never find our way."

Harlow drew back, but the nape of her neck tingled as they rode. Something about the weather felt unnatural, and she sensed someone watching their progress.

"I feel it, too," her father said quietly. "Just keep riding. It will pass."

Evara rode beside them, her face tight and pale. She said nothing, but her eyes were sharp, sliding back and forth across the horizon in search of whatever might be hunting them.

Harlow's neck hurt from how stiffly she held herself, her knuckles whitening as she held tightly to the reins. She didn't know how long they rode through the oppressing fog, but it felt like hours.

Soon, all evidence of civilization faded away, and they rode on a poorly made dirt road. Tall trees lined each side, the forest cover so heavy, Harlow couldn't see anything through it. Any number of things could be hiding in there waiting to ambush them, but Magnus didn't seem worried. Alert, yes, but not alarmed.

Eventually, a sliver of sunlight broke through the fog. Harlow let out a slow breath. Evara's shoulders dropped, and Magnus sighed. Luci sped up, heading toward that sliver like it was her salvation.

"I know," Harlow murmured soothingly, patting the side of the mare.

Eventually, the fog was a distant memory, and the road was covered with dappled sunlight. The temperatures warmed enough for Harlow to slide her cloak off, though there was still a chill in the air, but it was comfortable enough that she rolled up her sleeves.

"What was that?" Evara finally asked.

Magnus shook his head. "Unfamiliar magic. Not Thornewood, but someone was definitely keeping tabs on us."

"I didn't feel any strong magic when we were there," Harlow said.

"They must have stayed far enough away to escape our notice," Magnus said. He was frowning and looked lost in thought.

"Do you know anyone powerful enough to cast something like it?" Evara asked.

Magnus shrugged. "I used to. Many witches could, but this magic doesn't feel like a witch. If I had to guess, I'd say it was a sorcerer, but I haven't seen one in a decade. Many died after magic fell in Thornewood. Those who didn't kept their magic hidden, if they still had any."

"Why were they watching us?" Harlow wondered aloud.

"Few people travel toward Thornewood these days," Magnus observed.

Indeed, he was right. They'd passed a few travelers on the road, but none were heading the same way as their party. A few had stopped to offer warnings about the direction of their travel, and Magnus had thanked them without confirming their actual destination.

But as the distance to their destination grew closer, they found themselves alone on the long stretch of road.

"We'll be there by dusk," Magnus said, his voice sounding too loud in the oppressive quiet. "We are about to pass through the heart of the Wolf Kingdom. Stay close and do not engage."

Harlow didn't know much about the woman who'd been her caregiver when she was young, but she'd accepted the duty and risked her life to keep Harlow alive. She owed the wolves a life debt and would like to meet them—if they didn't blame her for what happened.

"Should we camp away from the Thornewood border and go in when it's daylight?" Evara asked.

Harlow snorted. "I'm not afraid of the dark, but we'd be fools to wade into Thornewood during the dark of night when we have no idea what to expect."

Evara's teeth flashed. "That sounds exactly like you're scared."

"As she should be," Magnus chided. "While it's easier to sneak around under the cover of darkness, dangerous things venture out at night. It's already risky enough. We will camp close enough to the border to gather what intel we can, but we don't go in until morning."

Harlow shot Evara a dark look, but the guard was unrepentant. The urge to stick her tongue out was almost overwhelming. Instead, Harlow shook her head and focused on thinking about anything other than the screaming muscles in her hips and back.

They briefly stopped to eat some stale bread and cheese and let the horses rest. Harlow didn't care for the crumbly cheese the flirtatious woman sold Magnus at the market, so she handed him back her piece and rummaged through her bag for the cheese she filched from the kitchens back home.

Evara leaned against a tree idly munching on a piece of dry jerky, but her gaze felt like it was everywhere at once. Nothing would sneak up on them with her watching, so Harlow settled on a small patch of grass well away from the unnaturally dense forest cover and finished her meal before stretching her muscles out as best she could.

The Wolf Kingdom didn't look much different from the Witch Kingdom, but the flora was denser here. Thick forests rose high in the sky and the grass was soft as a blanket. Harlow stroked her fingers through it and wondered how many times she'd toddled through it when she was a baby. The thought sent a pang of longing through her and made her miss the mother she'd never met.

Sighing, she stood, brushing off the seat of her pants, and was about to fetch Luci when the forest went silent, and she had the unnerving feeling she was being watched again. It wasn't the same oppressive and evil weight as the earlier fog, but Harlow had the sense something was taking her measure.

She only hoped she passed whatever test this was. A frantic look around revealed nothing, but when everyone had mounted their horses and started back on their way, the sound of dozens of wolves howling shattered the quiet. Harlow squeaked in fear, almost sliding from her horse.

Magnus stopped his mount and looked around, his brows rising almost to his hairline. No fear crossed his face, only a small smile. With a thoughtful nod, Magnus clicked his tongue and spurred his horse on, coming up beside Harlow.

"They recognize you," he said, his voice raised loud enough to be heard over the unearthly sound.

Harlow glanced at him with wide eyes. "They sound terrifying."

"Make no mistake," Magnus said gravely. "They are terrifying, but we have their permission to pass."

"Will I see them?"

"Only if they want to be seen."

The howls went on for several minutes before dying down right when they dipped into a valley. Harlow glanced up, trying to tell the time from the sun's position, only to see a massive white wolf standing at the top of a grassy hill.

Her breath caught when she realized the wolf was staring right at her. It sat on its haunches, tipped its muzzle to the sky and let out a sole, mournful wail.

Tears sprang to her eyes. She lifted a hand in greeting as the howl died down.

And she could have sworn the wolf dipped its head before disappearing down the hill.

"We're about three hours away," Magnus said, his eyes on the place where the wolf had disappeared. "Plenty of time to set up bedrolls and start a small fire before darkness settles in."

"It's safe to have a fire?" Harlow asked.

"Safe enough as long as our intel is correct. Nothing prowls outside the Thornewood borders besides the normal things."

Harlow's eyebrows lifted. "Normal things?"

"Wolves, snakes, things like that. Though it's a little too cold for snakes to be out, so I wouldn't worry about those. Just make sure to shake your boots out in the morning."

Harlow sighed. Some Virago she was. Castle life had spoiled her if she was nervous about snakes.

Evara grinned at her from across the clearing. Harlow rolled her eyes and resisted the urge to laugh. While she'd kept up her training, and her calloused hands were evidence of the hard work she'd put into her skills, the allure of good food and a soft bed could not be overstated.

Soon enough, they were back in their saddles and galloping down the road, not another soul in sight. In the past, before things had gone so wrong, the roads were packed with travelers and merchants, all going about their day-to-day business. Now the silence was eerie and unsettling. An evil pall settled over their shoulders, driving their horses forward.

They couldn't battle something they didn't fully understand. Knowing what it wanted and why it wanted it was helpful, but its magic was still a mystery. If the Luna stones held any clues to help them, or the city itself, they had to find them.

Failing could mean all their deaths.

King Adama's words came back to her. How did the Luna stones belong to the Darkness? She couldn't figure out how everything fit together, and it was driving her mad.

JUST AS MAGNUS HAD SAID, three hours later, they approached a wall of absolute darkness. Evara sucked in a breath as their horses stopped.

Magnus's expression went grim as he beheld what the Darkness had wrought.

Harlow's stomach turned, fear skittering down her spine.

This wasn't the darkness of shadows. This was the darkness of absolutes. True night with no stars, no moon, no flickering fires or candlelight.

Even when Harlow closed her eyes, she still felt light behind her eyelids. Looking ahead, there was only nothingness, the type of darkness that became endless. There would be no way to navigate inside from what Harlow could tell. All she saw before her was evil.

"Is this a fool's errand?" Evara asked softly.

Magnus's lack of response made Harlow turn to her father. He sat on his horse like a statue, brow furrowed and eyes glowing.

"We have to know," Harlow whispered.

"And die in the process?" Evara shook her head. "Walking into that makes me feel like if we make it out, we will never be the same."

To that, Harlow had no response. Evara was right. One could not walk through the darkness without seeing the worst parts of themselves. But life required balance. There was no dark without light. No light without darkness. Whatever they found there had to reveal something. Even if it was total destruction.

Magnus let out a gasp of air and slumped forward. Harlow turned Luci and trotted over to him. "Father?"

Magnus held a trembling hand up. "A moment," he croaked.

Harlow waited, staying close beside Magnus until he dragged in a shuddering breath and opened his eyes. "The kingdom is overrun. Nothing inside remains untouched."

"You can see in?" Evara asked, her eyes sharpening at Magnus's revelation.

"Not exactly. I sent in a thread to see what I could feel. There are a few who fare better, but many people inside are corrupted." He slid off his saddle and led his mount to a tree. "We go in at first light tomorrow morning."

Any other questions remained unanswered. Whatever Magnus saw inside had shaken him to his core.

Harlow spent the rest of the night wondering if this would be their last night together.

CHAPTER TWENTY-ONE

THE VIRAGO RETURN

A rustling of limbs woke her. Stars shone high above them, casting a silver glow over the greenery. She looked over at Evara whose eyes were already open, though she lay still.

"Harlow," a voice whispered.

Evara's brow furrowed. She slowly reached down and slid a dagger from the sheath at her hip.

Harlow came to her knees and looked around. By now her father was on his feet, an axe held loosely in his hand.

A tall woman with ruined armor and dark, streaming hair stepped from the Thornewood forests.

Harlow peered ahead, eyes straining to make out who approached them. The woman had her hands up in a gesture of surrender. She had a deep limp in one leg, and moonlight shimmered over her left arm. Blood.

Harlow took a step closer.

"Stay here," Magnus said.

But as the woman came closer, and the shadows gave way, Harlow gasped and ran for her.

"Melara!"

A pained smile broke over the Virago's face when Harlow stopped before her, eyes wide with horror.

"Hello, Heir," Melara said, seconds before she collapsed into a heap at Harlow's feet.

Magnus swore and re-strapped his axe to his side as he hurried over. "You know her?"

Harlow nodded. "I trained with her. She—" How could she explain Melara? Bully, enemy, then tentative friend. "She helped me come to terms with my power." It was a lie in a way, but it would do for now.

Magnus gave her a long look. "You wish for me to heal her?"

Harlow blinked. Her father would let this girl die? "Yes."

Magnus nodded once before a golden light appeared in his palms. He held them over the unconscious girl and moved the light over her injuries, most of them unseen.

Evara crouched beside Magnus. "I don't see any evidence of corruption."

"There is none," Magnus said, extinguishing his magic. "She will sleep for hours yet." He dug into a small pack at his side and produced a long length of rope that he cut two pieces from.

Harlow gaped. "You're tying her up?"

"She came from Thornewood. Your friend might be here to kill us."

Harlow opened her mouth to argue but realized that technically, Melara *had* almost killed her several months ago. Even if her purpose turned out to be ultimately altruistic, it could have gone very wrong.

She nodded instead. "Will she be alright?"

"Yes," he said, as he tied her wrists and ankles into a complicated knot Harlow couldn't follow. "She'll wake up sore and hungry, but her wounds will be mostly healed."

"How do you know her?" Evara asked.

"She was one of the girls training for the Virago." Harlow knew Melara had escaped, so what was she doing back here?

A silvery shimmering light appeared a few feet away. Harlow jerked back in fear until she recognized the cool, comfortable feeling of Nova's magic. Astrid stepped through looking hale and hearty and extremely displeased with all of them.

When she spotted Melara, her reddish eyebrows rose. "She looks terrible," she observed.

Magnus rose when he saw her and grabbed the bard, crushing her to his chest. Astrid let out a soft puff of air before her arms went around him.

"I'm so relieved," Magnus said.

Astrid had the grace to look embarrassed. "Magnus," she whispered.

He let go and stepped away, but the embrace had told Harlow everything she needed to know. Astrid was ageless, or at least Harlow thought so. Bards aged slower than humans, and many of them claimed generations of age. Harlow had never thought to ask her.

The portal behind them had not yet closed, and someone else stepped out. A tall, dark-haired woman with a neater braid than Harlow's would ever be. She was beautiful and serene, and smiled when she saw Harlow.

"Bloom!" Harlow hurried to the Seer and brought her in a tight embrace. "Where have you been?"

Bloom rarely stayed in one place for any length of time though she always came back to the Shadow Kingdom. Harlow hadn't seen her for several months, and when she asked Nova, all her sister would say was that Bloom was fine.

"Here and there," Bloom said in her maddening way. Ever since her magic had come back, it was like Bloom's head was in the clouds. She didn't have the same sleeping sickness Miriam seemed to get, but there was a difference in her since she arrived in Nova's kingdom. Harlow saw the same thing happening within herself. One was not the same person when magic manifested inside them. It wasn't possible. Power had changed many things about her, and Bloom was no exception.

Bloom tugged Harlow's braid and grinned. "I see you're just as terrible at braiding as you were while we were in training."

Harlow laughed. "What can I say? This student will never become the master. I hope you brought hair ties."

Bloom smiled, but it faded when she spotted who was lying on the ground. She sucked in a shocked breath and fell to her knees before Melara, pressing two fingers against the girl's neck. Her shoulders fell when she realized Melara was still alive.

"It's a healing sleep," Magnus said. "She was gravely injured."

Bloom nodded. "Where did she come from?"

Evara jerked her thumb over her shoulder. "Thornewood Forest."

Bloom took in a hissing breath. "And she's still alive," she murmured in wonder.

"I expect her to be awake by morning," Magnus said. "We won't infiltrate Thornewood until she answers some questions."

The portal shimmered. Nova popped her head out and waved. "Astrid is pissed at all of you," she said with a chuckle. "Also, I'm keeping Shade here temporarily. If I finish with him by morning, I'll send him through." Her expression sobered for a moment. "Come home to me." She lifted her hand in a wave before ducking back inside. The portal popped out of existence leaving us staring at the angry bard.

"You're very lucky your sister has a fast travel method. If I had to ride all the way here after that last trip I took on horseback, I was going to skin all of you alive." She rolled her eyes.

"And to think she was going to drop me off in the wolf kingdom if I hadn't told her where those shadows were!"

Harlow winced. "It's my fault."

Astrid snorted. "There's no need for you to confess. I assumed you were at the heart of this."

Harlow frowned.

Magnus chuckled. "I caught her in the stables with a week's worth of stolen food."

Bloom grinned. "She has quite the knack for thievery."

"I am *right* here," Harlow said through gritted teeth.

Bloom leaned forward and swore. "Why is Melara tied up?"

"Because I'd rather her not try to kill us all in our sleep tonight," Magnus said.

Bloom jerked her attention to him. "What? Why would she do that?"

"She's been in Thornewood for who knows how long. The entire kingdom is corrupt. There's no way to know where her allegiance lies."

The Seer gave Magnus a long, disapproving look. "Her allegiance has always lain with the Virago."

"Which no longer exists," Magnus reminded her gently.

Even Harlow, who'd been away from the fractured Virago for months now, bristled at his words.

"The Virago will always exist," Bloom snapped. "Whether we are loyal to Desminda or another worthy ruler, or if we are fractured and scattered across the worlds, we will always find each other."

Harlow looked down, her heart breaking for Bloom. There was a time when she'd felt the same, but time and circumstance had changed her mindset. The Virago held an important place in her heart, but she would never be allowed to rejoin it—not with the truth of her birth discovered.

Magnus laid a hand on Bloom's shoulder. "I am sorry. I

meant no offense. The Virago are fractured, and the last news we heard—"

Astrid crouched beside Bloom. "Most of the others are corrupted by the Darkness. Kalen was still holding on, but it's been months since I've seen her."

Everyone heard what Astrid hadn't said. Any hope for Kalen was probably long gone unless the young Virago had found a miracle.

"Kalen is responsible for the destruction of the Virago," Bloom said quietly. "I've Seen it." They all knew Kalen had led the girls away from Thornewood and worked with Celestine to infiltrate the queendom. But most of them had never made it back from the forest to try.

Astrid nodded. "Then it is your decision what to do with her if we see her inside. Though I would leave no one to the Darkness's mercy."

Bloom's jaw tightened. Magnus rose and held a hand out to help Astrid to her feet. "It is time to rest. We don't have extra bedrolls, but you're welcome to share with someone."

Bloom shook her head. "I'll stay with Melara."

Magnus's eyes softened. "Then we shall leave you be."

He led Astrid over to his bedroll. Harlow averted her eyes. She sat with Bloom for a while before her eyes grew heavy. A gentle touch on her arm jerked her awake.

"Come," Evara said softly. Bloom had settled in next to Melara, though her eyes were still open.

She let Evara lead her back to her bedroll, not questioning things when she saw the guard's pushed next to hers. Harlow sank down and pulled the thin blanket over her. Evara settled beside her, close enough that Harlow felt her body heat against her back.

Within moments, Harlow sank into a deep sleep.

· · ·

MELARA WAS alert and awake before Harlow. Soft conversation roused her from an almost dead sleep, and Harlow groaned before rolling over right onto the hard ground. Her blanket had tangled around her waist sometime during the night, and the cool morning air made Harlow shiver.

Magnus, Bloom, Melara, and Astrid sat around a fire, warming their hands. Harlow made her way over, squeezing between Astrid and Bloom. The women moved over to make room, staying close enough to block the worst of the breeze. With a grateful smile, Harlow held her hands before the fire, sighing when the crackling heat thawed her frigid fingers.

Melara sat across from her, dark circles under her eyes. Despite that, she looked much better than yesterday. Her leather armor was torn in several places, but the wound in her arm had completely closed and looked almost healed. She held a small hunk of bread in one hand and a cup of steaming liquid in the other.

Magnus and Bloom spoke quietly. "We can use Melara's path to get inside. But I need to examine the stones."

Melara shook her head. "Impossible. Trying to get into the castle is a death sentence. Whatever that thing is has the entire castle under constant surveillance."

"If you want us to save Kalen, I'll need access to them. If I can cleanse the stones, it's possible I can break the spell trapping magic. Harlow is with me, and while her training isn't where I'd like it to be, she has a strong grasp of her power. With the Luna stones acting as a magnifier, we might be able to deal a serious blow here and save anyone who is still hanging on."

Melara's shoulders drooped. "There are no more Virago. They've all fallen. Everyone except Kalen. She's found a spot in the kingdom that keeps her safe from the thing's power."

Astrid nodded. "It's by the training grounds. Something lies beneath the ground that pulses with pure magic. It's one of the few uncorrupted places I saw when I was there."

"Kalen is sensitive to magic. She can sense when the thing is looking for her, giving her time to hide. But she can't be on the grounds for too long. Otherwise, she feels its pull."

"When's the last time you saw her?" Astrid asked.

"Two days ago." Melara finished the bread and wrapped her fingers around her steaming mug. "I don't think she has much time left."

Astrid's face sharpened. "What makes you say that?"

Melara shuddered. "Something is happening. I—I can't explain it. Things prowl through Thornewood that shouldn't exist. It feels like nothing is real anymore." She shook her head and sighed. "I must sound like a lunatic."

But Magnus leaned forward, intense curiosity stealing over his face. "You don't. Tell me some of the things you've seen."

Melara nodded and told the most bizarre story Harlow had ever heard.

CHAPTER TWENTY-TWO

THE FALLEN QUEENDOM

They all stood under cover of a magical shield, courtesy of Magnus Stonehand. After Melara's fantastical tale, Magnus deemed it unsafe to separate their party and declared they'd all go in together—everyone except for Astrid.

The bard had balked at the order until Magnus reasoned that someone had to stay behind to contact Nova if they didn't make it out. Nova couldn't risk opening a portal too close to Thornewood, and since the tainted magic was spreading, they needed someone with the magical ability to reach Nova as soon as possible.

Harlow did not know how to use messaging magic yet. Bloom was a Seer. Evara still kept her power a secret, though she shook her head when Magnus had looked her way. And Melara had no magical skill to speak of. Astrid, though, could communicate through music and sound waves. Magnus had tried to explain how fast sound could travel, but everyone's eyes had glazed over until Astrid laughed and told everyone it was an old bard trick, rarely used.

But Harlow felt Astrid's laugh sounded off, and there was a stiffness in her posture that wasn't there before. Was she mad at

Magnus, or was there more to the spell that the bard wasn't telling them?

Magnus's mind was on other things, though, and he didn't notice anything off about Astrid's behavior. With things settled, he went to double check their horses and supplies, leaving the women standing together. Harlow leaned close to Astrid.

"Are you okay?"

Astrid stiffened. "I'm fine."

"Is there something you don't want to tell us about the spell you are to use?"

Astrid slid a curious gaze her way. "Why would you say that?"

At Harlow's flat look, Astrid chuckled. "You are far more observant than people give you credit for."

Harlow crossed her arms over her chest and waited.

Astrid finally sighed. "The spell is not as simple as your father made it sound. It requires a great deal of magic and time. I will have to begin the spell as soon as you step into Thornewood, and I will be ... vulnerable most of the time. If someone happens upon me while I'm in the middle of creating the spell ..." Astrid shrugged. "I can only hope it is a friend and not a foe."

Harlow stared at the bard. "Are you insane?" she hissed. "Does Magnus know?"

"Lower your voice," Astrid urged. "No one knows. Except for you now. Bard magic is secretive for a reason."

"Then why are you telling *me*?"

Astrid laughed. "Because, little witchling, despite everything you've been through, you've never broken my confidence."

"Are you sure you should stay behind?"

Astrid nodded. "I am the only one who has a chance to contact the Shadow Queen."

"Can't she just reopen the portal in the same place as yesterday?"

Astrid shook her head. "It's unsafe. Opening it for me was a risky venture, and the shadows have spread even further this morning."

"I hate this." Everything hinged on chance, and Harlow liked plans. What if Melara misremembered where Kalen was? What if Magnus couldn't get into the castle? What if something too powerful attacked them and took one of them down? What if they couldn't find Kalen?

A hand landed on her shoulder. "I can see the worry all over your face," Evara said. "We are all competent warriors and mages." She winked. "Some of us more than competent."

Harlow snorted. "How can you be so calm when there's the potential for so many things to go wrong?"

"War is not calm or peaceful and never goes according to plan. War is not a *thing*. It is a concept. War is constantly questioning oneself because the other side has their own plans, and no one knows what the other will do. That's when emotion and strategy and battle prowess come into play. War is responding, Harlow. Just like this. We don't know what we will walk into. All we can do is respond in the best way we can. Worry is futile and bad for your health." Evara pushed a steaming mug of tea into her hand. "Drink this and calm down. You are with us, and we are with you. We are family, are we not?"

Harlow nodded and sipped from the mug, sighing when the scent of peppermint hit her nose. "You're right."

"Of course I'm right." Evara winked.

"But nothing you said really made all that much sense."

The guard chuckled. "But it made you feel better, didn't it?"

Harlow laughed. Magnus walked up to them, slinging a pack over his shoulder. "Is everyone ready?"

Harlow dumped the rest of her tea out and double checked

that her axes were strapped securely to her hips. She tapped the lids of the small bottles snapped in their respective holders to make sure they were closed. Her grandmother had altered her weapons belt to add the herb holders, and Harlow had never used them, but she knew how to. With the number of surprises sure to come, she didn't want to lose any of them on the way to the castle.

"Kalen is at the back of the castle, by the Virago training grounds. We get her first and infiltrate the area where the stones are," Magnus said. "Do not leave the party. The shield should hold unless we come under heavy fire." He looked around the group, stopping to thoroughly examine all their gear. "Are you ready?"

Nods all around. "Good. When we get in, I need a moment to examine the ground. Do not be alarmed if I don't respond right away."

The same thing happened to Harlow when she spiraled deep into her magic. Nothing seemed as important as the earth when attuning yourself to listen to the ground speak. The only way she could hear the words was to tune everything else out.

Magnus turned and walked toward the dark border. "Join hands."

Harlow stood at the end of the line. She reached for Evara's hand, the guard's fingers calloused and warm within hers.

"Do not let go of each other until we are all accounted for." Magnus took a deep breath and stepped over the border.

Disorientation hit Harlow like a punch to the gut. Darkness swept over her, an absence of light that sent all her senses into overdrive. Evara's hand tightened around her own.

"I am here," she whispered to Harlow when she whimpered. "Hold tight to my hand and know that I am real and solid."

Queasiness slammed into her, and everything spun. She

couldn't tell which way was up or down, and her magic burned in her veins, fighting against the overwhelming sense of evil all around them.

It felt like she floated in that space for hours, but it had to be seconds. The ground slammed into them, and Evara's hand tore from hers. Harlow groaned, her stomach heaving as she emptied her breakfast onto the dead grass.

It took several minutes before Harlow could lift her head without vomiting. When she did, she spotted Magnus not far from her, still throwing up. Melara seemed a little queasy, but otherwise fine. Bloom and Evara were in the same shape as Harlow and her father were. Whatever this was hit magic users much harder than humans.

The darkness wasn't so pronounced here, but the daylight had disappeared, leaving them in a land of eternal dusk. Shadows and fog swept around Harlow's body. She couldn't see more than ten feet in front of her, which would make navigating Thornewood extremely difficult.

She let her face settle against the cold ground as she dragged in air. Eventually, she rolled over and sat up, gasping when pain burst in her head.

Magnus came over and sat beside her, touching her knee. Warm, healing energy spiraled through her veins.

Harlow groaned in relief.

"Give it a minute and the nausea should pass," he said, his voice grim.

"Are you okay?" she croaked.

Magnus nodded. "I am now." He grimaced. "I've never felt anything quite like that."

When Harlow's breathing finally settled, he did the same for Bloom and Evara until they were all on their feet.

"We'll go in a minute," Magnus said, as he knelt on the

ground and sank his fingers into the earth. His eyes flashed gold and his face went blank.

Harlow moved closer to him and waited as Magnus communed with the earth. She wasn't sure what he would find, if anything. Everything felt dead or close to dying to her altered senses. All life had fled this place or at least buried itself so far down she could barely feel any spark of life.

When Magnus came to, his face was streaked with tears. He wiped his hands on his pants and used the back of his arm to wipe the wetness from his face. "Thornewood might be saved if we hurry. The earth here is close to death." He rose. "We need to make for the castle. Stay close to each other."

As one, they hurried deeper into the once great queendom.

CHAPTER TWENTY-THREE

REUNITED

Harlow's favorite part of Thornewood castle lay shattered on the ground. The once glorious stained-glass windows were ruined beyond repair, colorful bits of the painstakingly created murals scattered across the dying grass.

She was glad Desminda was not here to see it.

They hid behind a half dead bush in the former queen's gardens and studied the castle and its lack of activity. When Thornewood was at its greatest, there were guards surrounding the grounds at all hours of the day. They'd been there for half an hour and had yet to see a soul. Magnus's shield still held, and it seemed to protect them from the Darkness's far reach. Or the thing wasn't paying attention right now and hadn't swept the grounds for intruders. She hoped it was the first and Magnus had figured out a way to blunt all their magic from the power-hungry creature.

Melara pointed to the back of the castle. "Kalen is that way," she whispered.

There was little cover on the way, only a few sparse trees and a few bushes that would do a poor job of hiding them while they tried to find Kalen. Magnus nodded and sank his fingers into the ground again.

His eyes flashed golden. "There are four signs of life. Three are corrupted." His lips thinned. "The last seems to be dying."

"Kalen," Melara said grimly. "Can we get to her?"

Magnus nodded. "Only one of us should go. It's safer that way." His eyes flashed again. "My shield should cover you for the distance, but I won't be able to extend it to Kalen until she's in my field of vision."

"I'll go," Melara said.

Evara shook her head. "It should be a magic user."

"I'll do it," Harlow said.

Magnus glanced at her. "Are you sure?"

She nodded. "We know each other. I'm the most familiar besides Melara, and I can protect her if we run into problems."

Melara shook her head.

"No," Harlow insisted. "You've suffered enough. I will bring her back safely."

Melara's lips trembled, but she nodded once. "Thank you," she said hoarsely.

Harlow reached over and squeezed Melara's hand. "Don't thank me until I'm back here with her."

Magnus pulled his fingers from the earth. "Stay covered as much as you can. Do not dally to talk. Grab her if you have to and run."

Harlow nodded and crouched, doing one more sweep to ensure they were still alone. Seconds later, she sprinted from the cover of the bush over to the tree. She wore brown leather armor, which would help camouflage her, but she could do nothing about her golden hair. If anything were to give her away, it would be that.

She tucked her braid into the back of her leathers and swept the grounds with her gaze once more before hurtling toward the next damaged bush, and the next, and the next.

Harlow spotted Kalen sitting alone in a circle of undamaged earth. She was too far away to call out, so she moved to a space behind a large barrel close to the training grounds.

"Kalen," she hissed.

The Virago jerked and looked around, her eyes wild.

"Kalen!" Harlow called again.

When Kalen's eyes finally found her, they widened in shock. She slowly shook her head and rubbed her eyes. "I'm hallucinating," she croaked.

Harlow motioned her over. "Melara is with us. So are Bloom and my father."

"Melara?" Tears filled her eyes.

Harlow nodded, sympathy crushing her chest. "We don't have much time. Follow me."

Kalen slowly stood up, wincing with every movement.

"Are you injured?"

Kalen shook her head but frowned. "No." She paused. "Maybe. I haven't felt right for a long time." She pressed a dirty hand to her stomach.

"My father will help. We need to hurry."

Kalen looked around and bolted to the barrel, reaching out to touch Harlow as if to ensure she was real. A soft sob broke from her throat when her chilled fingers made contact with Harlow's skin. "It's really you."

Harlow nodded.

"Why would you save me after all I've done?" Guilt and horror lay etched on Kalen's face, and suddenly Harlow realized what had come before didn't matter anymore. She'd ask the reasons for Kalen's decisions later, but this Virago, this young girl, had suffered enough.

"You can ask all the questions you want when we're out of here." The tense quiet was making Harlow nervous, and she itched to leave this place forever.

"I've never been able to find my way out."

"That's why we brought Magnus," Harlow said firmly. "He has to go into the castle—"

"No." Kalen jerked her hand away. "We'll die."

"He needs to see the stones."

"They're corrupted. *Everything* is corrupted." Kalen looked down. "Please don't make me go in. That thing is there."

The poor girl was filthy and smelled horrific, and she looked like she'd lost twenty pounds from her already thin frame.

Harlow took a firm grip of Kalen's wrist. "If you stay here, you will die. If you come with us, you might also die, but at least you tried."

Kalen gave her a wide-eyed look. "You are a terrible motivator."

Harlow shrugged. "We have no good options. Either stay and die or go and maybe die."

Kalen sighed. "Melara is much better at this than you are."

Harlow gave her a dark look. "Yes, well, I'm the one here risking my ass to get you home, so that should be worth something."

She poked her head over the top of the barrel, saw no one, and jerked Kalen with her as she launched herself from her hiding spot. Kalen stumbled but quickly caught herself, following closely behind Harlow as they hurried from spot to spot.

Harlow's breath was harsh and rapid, and heart beat wildly as they inched their way back. A crack of sound made them both freeze. Harlow shoved Kalen down behind cover and put her index finger over her lips, warning her to stay silent. They crouched there for several minutes until they were sure they were alone, finally making one last, mad and desperate dash to freedom.

When they made it back to the party, Melara gripped Kalen in a tight hug, her nose wrinkling at the Virago's stench. "When we get back to the Witch Kingdom, I'm tossing you into a trough of soap."

Kalen blinked. "Witch Kingdom?"

Melara's lips twitched with amusement. "Our little Stonehand is full of secrets. If we make it out of here alive, we have a lot to talk about."

Bloom's eyes flashed silver. She reached out for Magnus. "Wait," she whispered. "Something ..." Her face went blank, and her jaw slackened as the vision overtook her.

The ground rumbled underneath them. Magnus grabbed hold of Kalen. A shimmer of magic rolled over her, his shield encompassing the last Virago. Abruptly, the shaking stopped.

"That was a close one," he muttered, looking at Kalen. "That thing knows where you are every time you step away from that spot?"

She swallowed hard and nodded. "I haven't eaten in two days. Every time I step out, he's looking for me."

Magnus swore and dug in his pack, shoving a hunk of cheese at her. "It's not much, but it's all we have time for."

Kalen looked at the cheese like it was her saving grace. Perhaps it was. Starvation could drive someone to eat pretty much anything if it had gone on long enough.

Bloom's head dropped. She sucked in a breath and shuddered as she came back to consciousness. "It knows something has disturbed its grounds. The thing is—" She swallowed hard. "Celestine but not Celestine. It's a gross caricature of what she used to be. We must be extremely careful. It searches for its next vessel. Yet ..." she paused. "It feels like more than one presence. But that doesn't make sense." Bloom's face went deathly pale.

Magnus's nostrils flared, but he nodded. "It's less risky if only a couple of us go in."

"It shouldn't be you," Harlow said.

"And why not?" Magnus demanded.

"You and I are the strongest magic users. Someone needs to stay back to protect everyone, and we both know this thing can be weakened by our magic. If we're both inside, everyone out here is more vulnerable."

Magnus's lips thinned. He didn't like her logic, but he gave one sharp nod. "You're right, but I have to be one of them since I set the original spell to bring magic down. I will take Evara. You stay here with everyone and protect them if something happens. My shield will hold. He thumbed through his pockets and pushed Queen Moira's trinket at her.

"Wait no more than half an hour. If we aren't back, get everyone out and use the portal."

Surprised, Harlow took the trinket but shook her head. "We won't leave without you."

Magnus took Harlow's chin in his hand. "Get everyone out of Thornewood. If I am not alive, you are the best hope to defeat this thing. You must think of more than me now, daughter. All the kingdoms are at the Darkness's mercy, whether they know it or not. Promise me."

She wanted to rail against him and insist they would wait for however long it took them to return, but she knew he was right. All she could do was nod. "Do not die," she whispered.

Kalen snorted.

Evara reached over and tugged Harlow's braid. "You and I have unfinished business," she said roughly, grinning when Harlow's cheeks heated. "We will return."

Magnus shook his head, amusement glimmering in his eyes

before he nodded at Evara, and they slunk away from their hiding spot toward the castle.

"What was that all about?" Melara murmured.

"None of your business," Harlow said hotly.

The last Viragos all laughed.

CHAPTER TWENTY-FOUR

MAGNUS AND THE BEAST

He had not often worked with Evara, but he felt the guard's power beating against his skin as they crept inside the ruined castle. Magnus still didn't quite know what she was. Part of the Beast Kingdom for sure, but maybe part witch, maybe part something else ... he couldn't put his finger on her magic. All that mattered was them both getting out of here alive, so whatever it was, he hoped it worked if he failed.

She stayed close behind him, silent as a mouse. Magnus felt the corruption pulsing at the heart of the castle, the Luna stones, once pure magic, leaking darkness. Dissonance jarred his senses, but it made the stones easier to find. The castle had once stood as a beacon of power. Now it was a reminder of what evil could do. All the stained-glass windows were blown out from the inside, as if someone's rage had gotten the better of them. Furniture was tipped on its side, the once gorgeous, expensive fabrics shredded, internal stuffing littering the ground like fallen clouds.

Jagged scratches had ruined the walls. Claw marks scraped all over the stone floor, marring the once perfect white marble.

A coppery scent tinged the air. Blood and something else. Something inhuman.

They carefully avoided the obstacles littering the floor and crept toward the back of the castle, the rotten allure of the Luna stones screaming a distress call to Magnus's magic. Soon enough, they stood in front of two massive mahogany doors, gouged down the middle with those disturbing claw marks.

The doors stood ajar, black magic seeping from the opening. Magnus raised his index finger to Evara, urging her to be silent, and peered inside the room.

Silence, except for the screaming stones, a sound only he could hear. He motioned for Evara to follow and stepped inside, careful not to touch the doors. Magnus stopped abruptly, his nature magic recoiling at the abhorrent stain upon the heart of Thornewood's magic.

Evara sucked in a horrified gasp as she crept in behind him, her fingers reaching out to brush the stones. Magnus slapped her hand away and gave a sharp shake of his head. "Touch nothing," he whispered. "One of us needs to walk away from this."

Evara gave him a withering look. "And you'd have me tell your daughter I left her father to die?"

"You'd have me tell my daughter I did the same to the woman she may love?"

Evara blinked and stepped back, dropping her eyes in surprise. Whatever she expected him to say, it wasn't that. But Magnus couldn't miss the tension between the guard and his daughter. The gods knew Harlow deserved to find love and not with that manipulative, golden-eyed princess.

Evara shook her head and looked up at him. They glared at each other before Magnus rolled his eyes and turned to the stones. Their once shimmering iridescence was barely visible. Black rot pulsed where they were once a milky blue white color, flashing with power. Underneath the black ran veins of red, the color of poisoned blood.

"Can you heal them?" Evara whispered, looking through the crack in the door to ensure they were still alone.

Magnus shook his head. "No. I'll need Harlow's power to heal them." He stared at the stones for a long moment, rethinking all the plans he had. "I don't think the land is salvageable any longer."

Evara stared. "I—" She blew out a breath. "I'm not sure what you're saying."

Magnus's lips pressed together in a thin, grim smile. "I think we should transport the stones."

Evara's jaw dropped. "What?" She snorted and rubbed a hand over her face. "If such a thing were even possible, where would we put them? We can't take them into the Shadow Kingdom, or anywhere our allies are, for fear they'd poison the rest of the other stones."

"Contamination is possible, depending on how the poison spreads." Magnus scratched his chin. "I can contain the rot until we figure out how to heal them."

"What if it doesn't work?"

At that, Magnus gave her a quelling glare. Evara waved her hand. "Yes, yes, we all know you're the most powerful mage in the world, but what if it doesn't work?"

Magnus thought for a moment. "I don't know how we'd be in any worse shape than we are now."

"Except by moving the rot, it could stifle magic in the new place?"

Magnus edged closer to the stones, crouching on the chilled, cracked floor. "No. I'm responsible for the spell stifling magic in this kingdom. The stones are only part of the magic. An important part, but if we take them away, it's possible we will land a blow against the Darkness's power."

Evara's face grew thoughtful. "How do we move them?"

Magnus stood and held his hand up, palm facing the stones. "I will perform the spell, but I'll be magically tapped once it's complete. Can you get me out of the castle?"

Evara nodded. "I will do my best."

Their eyes met. "This will attract attention. Once I'm trapped in the magic, I can't protect myself. Are you prepared for what that means?"

A black shadow rolled over Evara's irises. "I am."

Magnus's eyes sparked gold. "Then let's begin."

Their hiding place afforded them a view of the castle, but Harlow could no longer see Magnus or Evara, and her mind ran wild with terrible possibilities. They'd only been gone for ten minutes. She'd heard no noise and felt no magic other than the corruption, so either they hadn't found what they were looking for or something else had happened.

Bloom, Melara, and Kalen had fallen silent, their bodies huddled together as they waited. Her father's shield still held over all of them, keeping them in a magic-proof bubble, but Harlow felt that shield pull a moment later when the familiar feel of his magic saturated the surrounding air.

Bloom's eyes flashed silver. "What's happening?"

Kalen went still, her eyes traveling over the castle, brow furrowed as she tried to figure out what she was sensing.

"Big magic," Harlow breathed. Larger than she'd ever felt her father perform, except for the time he'd found her during her astral travel. What was he doing? And did he need her help?

Twenty minutes had passed by then. Ten more until her father told her to run. Harlow sank her fingers into the dirt and closed her eyes. Magnus wasn't that far away, but her senses weren't as sharp as her father's, so she couldn't tell where in the castle he was.

A golden haze seeped from under the castle floors and out

the castle windows as a stillness settled over the land. Every muscle in Harlow's body tensed. Melara crept closer, eyes skating over the horizon in every direction.

A rage-filled scream shattered the silence, followed by the oppressive weight of rotten magic. The ground underneath their feet rumbled. Harlow jerked her fingers from the earth as her father's shield wavered.

"Get closer to me," Harlow whispered. The girls huddled up, bodies touching as Harlow readied her magic. Her shields were not as powerful as Magnus's, but it could still offer protection if his were to drop.

Five minutes before they ran. "Get ready," Harlow breathed.

The other girls gave sharp nods. All of them stared at the castle as dark magic raced to cover her father's gold.

What was he doing? And would he make it out alive?

THE STONES SHIFTED at Magnus's urging, breaking away from their birthplace in the mountains, groaning as they ripped from their stone coffins.

"It's coming," Evara breathed.

Magnus barely heard her. It was taking everything from him to lift the stones. He'd forgotten how many Luna stones were inside those mountains. Tons ripping away from the walls and ground as he focused on where he wanted them to go, directing the spell as fast as he could.

The sound of tearing clothing registered in his senses, followed by a low, savage snarl. Magnus knew he should be worried, but if he focused on anything other than what he was doing, it might be the end of them all.

"WHO INVADES MY SANCTUM?" screamed a hideous, rasping voice.

The snarl grew in volume.

Magnus whispered the words of the spell in a frantic voice, sweat beading on his forehead. Magic beat in the air, the pressure pounding against his temples as the spell's intensity grew.

A furry head butted against his hip, urging him to hurry. Magnus swallowed, closed his eyes, and barked the command word to seal the spell. Pressure grew in the room, making Magnus grit his teeth. The beast beside him whined low in its throat.

Magnus swayed and threw his hands away, commanding the stones to leave.

Nausea roiled through him seconds before Magnus's eyes rolled to the back of his head, and he sank like a stone.

MAGNUS'S BODY jerked like a marionette on a string. His eyes peeled open to reveal the world upside down, his body swaying in mid-air. This morning's terrible breakfast threatened to rise, and he inhaled a breath of stale air.

"Don't throw up on me," an inhuman voice whispered.

Magnus froze for a moment before realizing an enemy wouldn't say something like that to him. He twisted his head around only to see a leathery, clawed hand splayed over his hips.

"Evara?" he croaked.

"Can you run?" the voice hissed.

Magnus thought about it. "I think so."

She unceremoniously dumped him to the ground, then hauled him to standing by his upper arm. "Run," she barked.

Magnus didn't bother to look behind him. Evara dragged him until his brain caught up to his feet, and he took off toward the castle's door.

Evara's beast form was ahead of him, loping swiftly on four legs. Magnus sucked in a breath at her dark, leathery skin and membranous wings. He'd never seen such a creature before, but whispered a thank-you to the gods that she was on their side.

Dust poured all around them as plaster and stone crashed to the ground.

The Darkness had found them, and it was extremely displeased.

"Now," Harlow barked, shooting like a star from their hiding place. Magnus's shield had fallen only seconds before, forcing her to quickly build a shield of her own.

"Don't let go," Bloom warned, sensing the fragility of Harlow's hastily built protection, as they ran with their hands joined together.

Each girl kept pace with the others as they raced for the border, and Harlow prayed she could remember where they were once they reached the disorienting darkness that lay ahead.

Thornewood Castle and the grounds collapsed around them, the buildings and gardens disappearing deep into the earth, sucked down like they'd never existed. A pang of grief struck her as Desminda's favorite roses disappeared below ground, but there would be time later to mourn what they had lost.

They had to make it out alive first.

And Harlow had to pray her father and Evara would make it out too.

She wished she could use the trinket her grandmother had given her, but knew it would be foolish to use it where magic had been both broken and so ruthlessly corrupted. But as she ran, she remembered something Queen Moira had said and almost stumbled in horror.

The portal stone could only take five. Astrid's presence and rescuing Kalen had added two more to their party. Astrid was competent enough to find her own way home, as were

Harlow and Bloom. Melara and Kalen might be another story, though.

She swallowed hard, gritted her teeth, and kept running. They could figure it out later. Nova would find her once she made it far enough away from the border.

"No matter what you see, do not let go," Harlow warned again as they reached the shadow border and leapt inside. The girls plummeted into total darkness.

Melara, or was it Kalen, gasped in horror. Bloom sucked in a breath, and Harlow squeezed her eyes tight waiting for the disorientation to subside.

Seconds or hours later, they landed in a heap just outside the border. Harlow groaned and dragged in a ragged breath of fresh air. Someone close sobbed in relief.

Harlow closed her eyes and pressed her face against the fertile ground, her magic settling inside her body once again.

When she felt mostly human, she rose to her feet with a groan. Bloom held a sobbing Kalen against her shoulder, stroking the girl's dark hair. Melara still lay on the ground, arms and legs splayed out like a midnight star.

"Let's get farther away from the border," Harlow urged.

No one argued, even if Melara let out a pained groan as she rose to her feet. Kalen's sobs of relief had subsided, and she walked close to Bloom, her head down, staring at her worn boots as she followed Melara and Harlow.

They moved far enough away that they no longer felt the pulsating darkness of the border but could still see it once Evara and her father made it out.

And they would.

They had to.

CHAPTER TWENTY-FIVE

TRAPPED

Every muscle in Magnus's body hurt. Evara had given up and tossed him back over her shoulder as she raced to escape the castle, but something was wrong.

They should have been out several minutes ago, but every time they thought they were close, the distance grew.

"Magic," Magnus croaked.

Evara stiffened, then slowed. "We can't get out."

"Looks that way."

Evara set Magnus down and shifted back to human form, her eyes shadowed with her beast form. He said nothing about it. Her magic wasn't his concern, and she'd saved his life. Whatever she was interested him, but now wasn't the time to try to dissect how her magic worked.

The Darkness hadn't made itself known yet, but Magnus felt its presence pulsing around him. He didn't think the thing realized what Magnus had done to the Luna stones, but it might soon, once it tried to launch a spell.

As it turned out, they didn't have long to wait. From a doorway on the other side of the corridor, smoke swirled, illuminating the luscious curves of a young woman, but Magnus sensed the wrongness in her even before she'd finished forming.

"Celestine," Evara said, her voice still holding some of the raspiness from her beast form.

The redhead woman tilted her head to the side, studying them. Her face was mostly in shadow, but as she moved closer, Magnus barely contained his shocked inhale.

This person was Celestine, the second heir to the Rose crown, no longer. Once a stunning beauty, part of her face had morphed into a terrifying visage with fiery red eyes and sharp fangs, while the other side was just as pristine and human as it used to be.

"So we meet again," the thing spoke with Celestine's sweet voice. "I did not expect you to drop into the heart of my kingdom."

"Your stolen kingdom," Magnus said.

The thing's eyes flashed. "Are you here for the girl?" it asked. "Or to steal more of my magic?"

Magnus grinned. "Both."

The Darkness hissed a laugh. "I don't care about the girl. She had barely enough magic in her bones to sustain me for more than a moment. But the stones are ours."

An odd way to phrase things. Ours instead of hers. "Are they?" Magnus asked lightly.

"Stolen from us," it continued. "Ours by right. By law." Its voice trembled.

"Then why were they so easy to steal?" Magnus said.

Evara's attention snapped to him, her eyes wide at his confession.

It seemed foolhardy to tell this thing what they had done, but how were they to know how it affected the creature without angering it into action?

The Darkness's body stilled before its head snapped in the direction of the Luna stones.

Magnus touched Evara's elbow. "Run." His whisper was barely audible. Letting Evara take over for a little while had allowed his magic to replenish some. At least enough to blow a hole through whatever magic this thing used to keep them trapped.

Evara didn't hesitate. She took off with Magnus close behind.

"Get ready," he warned. Golden magic flowed through his body and into his hands. Magnus gathered as much as he could before a word ripped from his throat.

"*Sunder.*" The command made the ground shudder.

A cry of rage and a lash of dark magic tore through the air, slashing into his back. Magnus's bark of pain made Evara skid to a stop, but even with the agony slamming into him, the surrounding illusion broke, revealing the broken castle doors just ahead.

Magnus swayed on his feet, exhausted beyond belief, but Evara grabbed his hand and dragged him toward the door.

They plunged into shadow the second they stepped outside.

"WHERE ARE THEY?" the thing possessing Celestine's body demanded.

"Don't stop," Evara commanded.

"It worked," Magnus rasped. "We aren't dead, so there's no way the thing has command of all of its power."

"We can throw a party later," Evara barked. "Move your ass."

Magnus huffed a laugh but hurried after Evara. The wound in his back pulsed in agony, and he pushed the pain down. He had to keep moving. If he stopped, they would die. Even if the creature didn't have all its power, based on what it had just done, it had enough to kill them if it caught them.

Catching them couldn't be an option.

By the time the shadows appeared, Evara was all but dragging a bleeding, exhausted Magnus. Without hesitation, she turned, wrapped her arms around his waist, and dragged them both into the darkness.

THEY FOUND Astrid not too long after. The bard sat on a large stone, idly strumming a lute she definitely didn't have when she arrived. Astrid stood when she spotted them and smiled, but the smile faded when she realized Magnus and Evara were not with them.

"Where are they?" she demanded.

"Still in the castle." Harlow sank to the ground and settled with her back against the stone. She drew her knees to her chest and watched the border for any signs.

Astrid's lips tightened. Her gaze settled on Kalen. She nodded at the Virago and dug into her satchel to find a hunk of cheese to toss at her.

Kalen caught it one-handed and nodded her thanks before she turned and devoured it in two bites.

"I need to speak with you," Harlow said quietly. "Alone."

Bloom gave her a long look, but took Melara by the elbow and led her over to the other side of the clearing.

Astrid settled beside her.

"The portal stone will only take five of us," Harlow said.

Astrid didn't seem too concerned. "Nova will find us. Now that you're back, I can start the spell. Since you're here to protect me, it should go faster than normal."

Harlow let out a sigh of relief. "Please do."

Astrid reached over and squeezed Harlow's shoulder. "He will find us. Your father and Evara are tough. They will make it through."

Harlow's lower lip wobbled. All she had the energy for was a small nod.

Astrid reached over and gave her a one-armed hug before rising and settling back onto the rock, this time in a cross-legged position.

When she plucked the lute strings this time, magic hummed through the air.

Harlow watched as Astrid settled into a trance, unique to the bards. Her fingers continued to play without a hitch, but when Astrid opened her mouth and an ancient song poured from her lips, the hair on the back of Harlow's neck rose.

The other Virago watched the bard with awe, and Harlow shifted to keep an eye on Astrid.

The bard's magic wasn't visible, but her power swept over Harlow's skin, cleansing her weary soul with every word Astrid sang. Tears filled Harlow's eyes and slipped down her cheeks. She drew in a shuddering breath and sank back onto the rock, keeping her eyes open for Astrid but wishing she could sink into a peaceful sleep.

Melara, Bloom, and Kalen came closer until they sat at the base of the rock by Astrid's feet. From Harlow's viewpoint looking up, the bard looked like a goddess of old. Her fingers flew over the lute strings, the melody pouring from a place of ancient magic deep inside her. A gentle wind blew Astrid's red hair away from her face like a bloody banner.

Like all magic, time passed slowly and quickly until Harlow snapped back into the present when she felt Nova's cooling magic touching her cheek.

A portal lay open, and her sister stepped out, brows drawing together when she spotted Astrid, whose fingers still kept playing even though the spell had reached its conclusion.

"Harlow?"

"Magnus and Evara are still in Thornewood," she blurted.

Nova's silvery eyes flashed. "How long?"

Harlow opened her mouth, but she realized she didn't know. "I-I'm sorry. Astrid's spell made me lose track of time." She peered up, and the suns had shifted position just slightly. "Maybe an hour," she breathed.

Nova's expression turned grim. Shade stepped out of the portal behind Nova, eyes sweeping over them.

"Where?" he asked.

Harlow pointed in Thornewood's direction.

Nova lay a hand on Shade's arm. "Wait a moment." She reached for Harlow, helping her up. "Go through the portal. I'll wait for Magnus."

Harlow shook her head. "Let them go first. I'll go with Shade."

"No."

"Yes," Harlow insisted. "Thank you for coming for us, but I am not leaving my father."

She jerked her head at Bloom and the other girls. "My grandmother is through there. Tell her who you are and let her know I'll be home as soon as we gather my father."

Melara nodded and helped Kalen through the portal. Bloom stopped by Harlow's side. "I will wait with you."

Harlow's smile didn't reach her eyes. "I'm not going to wait." She glanced at Shade. "Ready?"

He bared his teeth in a savage smile. "Ready, Virago."

Bloom shrugged. "In for a penny," she murmured.

"That's the spirit," Shade said. He brushed a kiss against Nova's cheek. "We will be back as soon as we can."

"I'll hold the portal open as long as I can. Magnus has the stone from Queen Moira. If I am not here, you can use it to return."

"Very well. Let's see how much of their training these two

remember." Shade started the short walk back tc the Thornewood border, Bloom and Harlow following close behind.

Not a moment later, the shadowy border heaved and spit two lifeless humans out.

"WAIT," Magnus rasped. "I want to see if I can take it down while she's weak."

Evara turned on her side and coughed up liquid. She groaned and waved a hand at him that he took to mean *carry on*.

He studied the border one more time, looking for weak spots, before nodding to himself and sinking his fingers into the earth. The Luna stones weren't long gone, but their absence even in this short time had weakened the Darkness. Magnus's spell dampening magic in Thornewood still held, and since the creature couldn't bolster its power with the stones, it was close to being helpless.

He had to make his move now before the creature moved to other kingdoms still rich in magic. Magnus took a deep breath and let himself sink into the earth feet first. Rich, fertile soil covered his feet, then his ankles and calves, until Magnus was submerged to his chest.

He didn't often sink so deep into his magic, but if this worked, it would solve their problems before anyone else had to die. Magnus closed his eyes and used the world's magic to strike at the heart of Thornewood's poison.

"FATHER!" Harlow shouted, skidding toward Magnus cn her knees. She touched his face and found it was cooler than normal. Her accusing eyes shot to Evara who sat on the ground beside him.

"He's fine," Evara said. "I'm not sure what he's doing, but it has to do with the border and that thing eating away Desminda's kingdom."

Shade lay a heavy hand on her shoulder. "Be careful not to go too deep," he warned. "Your father has years of experience on his side."

Harlow ignored his warnings and sank her fingers and wrists in the earth, seeking her father.

They stood in a barren field once more, but this time the Darkness knew where they were. Harlow's eyes widened when she saw what it had done to Celestine, but she stepped closer to her father.

"You shouldn't be here," Magnus breathed, "but I'm glad you are."

"What do I do?" she whispered.

"We strike at it with everything we have. Use everything in your arsenal, Harlow. This is not the time to be afraid."

I know you, a voice whispered inside her head. *Heir of Magic.*

The Luna stone in her pocket and the one she still wore around her neck pulsed, warning her.

This time, she didn't stop to talk. Magnus grabbed her hand, and their power merged, an unholy combination of raw earth magic and the seductive power of the witches.

A scream tore from her throat as they sent their combined power at the creature that was once Celestine. The ground shattered underneath Celestine's feet, deep fissures cracking up everywhere.

I smell the healer, it continued, though Harlow heard an unsteady tremor in its voice this time. *She is mine. I will have her. And you will be the one to bring her to me.*

Harlow exhaled and shoved the seductive voice from her

mind, willing herself to listen to only her father and her own voice.

The two halves of her power rubbed against each other, seeking a way to combine. Harlow focused on it, willing herself to let go. With the earth, she was an unbreakable stone. With the witches, she was a willow tree in the wind, flexible but strong.

She let go of Magnus's hand, ignoring his bark of protest, and tilted her face up to the desolate sky. Her powers should complement each other. Witches were of nature. They studied herbs and plants and the wind and the rivers and earth, so why couldn't she bring those two halves of herself together?

A lash of black power cracked against the sky and headed straight for her. Magnus's scream shattered the landscape, but Harlow didn't move. Her feet grew roots, stretching deep into the dry, lifeless soil beneath her boots. Her heart opened like a bloom, and her skin became hard as a rock. Nothing could bend her. Nothing could break her.

Unless she wanted it to.

Harlow reached inside herself and pulled out a small bead of magic—the witchlight her grandmother told her about—a powerful kernel of raw magic to be shaped and used as Harlow willed it.

If she could cage this thing, she could delay it. Harlow studied the kernel of her power. It looked like a seed of pure gold. She lifted her hand, and the kernel floated above her palm. She smiled at it and sent it straight for the Darkness.

The creature laughed. *You think to capture me with a seed? Stupid girl. I'm ageless. Immortal. I'm*—its words broke off as the seed grew and grew as it sped toward the Darkness, its power reaching out as it formed a cage of molten gold seconds before it slammed over the creature, sealing it within Harlow's power.

A howl of rage shook the earth. Black, monstrous hands

reached around the bars and shook them, and the smell of burning skin reached their noses.

Magnus swore under his breath. "Witchlight," he breathed a second later, before he pulled her to him and pressed a desperate kiss to her temple. "Well done."

Harlow's eyes rolled to the back of her head, and she fainted dead away, exhausted by what she'd done.

CHAPTER TWENTY-SIX

HOMECOMING

She came to on a soft couch with several pairs of eyes staring down at her.

An undignified squeak came from her lips as she struggled to comprehend what she was seeing. But one pair of eyes looked familiar. The similar blue to hers crinkled in a smile of relief.

"Welcome back," Magnus said.

Harlow blinked up at him, the rest of the room slowly coming into focus. Once she realized where she was and that she was safe, she closed her eyes for a moment and sank into the cushions.

"Everyone make it back?" she asked, her voice raspy. Harlow swallowed, her dry throat clicking.

Her sister smiled. "Everyone is here. Though Evara grumbled a bit at having to carry you all the way back to the portal."

Evara, not in the circle of faces around her, snorted. "Someone should have reminded me she had the portal stone!"

Magnus winced. "In my defense, there was a lot going on."

"She wasn't *that* heavy," Evara mumbled.

Harlow hid her smile and used her elbows to lift herself up. "Did we get the creature?"

"For now," Magnus said. "You pulled off a clever trick. Your grandmother hasn't stopped gloating about it since we returned." He rolled his eyes but smiled as he said it.

"How long will it hold him?"

"A few weeks at most," Nova said. "Long enough for us to figure out how to cleanse the Luna stones and see if Desminda's magic can cleanse Thornewood of the creature's corruption."

Her father poured her a cup of steaming tea and pushed it into her hands when Harlow was upright.

She inhaled the fresh scent of mint and lavender and took a sip, sighing when the warmth hit her throat. Nova sat beside her, propping her feet up on the table. Shade perched on the edge of the couch close to his wife.

"Where are the stones stashed?" Harlow asked.

"On the border between the Shadow and Wolf Kingdom." Magnus poured her another cup of tea when he noticed hers was almost halfway gone. "Once you are fully recovered, we need to return to Nova's kingdom to finish the work."

Harlow's hands froze in the middle of lifting the tea cup to her lips. "Will the queen approve it?"

Nova scoffed. "You are still my sister, Harlow. And you are an adult. Queen Moira doesn't have to approve anything."

Shade put a hand on Nova's shoulder. "Harlow is still the heir," he said quietly. "Moira will have a say whether she goes or stays."

Nova's lips tightened.

"I'll talk to her," Magnus interjected, his eyes bouncing back and forth between his friend and the queen he was loyal to. "Harlow's magic is necessary in the spell work to cleanse the stones of their corruption. If I'd gotten to them sooner, I could have done it without her help, but they've been exposed to the Darkness's rot for too long."

"I will go," Harlow said. "Regardless of what she says. If I don't, we may not have a kingdom for me to inherit."

"Wise," Shade said, pride glimmering in the depths of his dark eyes. "But you should still hear your grandmother out. It costs nothing to keep the peace."

Harlow dipped her head. "How are you keeping the stones hidden?" she asked Magnus.

He smiled. "Let's just say I had volunteers."

Shade snorted. "Cryptic as always."

The door opened, revealing Queen Moira. Her face lightened when she saw that Harlow was awake.

She hurried over to the couch and pressed the back of her hand against Harlow's forehead.

"I don't have a fever," Harlow protested.

"It doesn't matter. I am your grandmother and will care for you however I see fit." Moira fished through her pocket and pulled out a small sachet of herbs. She handed it to Nova. "Please see that she brews and drinks this at least twice in the next few hours. It will speed up her healing."

Nova didn't question it, only nodded and put the herbs in her pocket. Harlow frowned, but Nova winked.

"What is it?" she asked her grandmother.

"An old family recipe. One I used to give your mother all the time. I'll teach it to you once this is all over." Moira sighed. "From the looks on all your faces, I can only assume you're going to take Harlow away from me again." She crossed her arms and waited.

Magnus winced. "Not tonight. Or even tomorrow. But I need her power to help cleanse the Luna stones."

Moira's eyebrows rose. "How many stones did you bring back?"

Nova and Magnus exchanged a glance that made Moira's lips purse. "Let me guess," she said wryly. "A lot?"

"All of them," Magnus admitted.

Moira slowly blinked. "Excuse me?"

"Thornewood no longer has any Luna stones. Unless they're sole stones owned by solitary mages."

Moira sank onto the couch next to Harlow. "How in Lunamoor—" She cut herself off with an abrupt shake of her head. "No. I won't even ask." Peering at Magnus with a strange expression, she chewed her bottom lip for a moment. "What do you plan to do with them when they're cleansed?"

"Distribute them equally," he said with a shark's smile.

Moira laughed. "A good and noble plan, but won't our creature have something to say about it?"

Harlow's eyes bounced back and forth as they talked. Obviously, no one had briefed her grandmother since their return, and every revelation had Moira's eyes growing wider and wider. But when Magnus mentioned Harlow's witchlight, her face lit up in joy.

"Witchlight!" she breathed, grasping Harlow's hands. "We barely covered it during your lessons."

Uncomfortable with the praise, Harlow shrugged. "I was under a lot of pressure."

"Strong emotions can power magic in a new witch. But it's important enough to harness your powers in such a way that you don't lose control of them." She paused and stroked Harlow's cheek. "Or yourself."

Every time Harlow had done something amazing or destructive with her magic, strong emotions were involved. While she was gaining control of her power in many other ways, the fact remained she couldn't summon feats of incredible magic yet, unless she or someone she loved was in immediate peril. It was maddening she couldn't break through whatever barrier she'd erected within herself, but Harlow knew she was close. So close.

"I know, Grandmother," she said, bowing her head.

Moira turned her attention to Magnus. "How long will you need her?"

Her father shook his head. "After dinner, and with your permission, I plan to do some research in your library. I have a few ideas, but I'd like to see if I can find anything in the older texts. I hope not to have her for more than two weeks."

Moira inclined her head. "Two weeks, then. If you have need of her longer, have Nova send her shadows to me." The queen rose and exited the room.

"You're going to have her longer than two weeks, aren't you?" Nova said with dry amusement.

Magnus rubbed a hand over his face and chuckled. "Yes, but I figured that's all she'd give me if I asked outright. Once we get her there, we can keep delaying if we need to."

Harlow shook her head at their antics. "Is it almost dinner time?"

"Yes," Nova said as she rose. "But you'll take dinner in my chambers this evening. With Evara if she's alright with it."

The guard nodded.

"And then you'll go right back to bed," Nova ordered. "We'll determine when we leave tomorrow once you wake up and we see how you feel."

"I feel fine," she grumbled.

"Until you get up and fall on your face," Nova argued. "Stay here and rest. Everyone needs to get ready for dinner."

Shade smiled at his wife and followed Nova to her dressing room while everyone except Evara filed out to head to their own rooms.

Harlow slunk down and turned sideways, face planting into the softness of the couch cushions. She might have trapped the Darkness, but all it did was buy them time.

Harlow abruptly sat up. "Where are Melara and Kalen?"

Evara lifted an eyebrow. "In their guest quarters sleeping off some trauma, if I had to guess."

Harlow grimaced. "Sorry. I don't remember anything after the cage."

"I can't imagine why," Evara said, her tone dry. "We felt your magic a mile away." She studied Harlow. "Have you ever asked your father how powerful your mother was?"

Harlow rubbed the sleep out of her eyes. "I never thought about it, but I don't need him to tell me. My veins hum with their magic."

"I want you to start training with me," Evara said suddenly.

Harlow blinked. "I already do."

She slowly shook her head. "Not with weapons. I want to help you with your magic."

Harlow frowned at the guard. "You've never divulged your magic. What's changed?"

A slow smile curved Evara's lips. "I can help you manage your emotions, which I think will help you control your bigger magic."

She didn't think much of anything besides time could help her, but she shrugged. "I guess, but I don't think it will help. I've had some of the best trainers and I haven't managed to call it up yet."

"Let's give it a try. If it doesn't work, it doesn't work. No harm done."

Harlow stared. Evara sounded so sure she could help her that it was making Harlow nervous. What did Evara know that she didn't?

"What kind of magic do you have?" Harlow asked, before she agreed.

"You'll find out."

"That's not fair. You already know about mine. Why can't you tell me about yours?"

"Because I need the element of surprise."

"You think surprising me will help?" Harlow snorted. "I don't react well to surprises."

"That's what I'm hoping for. Once I see how you react, maybe I can help desensitize you to fear."

Harlow said nothing for a long moment, her mind whirling with the possibilities of Evara's magic. But she couldn't come up with a single thing that Harlow thought would help, so she nodded. "Fine. Maybe we can start tomorrow."

"If your grandmother approves," Evara said, walking across the room to retake her post by the door. She smiled again, and this time the sight sent a lurch of nerves through Harlow's stomach. "This is going to be fun."

HARLOW FELT MUCH BETTER the next morning, so after breakfast, Evara told her to meet her at the training area farthest away from the castle. The location didn't bode well for Harlow's training, but she agreed. Now, standing across from the guard, Harlow wondered if there was anything at all to be nervous about.

Evara stood before her clad in a tunic and leather breeches, her boots discarded by her vest and sword. Harlow had to bite down her smile. She'd never seen the guard this undressed during daytime. What could she possibly show Harlow that would scare her? And not only scare her, but help steady her magic so she could always use it?

Harlow tried never to be dismissive when anyone wanted to help her, but this seemed like a colossal waste of time. Not wanting to hurt Evara's feelings, Harlow reached for her ex and planted her feet in the dirt. Every time the guard attacked, she launched herself at Harlow in a direct assault. Frightening at first, but Harlow had grown to expect it.

Standing there now, she could understand Evara's logic, but since she was already desensitized to Evara flying toward her, Harlow didn't know how this would help her. Just as she was about to dodge out of the way, Evara's skin bubbled and moved.

Harlow froze in place, mouth agape. She lifted her hand to point, but in that moment, the guard's skin split open, clear liquid gushing from the wounds, revealing a ...

A low, moaning scream came from Harlow as Evara morphed into something straight from a nightmare. Harlow flung her hands out, golden magic touched with green streaming from her fingers. The thing that used to be Evara twisted, its sinuous limbs moving gracefully like water, avoiding the strike.

Harlow stumbled back, tripping over her feet. She landed hard on her tailbone and rolled out of the way as Evara crashed to the ground where she was only a second before.

A screeching roar rumbled from the monster, saliva dripping from its fangs. Another hoarse scream tore from Harlow's throat as she scrambled to her feet.

"Hurt me," the beast said, the sibilant voice crashing through Harlow's skull. It sounded nothing like her friend.

The earth rumbled underneath Harlow's feet as Evara prowled toward her.

"N-n-no." She flung her hand out toward the monster as Harlow backed away.

Evara's blackened lips pulled away into a fanged smile. Her haunches tensed.

Harlow turned tail and ran away, frantically looking over her shoulder as Evara leapt.

Claws slashed Harlow's leather vest. She veered left, stumbling again.

Harlow fell, her fingers brushing the earth, tingling at the contact. Her mind spun as she tried to figure out what to do, but earth's magic snapped to her fingers.

"Use it," Evara hissed.

Harlow hesitated.

"USE IT!" she screamed, claws scraping against the ground.

When she hesitated again, Evara snarled, muscles coiling as she poised to leap. But even though Harlow's heart pounded with fear and her mind screamed at the wrongness of Evara's other form, she still hesitated to hurt her, even though she might die.

So swift she was a blur, Evara's claw-tipped paw swiped toward Harlow's face. Pain bloomed in Harlow's cheek. She gasped as blood poured from the wound, spilling onto the earth.

The ground greedily drank the offering, feeding on Harlow's shock and anger. Its power rose through her feet and calves, soaking her veins with magic.

"You—" Harlow whispered. "You *bitch.*" She called up her magic without a thought, flawlessly melding gifts from both her mother and father, and threw them at the slavering monster before her.

A savage laugh broke from Evara as Harlow's magic rolled through the air, followed quickly by an agonizing scream of pain as power slammed into her. Evara flew through the air, slamming into the side of the weapons area. Wood and metal snapped under the impact, and Evara lay still.

Harlow, still furious, stalked toward the guard, her power still sparking at her fingers.

Evara rose on trembling legs and waited until Harlow was a few feet away.

"Again," she snarled.

"Gladly." Harlow lifted her right hand, commanding the earth to rise under Evara, rippling under her paws and throwing her off balance. Evara slammed onto the ground, but Harlow didn't give her time to get up. Vines and roots burst through the soil, wrapping around Evara's hind end. Flame rose from Harlow's other hand.

Fear flared in Evara's eyes, but Harlow was past caring. She threw the fireball at Evara's vulnerable form and—

"STOP!" commanded a booming voice. Harlow's fireball halted in mid-flight and fell, extinguished by a phantom hand.

Magnus Stonehand stepped into the training ring, his face a mask of fury. "What is the meaning of this?"

Harlow trembled with anger even though Evara was trussed up like a roasting pig unable to move.

"She—she—" Harlow's lower lip trembled.

Evara's body shimmered, her oversized haunches and limbs shrinking and re-forming until a naked woman lay on the ground, still trapped in the maze of Harlow's magic.

Magnus's eyes flicked over the guard, his lips tight with anger. With a downward slash of his hand, the roots and vines fell away, leaving a trembling Evara shivering in the dirt. He stalked over to her, shrugged off his cloak, and tossed it over her before turning to Harlow.

He crossed his arms over his chest and waited.

Harlow still hadn't extinguished her magic, and as she stood there, she realized the magic was waiting for her command. Evara's wild, almost deadly gamble had worked.

She closed her eyes and dragged in a shuddering breath. "Damn you," she hissed, stalking toward Evara.

"Harlow—"

She ignored her father and crouched at the guard's side. "Are you okay?" she asked softly.

Evara smiled through bloody teeth. "Told you," she whispered.

Harlow sank onto the ground and buried her face in her hands, relief coursing through her body.

CHAPTER TWENTY-SEVEN

THE CLEANSING

Two days later, Nova, Desminda, Magnus, and Harlow stood close to the border of the Shadow Kingdom, staring at the pulsing, rotten heart of the Luna stones. Prince Naiam had elected to stay behind, and no one argued. He'd closed himself off from everyone once he arrived, and none of them had the heart to force him to accompany them. Losing one's father and their kingdom were two blows few recovered from, Desminda notwithstanding. Eventually, they'd have to do something about his presence in the Witch Kingdom since he was a monarch, but Queen Moira didn't seem overly worried.

Desminda said little about it, though she'd retreated even further into her shell. She gave short, one-word responses to any questions asked, though from everything the others said, she'd taken to her new magic lessons like a duckling to water. Harlow and Shade were the only ones unsurprised. For all her faults, Desminda had a sharp mind and a thirst for knowledge.

Her mother had failed her by not providing her the means to use her magic earlier, but since the queen was responsible for its downfall, no one was surprised Desminda only had rudimentary knowledge of how her gift worked.

Nova grimaced and took a few steps back. "I can barely stand close."

Evara rubbed her hands over her crossed arms and stared intently at the stones, her eyes haunted.

Desminda's lips curled in distaste, and she moved closer to Nova.

Harlow still carried the stone her sister had given her and the one the mysterious woman in the marketplace had insisted she'd come back for one day. But she never had, so Harlow took to wearing that one on her neck and keeping her sister's stone in her pocket.

The difference between the stones she wore close to her body and the stones a few feet away felt like night and day. Her magic threatened to leap from her body to cover the stones and snuff out the rot. Magnus stood next to her, his face a grim mask as he studied them.

"Where should we start?" Harlow asked.

"Let me see if there are any untouched stones I can separate," her father said.

The size of the pile was mountainous, a towering, haphazard tangle of black and iridescent stone. Harlow admired his ability to sort meticulously through it with his magic, to figure out what he could extract and what had to stay.

"Take a few steps back," he warned.

Harlow didn't hesitate. She and Evara moved close to Nova and watched as Magnus lifted his hands. The tower of stones rumbled and cracked, some at the top breaking off and plunging down the pile to land at Magnus's feet.

Sweat broke out over his forehead, and they watched as a large pile of stones floated from the back of the pile over to where he stood. Clean stones, and not even a tenth of what lay before them.

He gently moved them far away from where they stood and set them on the ground.

"Everything else is corrupted?" Harlow asked.

"Unfortunately." He jerked his head toward the stones. "Desminda and Harlow. Come stand beside me."

Desminda hesitated, but came when Magnus turned and gave her an annoyed look. "These are the stones your kingdom stole from its people and the rest of Lunamoor. If you don't help us, I will inform your people who became their salvation."

Desminda's cheeks colored. She bowed her head and scurried over, coming to stand next to Harlow.

"Fear does not become you," Harlow said under her breath. "What happened to that girl who was scared of nothing and no one?"

Desminda's brows drew together. "The Darkness spoke to her and tried to make her his."

Harlow shot her a look of alarm, but Magnus took a step closer, dragging Harlow by the hand. She grabbed Desminda to come with her.

"I want you to reach out and tell me what you feel," he said to Desminda.

She grimaced, but did as she asked. Her palm went up and a gentle pink light flowed from her hands to the stones. Desminda gasped when her magic touched the corruption, and tears slid down her face.

"They're sick," she whispered. "Begging for help."

"Can you heal them?" he asked.

Desminda glanced at him in surprise. "I-I'm not sure."

"Try," Magnus commanded.

Desminda frowned, but turned her attention back to the stones. She blew out a breath and sank to the earth, folding her feet under her as she placed her hands on the earth. A gentle wind began to blow, sending Desminda's dark hair flowing away from her face like a ribbon.

Her magic rolled over Harlow's skin, a sensation that reminded Harlow of morning sunshine. A smile slid over her lips, gentle and serene as Desminda reached out for the corruption. The stones flared pink, then gold, until they became the deep, glossy green of shade plants in a dim forest. Sweat broke from her upper lip and forehead, and her smile became strained.

"Come," Magnus whispered to Harlow. He motioned for her to crouch on the other side of the healer and when they were situated, he touched her shoulder and closed his eyes. Harlow did the same, jolting when Desminda's power mingled with her own.

Harlow's magic always felt destructive in a way, never this gentle pool, like a bubbling stream, that came from Desminda. She felt her father's power soaking into the healer, and Harlow followed suit, opening herself up and allowing Desminda to use their power to fortify hers, sending it through the stones to cleanse them of the dark magic that had almost destroyed them.

As soon as their combined power touched the rot, Harlow sucked in a harsh breath. Everything inside her told her to pull away, to retreat, to run away from it and never return, but Desminda held steady, chipping away at the black rot until each stone was cleaned. She worked methodically, checking all angles to ensure not a speck of black was left before moving onto another.

She wasn't sure how long she knelt by the princess, but sweat poured from her, down her hair, sliding underneath her shirt and down her bare back. Breath hissed from between her teeth as Desminda took more and more. Opening her eyes felt like a chore, so she kept them squeezed tightly shut, allowing the former queen to direct their commingled magic.

A rumble shook the earth, and silence fell a second before

the world shattered with the high notes of a pure song of power. Desminda gasped and reared back, breaking the connection.

Harlow sagged to the ground just before Desminda slumped into an unconscious heap.

Magnus swore and reached for her, but Harlow wasn't sure what happened next because sleep overtook her.

A GENTLE SLAP on her cheek brought Harlow around. She blinked and put a hand to her aching head.

"How long?" Harlow croaked.

"Only a few minutes this time," her father said with a grin. "You're getting better."

"Desminda?"

"She's still out." Magnus held a hand out to help her up. "I don't think she's ever used that much power at once."

Once she steadied herself, she turned to look at the Luna stones. Her jaw dropped and tears sprang to her eyes. The mountain of stones had collapsed on itself, sending them scattering as far as the eye could see. They lay around them in random piles, thicker than Magnus's arms. But the best thing was the absence of the haunting, dark magic that had clung so tenaciously to the stones.

She opened her senses, and her magic sang. "Oh,' she breathed. "It's beautiful."

Her sister moved through the stones, careful not to step on any. "This is how it should always feel," Nova said quietly. "The creature is anathema to magic and corrupts everything it touches."

"What will you do with them?" Harlow asked, reaching down to scoop up a handful of glittering stones.

Magnus smiled. "I will return them to the kingdoms, but before I do, we have one more spell to perform."

Harlow's shoulders slumped. The thought of doing more magic after cleansing the stones made her want to curl into a ball.

Magnus laughed. "But not today. We'll come back here tomorrow and give Thornewood its magic back."

"What about the Darkness?" Harlow asked. "It possesses magic, too. Will it grow more powerful if we break the spell?"

Magnus nodded. "I believe so, but it's our best chance to win. We need everyone at their full power if we hope to stand against the creature. There's still time for us to break the spell's hold and return to Thornewood to destroy it while it's still caged."

Desminda stirred at our feet, her hand swiping through the stones. Her eyes flew open, and she abruptly sat up, wincing as she lifted a hand to her head. "Ouch," she moaned.

"Don't get up yet," Magnus warned. "The first time depleting dark magic is the worst."

Desminda gasped when she saw the stones littering the ground. "They're free?" She lifted wide eyes to Magnus.

He smiled, true delight brimming in his eyes. "Yes. We will come back tomorrow to break the spell on Thornewood."

Tears shimmered in Desminda's eyes. "And everyone will get their magic back?"

Magnus nodded. "As long as everything goes correctly."

Harlow glanced at him, but Magnus didn't seem worried.

Desminda smiled a true smile, the first one to grace her face in a while. "That would be wonderful."

Harlow looked for Evara, finally spotting the guard several feet away, scooping up handfuls of the stones and sifting through them like sand. She wore a strange smile, and Harlow could have sworn her eyes flashed an odd green color. Of all the magic Harlow expected Evara to have, the beast she'd turned into was not one of her choices. She still hadn't brought it up or even thanked the guard for her role in helping Harlow's magic merge.

How did one thank someone for simultaneously scaring them to death while also helping them defeat a self-imposed barrier? She shook her head and waded through the stones toward the guard, practicing what she was going to say.

But when she got there and Evara was looking at her expectantly, all thoughts flew from Harlow's head.

"Err," she began.

One of Evara's dark eyebrows rose.

"Thank you for helping me," Harlow mumbled. "The other day. Umm. When you turned into ..." Her voice trailed off.

"When I turned into a hideous monster and scared the pants off you?" Evara said mildly.

Harlow sighed. "Yes. Well. Sort of. You know what I mean."

Evara crossed her arms over her chest and stared. "I'm afraid I don't," she said sadly.

Harlow snorted. "I hope I get to choose the next round of guards Nova hires so we don't bring on another like you."

Evara laughed. "I give it two weeks before they find you dead, then. Nova knew exactly what she was doing when she assigned me to her troublemaking sister."

Harlow rolled her eyes. "I can't help that trouble seems to find me."

"Exactly," Evara said. She slung an arm over Harlow's shoulders and leaned in to murmur in her ear. "You are welcome, regardless."

Harlow was dying to know where Evara had come from and why she'd never seen her magic before. She was mustering up the courage to ask when Evara pulled her away from their party and maneuvered her over to a large slab of rock. She climbed on top and sat down, motioning for Harlow to do the same.

"I don't know where I'm from," Evara began.

At Harlow's look of surprise, she smiled. "My parents are of mixed heritage, and I'm not sure where my beast form comes from. I've never met another like me."

"It's …" Harlow drifted off, unsure what to say without hurting Evara's feelings.

"Terrifying?" Evara supplied.

Harlow nodded. "When did you shift for the first time?"

"My sixteenth birthday."

Just like Harlow. The sixteenth birthday was sacred in the lands of Lunamoor. Most came into their magic that day, though the teenagers of Thornewood didn't have the option, thanks to Desminda's mother. She wondered for a moment what would happen when magic spilled back into their kingdom and what kind of chaos it would bring.

"Are you afraid of me?" Evara asked softly.

Harlow blinked. "No. When I first saw you, I was," she admitted. "But not after it was all over. You aren't different just because you have another form."

Evara's hazel eyes bore into Harlow's face. She reached out and tipped Harlow's chin up. "When this is over, I'd like to spend some time with you. Properly. Without the threat of death or war."

Harlow lowered her eyes. "I'd like that."

"Good."

Magnus called everyone over. Nova's magic tingled in the air as she opened a doorway to the Shadow Kingdom to let everyone in.

When Magnus lingered behind, Harlow stayed with him. He murmured a few words and lifted his arms in the air before slowly lowering them. The Luna stones trembled before the earth opened up and swallowed every single stone whole.

Harlow sucked in a breath. "Why did you do that?"

"So someone doesn't come along and stumble over these and think they've earned themselves a fortune," he said dryly.

Harlow looked and couldn't find a single stone. "Where did they all go?"

"Deep within the earth. Not a single one should go missing tonight." He winked and headed into Nova's kingdom.

Harlow took a minute to marvel at her father's power before she hurried inside after him.

CHAPTER TWENTY-EIGHT

THE SUNDERING

Nova's shadows danced joyously at their queen's return. Unlike the Witch Kingdom, Nova's people lined the streets in anticipation of a glimpse of their queen, and Nova granted it, choosing to walk the main streets through town instead of taking the shadowy passages back to the castle.

Harlow marveled at Nova's welcome, and a pang of homesickness hit her that was so strong it humbled her. As much as she loved her grandmother, she missed the Shadow Kingdom and its citizens. Their love for Nova knew no bounds, and Harlow's posture straightened as she walked beside her sister, knowing Nova deserved it.

The gates of the castle clanged behind them. As soon as they stepped behind the doors, Nova stopped and leaned against one of the stone walls, exhaling. Her shadows escaped and hovered worriedly over her shoulders.

She waved them away. "Worry warts," she said fondly, a faint smile curling over her lips.

"Are you okay?" Harlow held the door open for Evara and her father before allowing it to clang shut with a metallic boom.

"Just tired. I didn't sleep much last night and I've been

burning much more magic than usual." Nova pushed away from the wall. "Nothing a good night of sleep won't fix."

Harlow linked her arm through Nova's. "I'll walk you to your rooms. Shade's already there, I assume?"

Nova nodded. "I sent him back this morning."

Harlow waved at the rest of her party and led Nova back to her chambers, knocking softly when she reached the rooms.

Shade opened immediately, eyes flashing with concern when he saw his wife. He reached for her and took her hand, leading her inside.

"Everything go according to plan?" he asked Harlow.

"The Luna stones are cleansed and buried where no one can find them. We'll head to Thornewood tomorrow to break the spell hindering magic."

"We should be prepared for a full-scale conflict."

Nova, who had already kicked her shoes off, flopped onto the bed. "We will be. I've been making some house calls."

Harlow and Shade looked at each other. Shade shook his head and grinned. "We're skipping dinner. Tell the others, please."

Harlow nodded, but Shade had already slammed the door in her face.

She chuckled and went to find her rooms, exhaustion weighing her shoulders down.

THE NEXT MORNING, they stood just inside the border of the Shadow Kingdom. Harlow had left Astrid with the portal stone and should be outside waiting for them. Nova's magic was most powerful inside her kingdom, but her portal magic didn't work as well until she was outside its borders, due to all the protection spells she had up. Thus, the reason they were all gathered here.

Shade looked like wrath personified, dressed in all black and strapped with weapons. Desminda had given up the dresses she usually favored and wore head to toe earth-green leather. She wore a small blade strapped to her hip, one that looked familiar, and had her hair tightly braided close to her head.

Magnus wore dark brown leather armor but had kept his arms bare. He'd painted strange sigils all over his skin that made Harlow do a double take when she saw him at breakfast earlier. A massive sword was strapped to his back, and he looked every inch the powerful warrior of legend.

Harlow wore the armor she trained in, complete with two new straps for her axes that Nova gave her earlier. Her hair was woven, courtesy of Nova, into two tight braids down either side of her head. Her fingers twitched with anticipation. Thornewood had been devoid of magic since Harlow was a baby, and seeing it whole again filled her with hope. The kingdom and its people had the chance to flourish again. She could only hope there were people left to save, and they'd escaped before things had gotten so grim.

If they could destroy the Darkness and the chaos it had wrought.

"We have to portal farther away this time. There's no telling what's happened since you've left."

"I'd feel it if the thing had broken the cage, wouldn't I?" Harlow asked Magnus.

His smile was grim. "I've never seen magic performed quite the way you did it, so I'm afraid I can't say for sure."

Was that good or bad? Harlow grimaced only for her father to laugh and place a comforting hand on her arm. "Do not fret. Every magician is unique. You must find your own path. If I had done as you did, I would have sensed the cage break, but your magic is still untested. We will see when we get there. Regardless, you bought us the time we needed to free those stones. Releasing magic will come much easier now."

Harlow let out a sigh of relief, but her emotions were mixed. If that thing had gotten loose, who knew what would happen to the people they'd left behind.

Nova put a hand on her shoulder. "Do not worry about the things you cannot change," she chided. "Come. It's time to right a grievous wrong."

Nova led Harlow through the barrier.

Astrid stood with one other witch Harlow did not recognize, along with Bloom, Melara, and Kalen. The bard looked different somehow. Stronger, taller. She smiled when Harlow appeared through the shadows and stepped forward.

"Thought you could use some extra hands. The witch is courtesy of your grandmother." Astrid leaned forward. "Guess she thinks you still need supervision."

The witch gave her an exasperated look. "The witch has a name." She turned to Harlow and offered a bow. "Lyra. My specialty is healing. She thought Desminda might be busy, so she wanted me to come in case anyone needed help while you're in Thornewood."

"I don't think we've met before," Harlow said.

"I don't get out of the healing wing often," Lyra confessed. She was on the taller side, pale-haired and blue eyed. Lyra was slender but wore armor and a sword strapped to her back. "I'm decent in a pinch if we come under attack, but I'm much better used as a healer."

"We can always use a good healer," her father said. "I'm Magnus." He introduced everyone else. "If we're all ready to go, Nova can start opening the portal."

Everyone nodded. Kalen and Melara looked much better with some rest and proper food. Bloom started forward but abruptly stopped, her eyes flaring silver before freezing like a statue.

Nova had lifted her hands to start the spell, but lowered them when she saw Bloom fall into a vision. "I'll wait until she's coherent," she said quietly. "This might pertain to our trip."

Lyra gaped at Bloom. Surprising since Miriam was a Seer, but maybe her grandmother didn't use the healers for her.

"Should I do something?" Lyra whispered.

"No," Harlow said. "Bloom's visions usually don't last long."

Lyra didn't look convinced, but she made no move toward Bloom. Harlow settled herself on the ground, digging in the dirt with her fingers to see if she could find any of the hidden stones. But try as she might, Magnus's spell was effective. The only thing she unearthed was bits of mica and granite and not even a glimmer of a Luna stone.

Her father plopped down next to her. "You won't find anything," he said with a grin.

"How are you going to get them when we arrive in Thornewood?"

"They're already on the way."

Harlow jerked her head up to gawk. "Traveling through the earth?"

Magnus nodded. "Not all, but enough for the people of Thornewood to survive and thrive. The old queen hoarded the stones, and it almost became their undoing."

"I can't wait to see what happens when we get there," Harlow confessed. "It's been so long for those people."

Magnus nodded. "I will never forgive myself for my role in their pain."

Harlow leaned her head against her father's shoulder. "You had no choice."

"Maybe not, but I am still the one who ripped their power away."

"Why do you need me and Desminda to break the spell when you were the only one who cast it?"

Magnus bowed his head, grief etched into the lines of his face. "Safeguards I put in long ago so another mage or even myself couldn't return the power before it was safe to do so."

Harlow frowned. "And it's safe to do so now?"

Her father sighed. "No, but we need every available mage to help in our fight."

"And you think they will after all this time?"

"I can only hope they see their only salvation lies in fighting for their freedom."

Bloom snapped awake. "Gone," she whispered, her voice trembling. "Everyone is gone."

Harlow rose, but Nova was already by her side. She helped Bloom to the ground. "Sit down for a moment and gather your thoughts."

The Seer sank to the ground and buried her face in her hands, tears streaming through the cracks in her fingers. Everything went still, as if even the earth could sense her grief, and they waited to hear what terrible news Bloom had seen.

When she finally gathered the courage to speak, horrified gasps rang out through the clearing.

"The Darkness has claimed every person in Thornewood for its own. Everyone and everything once touched by the creature now bows to it. Or they are dead." Bloom drew in a shuddering breath. "I can sense no one left."

Magnus went to his knees, anguish written all over his face. His mouth worked as if he sought to come up with an explanation, something to negate what Bloom had said.

Nova closed her eyes and drew in a long breath. "Has it spread elsewhere?"

Bloom swallowed, tears still leaking down her face. "The Kingdom of Light has succumbed."

Nova waited.

Bloom's voice cracked again. "The Kingdom of Roses is gone, and the Kingdom of Crystal is almost overrun."

"The cage failed," Harlow whispered. "I—I felt nothing. No indication it had escaped." Her eyes found Magnus. "I—I'm so sorry."

Magnus's devastated eyes found hers. "You are still a new mage, Harlow. The magic you cast bought us enough time to remove those stones. It was enough."

But the truth was evident on everyone's faces. It wasn't enough. How many lives lost were worth cleansing the stones to return magic? Magic that maybe didn't matter anymore, since Thornewood was no more.

Harlow looked for Desminda. The former queen was on her knees, her face buried in her hands, silent sobs shaking her thin shoulders. Grief was a knife through Harlow's heart. She moved toward Desminda, sinking beside her and gathering the golden queen in her arms. Desminda didn't resist, sinking into Harlow's warmth. She shook with her grief, mouth open in a silent sob.

Harlow pressed her close, winding her fingers through Desminda's thick braid to hold her tight. There was no need to return to Thornewood to liberate a kingdom of ghosts. What were they to do now?

Everyone lowered themselves to the ground, their expressions of horror mirroring each other. The only sound was the soft sniffle of tears and a gentle wind rustling the trees.

Desminda's shaking died down, but she didn't stop clutching Harlow's vest, hot tears soaking through the linen shirt. But Harlow didn't mind. Grief expressed was grief eventually healed, and it was better than internalizing it. Shade eventually came over and sat down beside them, close enough for Desminda to feel his warmth. He pressed a hand to the top of her head and let out a sigh.

"I'm so sorry," he said quietly.

Desminda flung herself against him, and Shade took his turn providing whatever comfort he could until they all were quiet and numb.

The decision about what to do next was taken out of their hands when a mournful howl shattered the quiet. Harlow froze, eyes scanning the horizon, when several dozen wolves appeared from the woods.

Desminda gasped, scrambling closer to Shade, but Nova stood and raised a hand in welcome. Shade swore. "Nova," he hissed.

"They are our allies, Shade. The wolves are always welcome here."

Be that as it may, Harlow couldn't help the shiver of fear rolling down her spine. Wolves in the wild are large, but the ones standing before her ... she'd never seen the like.

She slowly came to her feet. These were the people who'd taken her in, protected her, and died for her. She owed them something more than fear.

Harlow walked up to her sister's side and slid her fingers through Nova's.

Together they walked up to the wolf who stepped away from the others, a creature whose shoulders came up to Harlow's waist. Her heart beat like a rabbit as the wolf came within a few feet. It stepped one leg forward and dipped its head. Nova smiled.

Harlow stepped away from her sister, so close to the wolf she could reach out and touch its white fur. She placed a hand against her chest and knelt.

"My name is Harlow Stonehand. My mother's name was Marion. Your people saved my life at the risk of your own. It's a debt I can never repay." She bowed her head.

A flash of light made her jerk in fright. When she raised her head, a tall, lean male with ash blond hair and piercing green eyes stared down at her.

"Rise, princess, and let me get a good look at the daughter of a witch and a mage." He held out his hand, and Harlow slid her fingers in his. The man's palm was warm and dry, calloused to the touch. A worker's hands.

Harlow came to her feet. He didn't drop her hand.

"My name is Cain. I lead the wolf people." He gestured to the wolves behind him. Flashes of light came with cracks of sound, and soon dozens of men and women stood before them. "I come with news and a request."

Nova stepped forward. "We have news as well, Cain. Would you like to come back to the castle for sustenance?"

"If it pleases you, Queen Nova. We've had a hard journey."

"Of course." Nova reopened the door to the Shadow Kingdom and escorted everyone inside.

Cain's news wasn't surprising. The Darkness was continuing at an unheard-of pace. If Cain's calculations were correct, by evening time, half his kingdom would be swallowed by corruption. He'd moved his people to the edge of the border, half to the Witch Kingdom, half to Nova's, and he was requesting food and shelter.

In return, he pledged his entire kingdom's aid in the fight against the Darkness.

Admittedly, Cain had already planned to help them and had sent troops to the Thornewood border in anticipation of their party's return trip.

"Where'd you get your information from?" Nova asked, an amused smile curving her mouth.

Cain grinned, his teeth a little too sharp and white. "We may not have the shadows for our eyes and ears, but our spies are still clever and quiet."

"Your information is correct. We planned to liberate Thornewood's magic this morning, but the kingdom has fallen."

Cain nodded, his face unsurprised. "How fare the Rose and Light kingdoms?"

Nova shook her head. "I do not know about their citizens, but the lands are covered by darkness."

Cain bowed his head. "I see."

"We cannot count on their armies," Magnus said. "Only three lands still stand."

Cain's brow furrowed. "The Crystal Kingdom?"

"I cannot tell you if their lands are free, but their king has bowed to the creature. He will stand against us," Nova said.

Cain let out a heavy exhale. "Our advantage is the magic richness of our lands. The other kingdoms have been in a weakened state since magic fell. I assume you have a plan on how to defeat this thing?"

"Normal armies won't do much. It feeds on magic and has to be defeated with magic."

I know who you are, princess. The voice slipped into Harlow's thoughts with ease. She jerked in surprise. *I know what your magic is made of.*

You know nothing about me.

The woman whose body I stole loathes you. I made a promise I would kill you first. The thing laughed inside her head, a hissing noise that made her quiver with fear. *But I don't want to kill you.*

No? Why not? Isn't that what you do?

Now who thinks they know me?

If you don't want to kill me, what do you want?

I have a proposition.

Let me guess. You want to slip into my skin and own me.

Not own, the thing said. *Coexist.*

You coexist with nothing. All you do is destroy things.

The thing scoffed inside her head. *I destroy nothing. I unmake.*

You twist reality to suit your needs. Unmaking is destruction.

No, child. It is unraveling something to its core to remake it into what it should be.

Is that what you did to everyone in Thornewood? Remake them?

Yes, to serve me. But I do not plan to keep them that way.

What will happen once they serve your purpose?

I release them.

Define release.

It chuckled again. Clever child. They will never be loyal to me unless I force them. No king wishes to begin his reign with disloyal subjects.

You're a tyrant with a stolen crown.

You have so much to learn. Allow me to teach you.

Get OUT of my head.

"HARLOW!" Someone gripped her arm in a bruising hold. Magic cracked through the room, a mix of her father's incredible power and her sister's cooling shadows.

She sucked in a breath of fresh air, a wheezing scream pushing from her lips.

"Thank the gods," Nova breathed, pulling Harlow's chin to face her. "Are you alright?"

She nodded, pressing her hand against her beating heart to ensure it was still there. Still hers. Harlow still felt the corruption crawling through her head, fingering through her memories for her secrets. The violated feeling shuddered over her skin.

Cain knelt at her feet. She blinked in surprise when he reached out and touched her on the knee. Strange magic flowed through her, not evil, just foreign. Cain's power swept through her veins, seeking for something.

"Gone," he pronounced a moment later. "How does it have a door?"

Magnus spoke. "I believe our magic stems from the same place. The earth speaks to us, just like it does to the creature. Where we heal, it corrupts."

"That's an issue," Cain said, rising to his feet. "How can we be sure it won't turn you against us when we are in the heat of battle?"

Harlow's cheeks burned. "How can you say that? We've fought against this thing before and won!"

Cain frowned. "When?"

"Several months ago," Magnus said. "We were traveling at the time. The thing sensed our power and snapped us into another realm."

"And now it's in ours," Cain said.

"The thing needs a body," Nova said. "One it received from Celestine."

Cain's brows lifted. "The Rose Princess?"

"The former Rose Princess," Nova said. "The Celestine we knew is gone."

"And Lucien?" Cain asked.

"Safe in my kingdom, working on gaining us allies across Lunamoor." Nova smiled sadly. "A mission I'm sure he has failed at after this morning's news."

"I wouldn't count the slippery redhead out too soon," Shade said. He'd been quiet almost the entire morning, silently listening to everyone strategize. "Have you spoken to Lucien recently?"

Nova turned a surprised look to Shade. "No. He's refused my invitations to dinner, claiming work."

A faint smile appeared on his face. "Perhaps we should find the new Rose King," he said mildly.

CHAPTER TWENTY-NINE

THE MIRACLE OF FLOWERS

The state of Lucien's room did not befit a new king. Food dishes lay piled up on a scarred wooden table. His desk was scattered with stacks of papers and pens, leather-bound journals filled with frantic scribbles, and candles burned down to the nub.

Bed clothes were arranged in disarray, half on and half off the small mattress, and several pairs of shoes were scattered under the bed.

An altar sat at the opposite side of the room, a large copper bowl full of water at the center filled with glistening rose petals. Climbing vines of all colors and sizes twined around the curtain rod and window and curled around the altar. Fat and glossy green-leaved trees sat on either side of the window, their healthy branches reaching for the faint light.

Nova's kingdom never received full sunshine, so it was a miracle Lucien's plants still lived, but his power was living things. The heady scent of roses and jasmine filled the room, but Lucien was nowhere in sight.

Harlow stepped deeper inside his quarters, marveling at the flora inside when a deep voice spoke.

"Care to share why you're invading my personal space, little princess?"

Harlow spun on her heel. The last time she'd seen Lucien, he'd come riding in with Astrid, filthy, terrified—the prince of a lost crown and kingdom. He'd been safe for months now, but Lucien didn't look much better than the last time she'd seen him.

"You look ... different," Harlow said.

Lucien snorted. "If you are to be queen, you need to work on your ability to lie." He stepped inside his room and went straight to his desk. "Why are you here, Harlow?"

"Nova and Shade wish to see you." They'd sent her in to get him, suspecting Lucien had a bit of a soft spot for her after their time together in Thornewood. Harlow thought that was insane, but she'd agreed to go. She'd never been afraid of the man, but they weren't close either.

If anything, she felt sorry for him. His sister was a wicked wretch, and he reminded her of Desminda—lost and alone, adrift in an enemy's kingdom.

Though Lucien had long come to realize Nova was far from his enemy. At least she hoped.

He'd lost at least fifteen pounds from his once leanly muscled frame. His once glossy hair had lost its luster, and dark purple shadows had moved in permanently under his eyes. Lucien had always been a sharp dresser, but today he wore leather breeches, boots, and his tunic half tucked into his pants, stained from something Harlow couldn't identify.

But even though he was a mess, she didn't spot a single pitcher of ale or discarded wine bottle. Whatever his vices were, they didn't involve drink.

Lucien didn't respond to her summons. She waited until it got too awkward, then sighed. "Are you coming?"

"I am waiting for one more messenger. They should be here today. Please let her Highness—"

"She said not to take any excuses and to drag you there if I had to." Those weren't Nova's exact words, but Harlow didn't like to curse.

"Did she, little rabbit?" His eyes sparkled with amusement. "Do you think you could drag me to the throne room without assistance?"

Harlow let her magic surface. All the glass in the room trembled, a high tinkling sound vibrating around them. Her hair floated around her and golden power crackled at her fingertips.

Lucien's eyebrows went up, and a laugh rumbled from his chest. He turned in his seat and studied her for a long moment. "It seems you are a rabbit no more. Very well, Harlow." He rose. "Bring me to your queen."

Harlow held the door open, and Lucien passed by her wearing an amused smirk. She might be a princess now, but she still felt like the same scared young girl she was the first time she'd met him. Resisting the urge to stick her foot out and trip him, Harlow let the door close and led Lucien toward the dining room.

Noise from the main foyer drifted as they walked. Lucien's steps hitched when he spotted Cain's people inside. Harlow bit down her smile when she noticed some of them had reverted to their wolf forms.

"We have guests," Harlow said.

"I see that," Lucien murmured, craning his head around for a final look as they passed.

Evara and Shade stood outside the dining room speaking in low voices. When they spotted Harlow, they broke away and opened the doors for Lucien to step inside.

"Queen Nova and the Wolf King await you," she said.

Lucien's eyes flickered, but he nodded and went into the room.

Harlow followed, taking a seat at the end of the table where no one else sat. Evara sat next to her and Shade took the opposite seat.

Maybe she should have told Lucien to change his clothes. Next to Nova and Cain, Lucien looked like a stable hand.

"Prince Lucien," Nova said, her silvery eyes taking his bedraggled appearance in. "Thank you for joining us." She introduced Cain. The two men shook hands, but Lucien was obviously nervous, which amused Harlow to no end.

They made idle conversation for a little while until Nova brought up the reason they'd called him in. Lucien went pale when he heard the news about the Rose Kingdom and the others, sinking into a seat with a harsh exhale of breath.

"We need everyone we can get. Has anyone responded to your summons?"

Lucien scrubbed a hand over his chin. "The Wolf Kingdom is already here, so I'll leave them out."

Cain gave Lucien an edged smile.

"The Crystal King ignored me, but I heard from one of his ambassadors. I don't know their current status, but he implied he would be defecting from the kingdom with hundreds of other residents."

That was news to Harlow. The way King Adama described it, his entire kingdom was on the side of the Darkness. The prince hadn't said a word about any defection. Perhaps he hadn't known.

"I have not heard from him in two weeks, so I do not know their status. The Light Kingdom never responded. I have several contacts in my kingdom who informed me they were under strict orders to not speak to me." Lucien's eyes darkened. "I told them as much as I could without giving away my whereabouts and told them to leave the kingdom if they knew what was good for them."

"The beasts will ally with us," Nova said. "As will the wolves and witches. There's no way to tell about the other kingdoms under the Darkness's rule. For now, we must assume they are our enemies."

Lucien's jaw tightened. "You cannot ask me to fight against my own people."

Nova's look was sympathetic but steady. "Will you fight against your people when they try to murder you?"

Lucien drew in a gasp of shock. "They would never—'

Cain held up a hand. "They can and they will. If this thing has its claws as deep in your people as it appears to, we must treat them as an enemy until they show us otherwise."

"And how will we know?" Lucien asked.

"If something is tainted by the Darkness, you will know," Nova said quietly. She inhaled and steadied her shoulders. "Regarding that, I must speak to you about your sister."

Lucien stilled. "Celestine was lost to me the moment she turned her back on our family."

"Be that as it may, it is still difficult to turn on one's own blood. My people have seen Celestine recently."

Lucien's eyes widened. "Truly? She lives?"

Nova's jaw tightened. "What has been done to her is no life."

His brows drew together.

"She and the Darkness have merged. Celestine is no longer the sister you once knew. The creature has possessed her body and is using her magic to feed on."

"She is dead, then." The finality in Lucien's words felt like a stab in the heart.

"I'm sorry, Prince Lucien," Nova said.

He tilted his head in acknowledgement. "I am sorry, too."

Silence fell in the room as Nova's words truly sank in, along with the meaning behind them. His head jerked back when he realized it. "No," he whispered. "My parents—"

"It won't be official until we can get inside your kingdom to see what damage the Darkness has wrought," Nova said.

"Until then, we must assume you are the new King of Roses," Cain said.

Lucien's nostrils flared. A crack of laughter escaped him, but it wasn't amused. The opposite, in fact. "All my life, I thought about the day I might be king. But Celestine always had the stronger personality of the two of us, and I'd resigned myself to standing in her shadow. And at first, I was devastated." He bowed his head. "Then a bard straight out of legend hauled me onto a horse and raced me out of Thornewood to this kingdom where my magic should feel stifled. And yet, it doesn't. It still works just as well as the moment I broke free from Thornewood's curse. You gave me freedom for the first time in my life, Nova. Is it wrong that I do not want to go back? My kingdom is in ruins, and I am not sure if it's even worth going back to pick up whatever shattered pieces might still lie there."

"It is not wrong," Nova said quietly. "I did the same thing when I found Harlow in Thornewood's ruins. But eventually our duties come to collect us, even when we do not want to go. For now, we will assume you are the king-in-waiting. We will travel to Thornewood tomorrow to break the spell that never should have been cast. Once magic is restored, we may find ourselves in the fight of our life. But if we walk away the victor, we can see about rebuilding things again, along with peace between all our kingdoms."

Lucien nodded and rose, bowing his head to Cain and Nova. "Then I will prepare for a journey, if that is all."

Nova dismissed him, and waited until he was long gone before musing, "I think he's keeping something from us."

"Something bad?" Magnus asked.

She shook her head. "No. Something he hasn't yet resolved and doesn't want us to know."

"Should I try to find out?" Shade asked.

"No. He has lost everything. Let him keep this secret." Nova sighed and stretched her feet out. "I will ask the kitchens to let us dine separately this evening to give us time to spend with our loved ones. We shall meet tomorrow morning at the border where we came in." She rose and smoothed her skirts, turning to Cain. "If you have need of me, catch a servant to call. One will be in shortly to see your people to your rooms."

Cain rose with her. "Thank you for your hospitality."

Nova chuckled ruefully. "You may curse my name tomorrow, but you are welcome for today."

They smiled at each other before a servant breezed in and escorted Cain away.

When he was gone, Nova turned, her expression grim. "We should plan for battle soon. Possibly as soon as tomorrow."

No one said a word. Harlow wasn't surprised and from everyone's face, no one else was either. With four kingdoms off the potential ally list, and the possibility of thousands of Lunamoor citizens dead or subverted, things looked grim for everyone still left standing.

Shade held the door open as they filed out, silent and pensive. Evara walked beside her, the soft scent of night-blooming florals floating from her hair. Harlow longed for a time when she could retreat to her room and invite Evara in. Maybe they would just talk about their favorite books or the places they would travel to one day soon. Maybe they would do other things. But it would be normal, something she hadn't had in far too long.

Nova stopped at her door and turned. "Harlow?"

Evara and Magnus kept walking, her father reaching out to

tweak her braid. "I'll come to your rooms later for dinner if that's all right."

Harlow smiled. "Of course."

Nova waited until they were out of earshot. "Are you ready for tomorrow?"

Harlow snorted. "Ready for my first war, you mean?" She sighed and leaned against the wall. "Do you think everyone in Thornewood is dead?"

Nova nodded. "If they aren't physically dead, their minds are. It's only a matter of time before their bodies follow."

"Do you really believe that?"

She blew out a breath and slumped. "I have to. Otherwise, I will not have the courage to do what I have to do to save the rest of us."

Harlow moved closer and bumped her head against Nova's collarbone. Her sister huffed a laugh and gathered Harlow into a tight hug.

"You're the bravest person I know," Harlow mumbled against her sister's skin.

"Says the bravest person *I* know," Nova said.

They stood like that for a moment before Nova sighed and pulled away. Shade waited with his arms crossed, a soft look in his eyes reserved for his wife.

Nova leaned in and murmured in Harlow's ear. "I've given Evara the night off. You should invite her for dinner."

Harlow's heart leaped before she immediately came back down to earth. "Father asked to eat dinner with me."

Nova's lips twitched. "Ah. Well, I think he would understand this time."

Her cheeks burned with embarrassment. "We will have time later."

Nova took both of Harlow's hands and pressed her forehead against Harlow's. "Time is too precious of a commodity to think you'll have more later. I will talk to your father." She exhaled. "Enjoy this night together. Be normal for at least a little while." Her sister pressed a kiss to her forehead and stepped away. Shade pulled her close and led her into their room. Before the door shut, Shade paused.

"Harlow?"

She'd already started to turn away. "Yes?"

Their eyes met. "Time is the one thing your mother never had. I know she would have set the world on fire to have a few more minutes with you."

Harlow's throat went thick with tears.

He smiled, his eyes sadder than Harlow had ever seen. "And I would have set it on fire to have a few more minutes with her."

Shade shut the door, leaving Harlow standing outside, tears streaming down her face. She drew in a shuddering breath, wiped her face, and hurried down the hall, away from her room to find Evara.

CHAPTER THIRTY

NORMALCY

Evara and Harlow sat on the floor, on opposite sides of the table with a large slice of cake between them. Their conversation had been halted and slow for the last two hours, and Harlow felt like she was on the verge of screaming.

The easy camaraderie they'd experienced over these last few months had suddenly evaporated into this odd tension-filled moment that neither of them could seem to break. Evara looked uncomfortable, and she picked at the cake, barely eating any of it. Harlow hadn't even picked up her fork yet.

Time, as precious as Nova and Shade had impressed upon her, dragged like molasses dripping from a spoon, and Harlow wanted to erase the last few hours and pretend they'd never happened.

"This is awful," Evara said, pushing the cake away. She set her fork down and plopped her head on her hands, staring at Harlow with an unreadable expression.

Harlow sighed. "You can go if you want to."

Evara's expression didn't change. "Do you want me to?"

How was she supposed to answer that? She couldn't say yes *and* no. Harlow just wanted the awkwardness to stop.

"What kind of books do you like?" Harlow blurted.

Evara smiled. "All kinds."

"But your favorite?"

"Military history and tactics."

Harlow barely suppressed her wince, but Evara noticed, chuckling under her breath. "Yours?"

"Fantasy. Romance sometimes," she confessed.

"Ah. I'm not surprised your tastes run toward the fanciful."

Harlow chucked a napkin at her. "Real life is difficult enough. When I pick up a book, I don't want to think about real problems."

"Fair enough." Evara took a sip of her ale. "Are you sure you want to spend tonight with me?"

Harlow blinked in surprise. "Why wouldn't I?"

The guard shrugged. "You're a princess."

Harlow frowned. "So?"

Evara snorted. "I adore how you refuse to see duty and ethics as something that applies to you."

Harlow burst out laughing. "Don't queens get to do what they want?"

"Within reason," Evara agreed. "But you aren't a queen yet, so I caution you to be careful."

Harlow waved Evara's words away. "Everyone thinks we're dying tomorrow, so for tonight, I can pretend I am a queen."

Evara laughed.

"Do you play chess?" Harlow asked.

"I do. I'm quite good at it, too."

Harlow came to her feet. "Let's play."

Evara rose and came around the table. She reached for Harlow's hand and linked their fingers together. Evara's calloused fingers slid over her palms, and warmth spread through Harlow.

They settled on opposite ends of the chessboard. "Blue or white?" Harlow asked.

"Blue," Evara said.

They played three rounds, Evara beating her soundly for two. And as time passed, this time much faster, Harlow finally relaxed. Someone came in and refilled their pitcher of ale, and the suns slowly set beneath the horizon.

They moved from the chessboard to the couch and ended the night curled around each other, Evara's fingers trailing lazily through Harlow's hair.

"I should leave," Evara said. She shifted to rise, but Harlow made a noise of protest and tightened her fingers around Evara's waist.

"Stay," she mumbled against her shoulder.

Evara's soft laugh made Harlow smile. "I shouldn't."

"We shouldn't have to fight a monster that eats magic, but that's what we're doing tomorrow."

"You are the heir to the Witch Kingdom." Evara's fingers still moved through her curls, and Harlow wanted to stretch like a cat.

"Not after tomorrow."

Evara's surprised laugh made Harlow chuckle. "Who knew you could be so macabre?"

"Stay," Harlow said quietly.

Evara's fingers stilled. "Harlow—"

"I am eighteen, Evara."

"I know. I'm only saying—"

"Do not tell me what I want or what I think I want."

Evara sighed heavily. "Things won't be this clear when we all survive tomorrow and wonder what to do next."

"That is tomorrow," Harlow said flippantly. "Not right now."

Evara huffed. "You are incorrigible."

"Yes. Does that mean you're staying?"

Evara shifted, pulling Harlow closer. "If you're sure."

"I am. As long as you want to."

"There's nothing I want more," she said.

Harlow sighed happily. "Good."

"I just want it known that I would make a terrible queen," Evara said when the room fell silent.

Harlow laughed. "So would I."

Their laughter rose, the last reprieve before the looming threat of war threatened their peace once more.

THE NEXT MORNING wasn't awkward. Evara and Harlow had moved to the bed sometime much later that night, though Evara had refused to take anything farther than a few kisses, much to Harlow's consternation.

But when the morning light cast Evara in a golden glow, Harlow brushed a lock of the guard's dark hair away and pressed a kiss to her temple. She curled close against her and closed her eyes, sending up a silent prayer to the gods that she and Evara and everyone else she loved would walk off the battlefield tomorrow.

When Evara's hazel eyes opened, and the warm light of the sun turned them into a blazing glow of green and gold, Harlow covered Evara's lips with her own, sending everything she felt about her into that one final kiss.

And soon, they had no more time with each other.

Their precious night had run out, and now it was time to save their kingdom.

CHAPTER THIRTY-ONE

MAGIC REUNITED

The wolves guarded their backs as they stood before the shadows stretching past the borders of Thornewood. Nova sent her shadows out as far as she dared and only felt safe enough to drop them closer to the edge of the wolf kingdom's borders, forcing them to decide whether to wade into the darkness and find their way to Thornewood, or wait for the creature to come to them.

"I say we go in." Evara studied the pulsating darkness, a slight furrow between her brows.

There was no way she saw anything inside. To Harlow, it felt like staring at a solid dark wall.

Magnus nodded his agreement. "We break the spell first, then go in."

Nova said nothing, keeping her shadows tight to her body. Shade stood close, his body almost touching hers. His face was unreadable, but his frame held a stiff tension, and his fingers twitched close to the daggers strapped to his hips.

Harlow felt twitchy, too. Something watched them from beyond the border, the same malevolent presence invading her mind from time to time. She closed her mind off, sealing all the open edges of her thoughts. For now, she needed her focus to go toward the spell her father created all those years ago. When the stranglehold on Thornewood's magic lifted, then she could turn her thoughts to the presence threatening to swallow them all.

Magnus touched Harlow's elbow. "Come."

They passed by Desminda who fell into step beside them and stopped at a place free of trees and bushes, with a perfectly smooth patch of green grass, still glistening from the morning dew. Magnus lowered himself onto the earth. Harlow followed, sighing as her skin touched the ground. As time passed and she grew more familiar with her power, she began to realize contact with the earth made her feel at peace. She resisted the urge to kick her boots off and push her toes into the cool, damp earth, instead pressing her palms flat to the ground.

Magnus smiled when he noticed. "When things are safe again, you should try to commune with the earth at least once a day. I go out in the morning or early evening for at least ten minutes. But lately, it hasn't been safe." He looked in the direction of Thornewood. "I hope soon it will no longer be a problem."

Desminda remained uncharacteristically quiet, her gaze drawn to her conquered homeland.

Magnus's eyes softened. "If there's anyone left, we will do our best to save them," he said quietly.

Desminda shook her head once, a sharp motion. "Nothing could survive it. If they did, they wouldn't want to live like that." She looked down, twisting her fingers in her lap. "I remember what it felt like, having a piece of that thing living inside me. I'd rather die next time." Desminda rubbed her breastbone. "It's better this way."

"Desminda—" Harlow began.

"No. Our family is responsible for grievous sins. Perhaps it is our due to suffer this. Losing everything still doesn't make what we did bearable."

Magnus's lips thinned. "We don't know if everything is truly lost yet. If it is, it doesn't mean it's lost forever." He held his hand out to both women. Harlow and Desminda both took a hand before grasping each other to make a circle. "Harlow, follow my lead."

Harlow nodded and tightened her grip.

"Desminda, keep your senses open and send us a warning if you sense the creature. We need to complete the spell uninterrupted."

"Do you think it would try to disrupt your spell when it needs magic freed?" she asked.

"If it sees the opportunity to kill us, it will take the chance," Magnus said grimly.

Nova walked over and stopped a couple of feet away. "I'll keep watch on the borders. Cain and his people will watch your back."

Magnus nodded, inhaled, and closed his eyes. Harlow followed behind, sending her power deep into the soil to await her father. The ground rumbled, soil shifting around them. The familiar power of the Luna stones surfaced, hurtling through the ground at unheard of speed, before Magnus sent them shooting up like a geyser.

The startled shouts of Cain's wolves made Harlow smile. Magnus's fingers tightened on her own as she felt him catch the stones mentally before sending them floating back to the ground, enclosing them in a circle of power, boosted by their innate magic and the stones' natural resonance. Her magic leapt in joyous response.

Desminda's power sank into the circle, pink and golden light flashing behind Harlow's closed eyes. Warmth poured over their shoulders, her healing magic sinking into Harlow's aches and pains, washing them away like they'd never existed. Desminda's magic felt like walking through a stunning garden on a cool spring day. A sigh escaped her, and her shoulders fell, relaxing for the first time in a while.

"Ready?" Magnus asked.

"Ready," she and Desminda repeated in unison.

Harlow twined her power with her father's as it sank deep into the earth, burrowing underneath the shadowy border. Wrongness hit Harlow's tongue when their magic streamed into the kingdom fueled by darkness. Her skin turned clammy as cold sweat dripped down her neck and into the back of her shirt. Though they still made progress, it felt substantially slower now that there was a barrier fighting against them.

But Harlow gritted her teeth and fortified her magic, and together, she and her father finally reached Thornewood's beating heart.

A heart in golden and green chains.

Harlow gasped when she saw it, a single, massive pulsing Luna stone wrapped in Magnus's power. Her father stopped before it, examining the heart from all angles. A few of the chain links were damaged, but it hadn't affected the spell. A wrongness pulsed from those chains, not evil, more of a sadness that had settled into the earth.

Harlow's heart broke a little when she felt it. Magic should always be free, never wrapped in chains like this. She squashed down her disappointment, knowing her father never had a real choice in the matter, but it was difficult. She held hands with the daughter of the woman who was responsible for Thornewood's downfall, but Harlow couldn't muster up the energy to hate her.

They'd all made mistakes, but what mattered was they were here now to correct them.

"Get ready," Magnus said.

Harlow steeled herself.

When Magnus landed the first blow against those mighty chains, it felt like a gong had sounded through the world. Her teeth rattled in her head, and when the first link fell, some of the sadness dissipated. She pushed more magic at Magnus as he chipped at the chains, allowing her father to mold her power and his into a weapon capable of smashing the horrific spell he'd cast all those years ago.

They were halfway through, when the sound of the gong turned higher and sweeter. Harlow sighed in relief. Though the darkness had yet to dissipate, and it still felt like they waded in black tar, every link they broke felt like a weight lifted from her shoulders.

Desminda continued pumping her healing magic into their bodies, keeping them from getting fatigued too quickly. Harlow didn't pay much attention to her, but she felt when some of Desminda's magic crept away from their circle to explore deeper into Thornewood. They were so tightly linked Magnus had to notice too, but he seemed to pay it no mind, so Harlow did the same.

Seventy-five percent of the way through, Harlow felt something ... off. She couldn't explain what she was feeling, but the magic's resonance changed to something darker. Magnus paused, stopping Harlow's magic like a spigot.

Father?

Hold for a moment. Desminda?

Something is there, she said.

Harlow felt her father's alarm. *We need to hurry. Give me everything you have.*

She stilled, unsure, but her father's urgent tone had Harlow settling deeper into her power, opening herself up to him, allowing him to take what he needed from her, and trusting he would take no more than that. Her mother and father's magic flooded away from her body.

Magnus sucked in a breath. *Good gods*, he whispered, pausing at the behemoth that was Harlow's power, before he returned to the task at hand.

Harlow tested one of the links, studying closely how her father had done it. When she felt his approval, she struck at the chain, marveling at how it shattered beneath her thoughts and the onslaught of the power she threw at it.

And when Magnus struck the last link and the terrible spell fractured, the backlash of magic tore their hands apart and sent their bodies hurtling through the air.

She expected impact any moment, but something snatched her from mid-air, flinging her away from her allies and right into Thornewood's darkness.

She floated in an absence of light and sound, utter darkness surrounding her. It didn't matter if she closed or opened her eyes, she couldn't see a thing either way. It was the same feeling she had when she'd stepped into Thornewood's border the first time, but without the nauseating disorientation this time.

Harlow's fingers itched to connect with the earth, but nothing existed above or below her, only this odd space with an absence of light. She felt the magic surrounding her, but she couldn't reach out and touch it.

I told you we would see each other again.

Harlow stilled at the alien touch in her mind before sharply responding, *It's only fitting we meet at the end of your life.*

The thing chuckled, the sound reverberating even outside her mind.

You still think me a villain. I am what happens when magic is twisted, a natural product of your people's own folly.

Then why can't you fix yourself?

I don't want to, the thing said.

Harlow knew the words were a lie.

So you want to kill us all and do what? What will happen when you wipe us all from the face of this world? What will you have accomplished other than total isolation?

Freedom.

From what? You have no purpose without other people. No one does. Our lives mean something because of others.

I am not meant to have a purpose. I am life, but I am death. I am hope, but I am sorrow.

If you are not meant to have a purpose, then why do you insist on destroying everything?

Because you destroyed me.

I destroyed nothing.

Your kind. Humans.

Maybe. But holding the children responsible for their ancestors' sins makes you just as guilty.

You are a speck of dust and know nothing about the world.

Maybe. But you have been imprisoned long enough to forget that the world didn't stand still when it happened to you. We've grown and learned, and we're trying to make things right.

It is too late.

For you maybe. Not for the rest of us.

Harlow landed with a harsh thump on the cold ground, the voice absent from her head. She sucked in a gasp of air and rolled to sitting. Just like before, a gray pall hovered over Thornewood, but the ground no longer felt so evil. She ventured a finger in the dirt and sent a pulse of magic through the ground. The Darkness was still there, but rich, natural magic pulsed through the earth as well.

She exhaled in relief. Since the thing had snatched her into its kingdom, she didn't have to sneak around, but she also had access to her full magic without the threat of being swallowed by the Darkness.

Harlow headed straight for the old Virago quarters, keeping an eye out for any survivors. Once she did a sweep, she'd try to get out the same way she came in, but Harlow suspected escape wouldn't be so easy this time.

The longer she walked, the more disturbed she felt. There were no signs of life anywhere. No people walking or talking. Thornewood's town square looked like a ghost town, the stalls boarded up and fallen into disarray. If their people were under control of the creature, where were they? Or had it just killed them all in one fell swoop?

She paused at the entrance and froze, craning to hear any sound, but there was nothing but oppressive silence. Reaching out, she pushed the scarred wooden doors open and stepped inside the quarters she'd spent so much time in.

The beds were still in the same position they were when she lived here, but the large room was in disarray. Clothes and armor were scattered on top of the beds and over the floor. Boots and slippers were strewn all over. She went over to her old locker and opened it, expecting to see some of the things she'd left behind, but it was empty—like she'd never been there.

Harlow walked through the halls and inspected the bath-rooms and closets before exiting the back. The once proud Virago were nothing but a memory now. She and Kalen, Melara and Bloom, that's all Shade and Desminda had left of the presti-gious guards they'd painstakingly assembled.

She exhaled a heavy breath and walked to the church back in the square. People flocked to the divine when trouble came. If there were anyone left, that might be where they'd gone.

The last time she was here of her own volition, she'd stolen some books and almost got caught. Her lips tugged in a smile at the memory. Back when things felt so complicated. Compared to now, those days were a walk in the sunshine.

She paused on the steps and looked around, but nothing but

a ghost town looked back. A shiver ran down her spine when she opened the church doors. Large stained-glass windows loomed behind the pulpit showing Desminda's one true god striking down the heathens still worshipping the older gods. While frightening, the artistry was stunning, before someone or something had thrown something through the face of the god.

Not many had taken kindly to Desminda's mother forcing them away from the path of their original faith into one few believed in. It might be funny if things hadn't turned out so terribly for everyone. Where was their god now?

Harlow walked the main aisle to check the pews but found nothing but grim silence.

Shaking her head, she headed back to the town square.

"What's your plan?" she said to the empty kingdom. "Keep me here until I die?"

The Darkness said nothing.

Harlow shrugged and headed for the shadow border. As she reached out to touch the shadows, the landscape blurred and something yanked Harlow right off her feet.

Her scream cut off abruptly as all the oxygen disappeared. She reached out through the darkness, mouth open in agony, before her body plunged into nothingness.

CHAPTER THIRTY-TWO

A LONG OVERDUE MEETING

She stood next to a tall, severe man dressed in scarred, dented armor. Long dark hair flowed down his shoulders, stirred by a honeysuckle-scented wind. His nose was large and sloped, and a fresh scar flowed from the top of his temple to the middle of his cheek.

Harlow thought him handsome in a way. Severe, but worthy of a second look. She glanced down at herself and started. Her leather armor was gone. In its place was a flowing, lavender dress. Her arms were bare, her hair loose and flowing. She wore no blades, no axes, nothing to protect herself.

And she had no idea where she was. They stood on top of a cliff, overlooking a vast, green canyon. The air smelled fresh and sweet, and only one sun hung in the sky, barely peeking above the horizon. Houses dotted the landscape, tiny animals that looked like moving dots grazed in the plentiful grasslands. Birds of prey shrieked their cries above them, swooping through the air to catch smaller animals for breakfast.

She closed her eyes and inhaled.

"It's beautiful here, is it not?" the man asked.

Her eyes flew open. The Darkness stood beside her, but this

wasn't the creature who'd come to haunt her dreams. This person was human.

A smile creased the edges of his eyes. "I was just like you once." He glanced at her with earth-green eyes. "Though my power is much different from yours."

"Why am I here?"

"I want you to see what I was, what the land I ruled used to be before your golden-eyed queen's family swept in and destroyed everything."

Harlow couldn't help what was done long before she was alive. "It's beautiful," she said instead. And it was. The land laid out before her was stunning. Green and natural, calm and cool, the earth's magic begged her to call it forth. She would have loved to live in this world.

"Yes," he agreed. "My name is Alaxar. I was once a great mage before your kind imprisoned me."

"You've killed Celestine?"

His chuckle was warm and amused. "My ... *companion* took Celestine over when she invited me fully into this world."

Were there two of them, or was he being cryptic for a reason? "Your companion?"

"He used to be a friend. Caius is not as powerful as I am. Celestine offered herself up as a willing vessel and Caius accepted."

"You haven't answered my question."

"She was dead the moment Caius touched her."

Harlow suspected Caius wasn't quite as separate as Alaxar claimed.

"And what happens when her skin fails?"

"Caius will revert to his shadow form."

"And you?"

"I'm afraid I'm here permanently." He held out his hand. "Come. Let me show you something else."

Harlow hesitated.

"I ask for nothing but your time."

She put her hand in his and the landscape shifted once more moving them from a cliff top to a stone castle. Alaxar sat on a metal throne, a small crown on his dark hair. Harlow stood beside him, her dress changed from lavender to green. Hundreds of people stood in the room, forming a long line before the throne. A male knelt in submission, crouched on the floor before him.

He reached out and touched the top of their head. "Your request is granted," his authoritative voice boomed. "You may rise."

The man rose, tears flowing from both eyes. "Thank you, Your Majesty."

Alaxar tilted his head in acknowledgment.

It went on for what felt like hours. Just when Harlow was about to try to find her own way out of this odd vision, Alaxar swept his hand out, and the throne room disappeared.

They stood in a nursery next, Alaxar's hand brushing the top of an infant's head. He bent over the crib and pressed a gentle kiss to the baby's forehead. A woman stood next to the crib, small and beautiful. She reached for Alaxar's hand.

Harlow took a step back, tears filling her eyes at the scene. She didn't want to see this, didn't want to look at this creature, and see him as a man who had this life with a child and a wife who obviously loved him.

Hate was always the easier emotion, wasn't it? It was easier to grow and nourish, while love felt more like a plant that needed the perfect light, the perfect soil, the perfect amount of water to keep it growing.

She turned and left the room, blindly stumbling into the hallway to get away from the cozy scene. Pressing her hands against the cool stone of the wall, she sought the comforting feel of magic from the earth.

The sound of footsteps came from behind her. "It bothers you to see me as a man," Alaxar said.

Harlow pressed her forehead against the stone. "I'm ready to go."

Alaxar stood beside her, turning so his back was against the wall. "Together, we could remake the world back to what it was always meant to be. Your magic can unmake creation, Harlow. All you have to do is let me in."

She let out a strangled laugh. "Just like your *friend* did to Celestine?"

His expression turned disapproving. "Caius and I are not the same."

That wasn't quite the truth, either.

Harlow straightened. "You're close enough. You both feed on magic to sustain yourselves."

"We wouldn't have to if we weren't imprisoned in the first place. Those Luna stones you see all over your kingdom were never yours in the first place."

A horrible suspicion brewed in Harlow's mind. She watched Alaxar as clues began to click in her mind. How the Darkness said they'd stolen from him—both his power and his land, how he hated Desminda and her family. How could they have stolen his power unless ...

"The Luna stones are yours." It was something she already knew, but it didn't feel quite right.

Alaxar smiled, but it didn't quite reach his eyes. "Not exactly. The Luna stones are pieces of me and my family. Stolen pieces of my magic shattered into crystalized stone and scattered through the kingdoms."

Harlow's knees buckled. "H-how?" she whispered.

"The impostor queen wanted to take our magic and use it

for herself." He sighed. "Shattering my power into millions of tiny pieces kept her from doing so. The queen made it her mission to gather and store as many of the stones as she could, hoping to one day reassemble what she'd lost."

The magnitude of what he'd done sent Harlow reeling. "You started waking up when my father suppressed Thornewood's magic."

He nodded. "Your father's spell started my awakening, but I cannot return to my slumber."

"You seek to reunite your magic."

He held his arm out. "Walk with me."

Harlow curled her trembling fingers around the crook of his arm, Alaxar's metal armor cool against her skin. He led her outside and down a winding path dotted with yellow and white roses. They strolled in silence for a while before a massive garden came into view. Her heart clenched as the memory of Desminda tending her prized rose gardens assailed her.

A simpler time, but walking with Alaxar in this time and place, wherever she was, made her realize that even that simple, warm memory might be based on a lie. If he was telling her the truth, Thornewood's entire magic system was never based on the earth's innate magic, but the stolen pieces of a desperate mage.

And what would happen if Alaxar was able to put himself back together again? Would it mean their destruction? Could they allow it? Even more importantly, should they restore him to wholeness?

If Alaxar regained his magic, would it mean Thornewood's mages would lose their powers? She rubbed her temple.

They stopped at a bench. Harlow sat down while Alaxar moved from plant to plant, snapping off spent blooms and murmuring soft words.

"What will you do if you regain your power?" Harlow asked.

"*When* I regain my power," Alaxar corrected.

Harlow stayed silent.

"You still think to fight me, little mage? Even after everything I've told you?"

"You want us to suffer for ancient sins. Do you think that's fair to all the people who've never done anything to harm you?"

He glanced at her from between the fuchsia petals of a blooming vine. "Did anyone think it fair when they murdered my family and forced me to scatter my power across the world?"

Harlow huffed in annoyance. "No, of course I don't think so. But we didn't do it!"

"You are obsessed with things being fair. *Nothing* is fair. Someone has to pay for the wrongs I suffered." A branch snapped under his fingers. "Which is why you will work with me."

Harlow's brows drew together. "I never said—"

"Harlow. You are young and have much to learn. Your power remains untested, and your father coddles you by not letting you unleash yourself."

Heat spread across Harlow's face. "My father is training me how to use my power responsibly!"

"Magic is innate and should never be stifled." He dropped the flower and came to sit beside her. "Imagine the things you and I can do together. How much I could teach you."

Harlow shook her head. "No. I don't—"

Harlow!

Nova's voice screamed through her head. Alaxar's eyes narrowed, his head snapping around to look for her sister.

Nova! I'm here. I-I don't know where I am.

Trapped. We're trying to break the spell. Hold on.

I need to tell you something.

Alaxar's iron grip wrapped around her wrist and yanked her to standing. He hissed a curse. She jerked her arm, but Alaxar's nails dug into her skin. Harlow grunted in pain and reached for her magic. The castle groaned as the stone shifted beneath their feet.

Alaxar laughed. "Try to unleash yourself, little mage." His hand tightened, snuffing out her magic like it never existed.

Harlow gasped in surprise, twisting away with a move Shade had her practice a dozen times, but Alaxar held tight. As long as he touched her skin, Harlow couldn't access her power.

Helplessness roared inside her as she fought, and a flicker of her mother's power uncurled inside her. Marion and Magnus Stonehand created a daughter unlike any the world had ever seen. A natural witch had loved a battle-scarred mage, a man whose power knew no equal, and she gave birth to a small child with a burning supernova of power in her heart.

Flowers burst into bloom on her skin, and at first Alaxar was confused before those flowers grew vines, and those vines grew thick, wickedly sharp thorns. Blood burst from Alaxar's hand as those thorns pierced his skin, the first time Harlow had scored a direct hit on his body. He sucked in a breath, but the thorns grew barbs and Alaxar couldn't yank away from her unless he tore meat and sinew.

His teeth pulled back from his lips and a low snarl rumbled in his chest. "The lowest of magics," Alaxar growled.

Harlow fought for her life, but his words almost made her laugh. The lowest of magics was currently saving her life. She grabbed his wrists, ripping Alaxar's hands from her body. Fire burst from her skin, burning the plants away and singeing the sorcerer's skin from his face.

A tortured scream ripped from him as Harlow's hands wrapped around his neck. She conjured the thorns once more, and they burst through his skin as they fell to the ground.

"Harlow!" Nova's voice broke through her haze of rage.

The earth shook beneath their bodies as Harlow gained the upper hand, but just as Alaxar's struggles grew weaker, they were plunged into darkness once more.

A small, cool hand found hers. "I got you," Nova said.

"Father?"

"Beside you," Magnus said, dropping his hand on her shoulder. "Hold on."

"Do you know how to get out of here?" Harlow asked.

"Hopefully the same way we got in," Nova said, her voice strained.

They hurtled through the darkness, shadows brushing across Harlow's face before the bottom dropped out, and they landed in a heap on the ground.

Magnus groaned. "Still in Thornewood," he managed, coming to his feet.

Harlow lay on her back gasping for breath, still covered in flowers.

Nova peered down at her. "I like the new look."

Harlow snorted. "It just happened. But Alaxar didn't like it."

Her sister reached out a hand to help her up. "Tell me everything."

Just as Harlow opened her mouth, a sharp crack shattered the quiet.

Magnus spun in the direction of the noise only for them to watch in horror as the rest of Thornewood's buildings collapsed and came crashing to the ground, as if a sharp sword had cleaved everything in two.

"That cannot be good," Harlow murmured.

The ground shook hard enough to set them off balance. All around them, trees came unrooted, buildings collapsed, and massive, ragged cracks in the earth appeared.

"He's wiping Thornewood clean," Magnus said grimly. "We need to get out of here."

A swirl of dust and shadow appeared before them, revealing a rotting corpse with long, red hair and a skeletal smile.

Harlow took an involuntary step back. "Caius."

Nova's head snapped toward Harlow. "Who?"

"Not Alaxar." She frowned. "Or, not quite Alaxar." she corrected. Harlow shook her head. "I'll explain later."

But there was no time. Ropes of putrid magic skittered across the ground toward them. Magnus grabbed Nova and Harlow and leapt into the shadows.

CHAPTER THIRTY-THREE

SALVATION

They landed in a heap outside the border, limbs tangled together. Harlow groaned, knowing she was going to be bruised from head to toe the next day. She opened her eyes and gaped at the sight before her.

An army stood several feet away, Shade at its head.

Magnus helped them both stand, steadying Harlow when she swayed on her feet.

"First order of business," Magnus said, "is tearing the wall down."

The thought of messing with those wards again and experiencing that overwhelming nausea and weakness made her close her eyes for a moment and wish it was all over.

At least a dozen witches stepped forward, some familiar, some not. Then soldiers from Nova's kingdom came forward, dressed in the armor identifying them as mages, followed by at least thirty mages from the Kingdom of Crystal.

Naima caught her eye and gave her a sad smile. Not useless after all, she thought.

Desminda also stepped forward, alone.

"Where—" Harlow began. "How—"

Lucien stepped up next to Desminda and gave her a small bow. "It might look like I've been idle during my time in Nova's kingdom, but no war has ever been won without allies." He gestured to the army standing behind him. "I'm afraid my people are unreachable." His eyes flickered. "Though I hope when we tear down this creature's walls, I will find them again."

Nova lay a hand over her heart. "Thank you, Lucien. Your assistance has been invaluable." She turned to Magnus. "Let's convene for a few moments before we tackle the border."

Nova took Harlow by the arm and led them to a quiet place away from the armies.

"Tell me what you've learned," she demanded.

Harlow hurriedly spoke, and when she got to Alaxar's secret, Nova's eyes widened. Magnus's expression turned thunderous as he swore under his breath.

"That changes everything!" he bit out.

"Perhaps," Nova agreed. "But it makes a lot of sense. The other kingdoms don't need Luna stones for their powers to work. What if Thornewood was never meant to possess those stones and possessing them had altered their people somehow?"

"What are you suggesting?" Magnus demanded.

Nova looked around at the gathered armies and closed her eyes. "I think there's only one thing we can do if we want this to stop."

Harlow's stomach lurched with denial as Nova spoke. This situation reminded her of her life all those months ago when she realized everything she'd ever known was a lie. How could they go forward with destroying the stones, knowing what it might do to those people still left alive?

But how could they not with Alaxar hell-bent on their destruction?

"The world was never meant to be this way," Nova said. "Righting Alaxar's and Desminda's family's wrongs might result in anger and more upheaval, but balance must be restored. There's only one way we can ensure it happens."

They fell silent as the magnitude of what they had to do sank in. Evara and Shade walked over, their smiles dropping when they saw the somber expressions Harlow and the others wore.

"What is it?" Evara asked, coming to stand by Harlow.

When Nova explained, no one said a word for a long moment. When Shade finally spoke, he said something no one else had thought of.

"We can't tell anyone what we're doing. They may revolt."

Harlow felt sick about the entire thing. "Are we sure this is the right way?"

"It's the only way," Magnus said.

"But we aren't sure it's going to work. Alaxar is a shadow of what he could be, and we still haven't been able to do more than scratch him."

"I think you were doing quite a bit more when I found you," Nova said dryly.

"Maybe," Harlow agreed, "but he caught on pretty quickly."

"What about Desminda?" Shade asked.

"I highly doubt she'll go along with this plan." Nova glanced over to where Desminda stood alone. She watched them but made no move to walk over.

"You'd be surprised," Shade murmured. "I'll speak with her."

"I'm not sure we should tell her," Evara chimed in. "We still don't really know where she stands."

"That thing invaded her body and mind," Shade reminded them. "I think she'll do whatever it takes to get rid of it." Without waiting for them, he jogged over and drew Desminda away from the others, speaking softly in her ear.

Harlow marked the moment Shade told Desminda their

plan. Her eyes widened, and she jerked away from him, shaking her head vehemently.

"Told you," Evara whispered.

"He knows her better than we do," Harlow said. "Just wait."

Shade reached for her again, eyes pleading. Harlow saw the moment Desminda softened to his proposition.

"Got her," Harlow whispered.

A few minutes later, Shade and Desminda joined their circle. Tears swam in her eyes, but she cleared her throat. "What do you need me to do?"

HAMMERING the Thornewood border took time they didn't have to spare. The witches lasted longer than the crystal mages, but even they were drawn with exhaustion, their power sputtering. Magnus finally called for Harlow and Desminda.

"I thought we could take it down without exhausting all of us, but Alaxar's power is unlike anything they've ever gone up against." Magnus studied the border, finally shaking his head. "Let's switch the order of our plans."

"Even if it drains the other mages?" Nova asked.

"It won't harm the witches, and the crystal mages are already wiped."

"Very well." Nova's gaze swept the field. "Every soldier here has some magical talent. Once the backlash hits, we might lose them."

"We have to try." Magnus barked a command at the witches who dropped their magic instantaneously.

"We'll try again in a little while," he said, reaching out to catch a witch swaying precariously. After helping her to a cleared area and giving her a canteen of water, Magnus jogged back over.

"We'll start with the stones I brought back over. If it

works, we'll do the other ones right after." He sat down and held his hands out. This time Nova joined their circle, clasping Desminda and Harlow's hands. "Once Alaxar realizes what we're doing, the border might drop without our intervention. Ready?" Magnus swept his bright gaze over the three of them.

At their nods, he called his magic. Harlow gasped as power swelled in the circle, more power than she'd ever felt him raise. A moment later, she closed her eyes and did the same, then felt Nova and Desminda call theirs.

Contained in their circle rested enough power to raze the world. In some ways, Harlow felt like that's exactly what they were about to do.

"Concentrate and let me guide you," Magnus said.

Harlow focused on the stones, the comforting, shimmering iridescence they provided. Grief filled her, and she couldn't tell whether it was for Alaxar's loss or how their actions would make it permanent. He was a villain, there was no getting around it, but sometimes life made someone a villain due to no fault of their own.

Harlow felt the moment Magnus's magic locked onto the stones. Desminda's breath caught as she realized exactly how many pieces Magnus had taken hold of.

"*SUNDER*," Magnus commanded. Harlow's eyes flew open, her mouth open in a silent scream of effort. Lightning cracked above them, the roll of thunder shuddering through the air. Tears rolled down Desminda's face as the first Luna stone shattered. Every crack of stone felt like a stab wound in Harlow's heart.

It took a while for the others to understand what was happening. First came the screams of dismay, followed by the thud of bodies as the absence of their magic shorted out their bodies.

Desminda's tears became sobs, but the healer held on, still pouring her magic through their bond.

A scream of pure rage reverberated through the lands, Alaxar's realization cutting through the earth with startling clarity as a massive crack ran from the border straight through their army, upsetting the soldiers still standing like an avalanche.

Magnus's eyes opened next. His face was drawn in a rictus of effort. "Hold on," he said through gritted teeth, the *pop, pop, pop* of the stones shattering a sound Harlow knew she'd forever hear in her nightmares.

The Thornewood border fell, revealing a shadowy presence wearing golden armor, its face cast in darkness. Beside him stood the rotting form of Caius.

Alaxar's gaze swept the land, falling on their circle. He lifted a hand, shadows tearing from his wrist. Harlow braced herself for the blow, but Desminda let out a defiant scream and a shimmer of gold and pink rose above them, blocking the blow.

Alaxar rose above the earth, shooting toward them like a falling star.

Pop, pop, pop.

Harlow felt the last stone shatter. Desminda swayed. Half their army dropped, dead or stunned they didn't know.

Alaxar screamed, his flight faltering. He clutched at his heart, dropping to the ground.

"Be careful," Magnus rasped. "The stones might be gone, but Alaxar can still draw power from the earth." He waved his hand, and a portal opened up, reminding Harlow of the moment she first realized Magnus was still alive. Iridescent dust rose into the air, controlled by Magnus.

Alaxar lunged for it, but Magnus swept it all inside that portal, shutting it off as soon as the last speck disappeared inside.

Alaxar collapsed.

Desminda swayed, her golden eyes rolling up before she dropped like a stone.

Nova dropped Harlow's hand, and called her shadows, sending them straight for Caius. The creature was affected by the lack of stones, but appeared better off than Alaxar, who lay still as death.

Magnus rose, helped Harlow to her feet, and walked over to Alaxar.

She felt no different now that the stones were gone, her magic still a vibrant hum in her veins. Her pocket that once held a Luna stone was empty, not even a speck of dust to mark its presence.

Harlow knelt beside Desminda, checking her pulse. She was still alive but unconscious. Harlow sent a pulse of magic through Desminda's body and found her magic still alive and humming. Relieved, Harlow rose and went to help her sister.

Nova had Caius wrapped in shadows, but as fast as she could conjure one, the thing destroyed it. Harlow flung roots from the earth, trapping Caius in place, and unsnapped her axe from her side.

"Don't get too close," Nova warned, her voice breathless with effort.

"Someone has to." Harlow added thorns, piercing Caius's, or Celestine's, rotting flesh. The thing screamed and thrashed, trying to break free from its prison, but every time it broke a root, another one sprang from the ground to replace it.

Harlow didn't try to talk or reason with it. She was past the point of caring. Nothing anyone said would change what had happened. What they'd all lost. Gripping her axe firmly in one hand, she raised it and swung through the air. Metal collided with bone and sinew with a sickening crunch and slid through it like butter, sending Caius's severed head flying through the air.

Nova sent her shadows after it, catching the rotting thing, and lowered it to the earth.

Caius swayed and collapsed, black blood spraying before its rotted body caved in on itself, nature's magic finally restoring itself to allow Celestine's body to return to the earth.

An agonized scream came from Alaxar as one of the final pieces of him died.

Harlow's attention turned to Thornewood. A sob bubbled from her lips when she saw the once mighty kingdom reduced to rubble. Everything was gone. The once majestic castle and all its surrounding buildings were swallowed by the earth. Trees, stables, the carts in the town square that once held pretty trinkets and shiny fruit—all gone.

A land of green had been reduced to a desert landscape, similar to the one where she'd first met the Darkness. *Alaxar.* Everything had been taken from him, so he'd taken everything from the land.

Desminda's family's legacy destroyed forever. Nothing green grew there any longer, the trees were brown and skeletal, and the grass had shriveled and died. A hellscape looked back at her.

Harlow swallowed hard, her dry throat clicking, and turned her back on the kingdom. It was no longer her home and hadn't been for a very long time. She headed toward Magnus, but the ground under her feet cracked. When she looked down, horror filled her veins.

Something was sucking the land past the borders dry. As she watched, trees cracked and split in half, all the moisture and life sucked right out of anything natural.

"Father!" she cried, gesturing frantically to the trees.

Magnus's brow furrowed before he realized what was happening. Alaxar's head rose from the ground, a slow, pained smile crossing his face before he abruptly disappeared.

Nova blew out a frustrated breath. "He can't have gone far."

Magnus's posture grew tense as he whirled, searching for Alaxar. "Agreed. He's too weak."

"It doesn't mean he can't hurt us," Harlow said. If he's draining the earth of its power, she should be able to spot him by—

"There!" she shouted, pointing at a spot behind the army where the trees were slowly dying.

"Wall!" Magnus commanded.

Those in the gathered army still standing, raised their magic simultaneously until a shimmering wall of power rose a few feet behind Alaxar, trapping them all in an impenetrable field.

Harlow was glad because she was beginning to wonder if the army had been a waste of time. Seventy-five percent of them still lay unconscious on the ground. Guilt speared her as soon as she had the thought. It was her fault. Destroying the Luna stones meant frying some of their magic, and they hadn't been given any time to prepare for it.

Just as the wall went up, the thundering of boots sounded.

Lucien's head snapped in the direction of the sound, and he took off running.

He ignored Nova's warning, raising his hand, as he flew toward it. He disappeared through a wall of forest, only to return a minute later with a massive wall of troops, all dressed in dark leather armor, wearing flower pins of different varieties.

"Lucien," Nova breathed.

Tears swam in the prince's eyes. "My people still live."

A woman with burnished copper hair strode up and saluted Lucien. "Where is it?"

Everyone knew what she was talking about. Lucien pointed, and the woman did a smart turn and started barking orders.

Seconds later, the once dead trees slowly perked up, and a scream of frustration came from Alaxar.

"This is it," Magnus murmured.

But before he could strike, a blast of pink and gold magic struck, revealing Alaxar. Desminda's magic wrapped around him like a rope, lifting him in the air.

The healer rose on shaky legs and gently floated him over, staring at him with glowing golden eyes.

Alaxar struggled, but those bands held him tightly.

Desminda's posture straightened. "For your crimes against Thornewood and its people, you are sentenced to death."

Strains of faint music rang through the clearing. Desminda's brow furrowed, but she didn't stop speaking.

"You will die by the hands of the people you've subjugated. Your rot will be purged from the world, your name forgotten."

"You did this to me," Alaxar hissed, thrashing against Desminda's power.

"For my family's role in your pain, I am sorry, but I wasn't even a thought when you shattered your magic to save yourself. All those wrongs have never made a single right. It is time to stop the death and destruction." Her lips pressed together as her hands trembled.

Harlow stepped up beside her, placing a comforting hand on her arm, sending her magic through Desminda to bolster her.

The princesses' posture straightened as the music grew louder. Astrid stepped from the trees, several other women trailing behind her. The bard's green eyes swept the field, grief turning her generous lips down. Her companions, all stunning women holding a variety of instruments, fanned out, heading toward their fallen compatriots, strumming lutes or playing reed instruments. Magic swept over the clearing, the bards' gentle music cleansing the rot from the air. As their music touched the fallen, eyes opened, and bodies stirred.

Harlow's bottom lip trembled. The bards out of hiding, their ancient magic healing their world ... it was something straight out of legend. Even implacable Shade gaped as Astrid walked over, joining her magic to Harlow's and Desminda.

The witches came then, joining hands as the first one touched Astrid's shoulder. On the other side, the crystal mages formed a line, as a woman with amethyst eyes touched Harlow's shoulder.

Harlow sucked in a gasp as clean, crystalline power flooded her body. Magnus came next, followed by Nova, then Evara, then each of the soldiers who held magic in their veins until Alaxar glowed with their combined power.

His screams were drowned out by the bard's gentle music and the hum of their combined magic. Tears streamed down Desminda's face as she carried out Alaxar's sentence, his body exploding into a million particles of dust. Magnus opened multiple portals, the first with dark skies and rivers of fire, another with a landscape of cold nothingness, yet another with ice-capped mountains and deadly avalanches, sweeping Alaxar's remains away from their world, into hundreds of others, never to reform again.

Silence fell in the clearing. Desminda broke away from the others and walked into Thornewood, her torn green armor trailing behind her as she stepped onto the barren lands of her once fruitful queendom.

Harlow followed close behind her, unsure what to say, but knowing she wanted to end this journey with her once friend, once almost lover.

Desminda stopped when she reached the place her castle once stood.

"I am sorry," she whispered.

Harlow looked at her in surprise and found Desminda's golden gaze captured on her face.

"I am sorry for all of it," Desminda said. She bowed her head and dragged in a shuddering breath.

Harlow gathered her into a hug. "You could not have foreseen this."

"No, but I could have done so many things differently." Her frail arms wrapped around Harlow's waist. The smell of jasmine rose through the air, tickling Harlow's nose.

"Maybe," Harlow said. "What matters now is rebuilding. You have the chance to start over, Desminda."

But doubt held Harlow in a tight grip as she looked at the ruins of Thornewood. Desminda's land was dead, not a trace of life left anywhere Harlow could sense.

Desminda pulled away and sank to the ground, her fingers digging in the rough, barren soil. She lifted her eyes to Harlow. "Tell my people I will return."

Harlow's brows flew together. "What?"

Desminda turned and stretched out on the ground, her dark hair flowing around her. She reached deeper into the earth, up to her wrists now, and closed her eyes. Magic rumbled from her body, sinking into the ground below her.

"Harlow!" Magnus shouted. His terrified face jerked her out of her confusion.

She took a step back just as Magnus reached for her, yanking her away.

Roots burst from the ground, thick and green, and laced with thick, thorned hooks, covering Desminda's body in an impenetrable cage.

"Run," her father breathed.

"Wha—?"

Her father's hand tightened around her arm, and he dragged her away, past the border where the darkness had once formed. A shimmering, transparent veil rose like a bubble, covering Desminda's queendom.

"What's happening?" Harlow whispered.

Her sister stepped up beside her, her eyes full of surprise. "She's attempting to heal her land."

Harlow's attention snapped to Nova. "Can she do it?"

Astrid came over and watched as the living thorned prison swallowed Desminda whole. "Gods-touched healers can fix anything," she said cryptically.

They watched for a while, but once the cage closed, nothing else happened. Disturbed, Harlow turned away and began helping Magnus and Nova as they escorted people home through the use of Nova's portals.

By the time everyone was gone, both suns had set, casting the land in a haze of silver as the moon rose. Harlow passed by the border one more time to whisper a goodbye she knew Desminda would not hear, but as she turned to go, she spotted a solitary white flower peeking up from the ground.

One bloom symbolizing hope and the potential rebirth of a new queendom.

At first, she checked monthly, then quarterly, then twice a year. As Desminda's magic healed Thornewood, the land grew lush and green, filled with towering trees and blooming flora. Eventually the animals returned, streams formed, and new species introduced themselves—animals and flowers Harlow had never seen in all the lands of Lunamoor.

When it became obvious Desminda would not awaken until she was good and ready, Harlow cut her visits to once a year. Today. She jumped from Luci's saddle, giving her mare a fond pat on the neck, and strode to the border. Evara dismounted with the same ease, following close behind. She linked their hands together and laid her head on Harlow's shoulder.

Harlow inhaled Evara's scent and smiled. They'd married last year, just after Harlow accepted her crown, following in the footsteps her mother had always meant to. Queen Moira was still alive and well, but she was tired of ruling and wanted to spend her days relaxing. Unfortunately, Miriam had never woken up after her last vision, passing away six months after Thornewood's fall, leaving the line of succession clear and open, leading right to Harlow.

She wasn't sure how she felt about the power dumped in her lap, but she'd done her best to be a good queen. When she faltered, Evara guided her back to the right path. They never spoke about children. It was a discussion that would have to come, but now they were trying to enjoy the peace their final battle had brought.

Magnus and Astrid had married two years after Thornewood's final fall, and Harlow was the proud new sister to a redheaded half-bard, who hadn't slept a full night since she was born.

She'd also become the aunt of dark-haired, silver-eyed twins, two peaceful children who'd stolen Harlow's heart the second Nova had lifted them up for her to hold.

The Rose Kingdom recovered. Lucien sat as king and had proved to be a good one, re-opening trade to the other kingdoms. Prince Naima was king now, and refused to speak of what happened to his father. Considering King Adama had stabbed them all in the back, no one begrudged Naima denying a little regicide. It helped that he, too, had turned out to be a good king.

The Kingdom of Light fared much worse than the others, but Desminda had included their kingdom in her barrier, choosing to heal their land too. No one knew what happened to their king or people, but Harlow had seen no one stirring since Desminda went under the healing spell.

She held a hand up and pressed it to the barrier. Even after all this time, it still felt warm under her touch.

"Where's she going to put a castle?" Evara murmured, making Harlow laugh.

"I'm not sure she'll rebuild the same way her ancestors did. After everything that happened, I think Desminda will start much smaller than before."

"Mmm," Evara agreed. "She's done a beautiful job."

Harlow had to agree. Thornewood looked like something

straight out of a fairy tale, complete with a trapped princess. Deer grazed only a few feet away, and rabbits scurried through the silky grass.

She started to lift her hand, but the barrier pulsed. Harlow gasped in surprise when the magic flared pink then fell altogether.

Evara pulled Harlow back, her hand hovering over the sword at her back.

"Wait," Harlow whispered.

The cage of thorns had been long covered with vines of blooming flowers, but as Harlow watched, the cage trembled and cracked, the thick branches returning to the earth.

Harlow took a tentative step over the border, Evara close at her heels.

Desminda lay still as death, her hair all the way down to her knees. Daisies rested on top of her eyes, until she shifted, and the flowers slid away.

Desminda's eyes opened, the burnished gold turned to liquid sunlight. She blinked several times.

"Harlow?" she whispered, her voice cracked with disuse.

Harlow sank to one knee and bowed her head briefly. "Queen Desminda."

Desminda shifted as she slowly sat up. She brushed blooming flowers away from her skin and looked around, her lips parting in shock.

Harlow grinned. "Welcome back to Thornewood, Your Majesty."

A tentative smile broke over Desminda's face. "How long?" she whispered.

Evara and Harlow exchanged a glance. Desminda frowned. "Harlow."

"Four years, Desminda."

The queen's eyes fluttered shut. Her nostrils flared as the

words penetrated. "Four years," she murmured, her voice trembling. "The land was almost dead. It took everything I had."

"We came," Harlow said, "all the time at first. This was our first trip back in a year."

Desminda reached out and grasped Harlow's hand. "Thank you. I'm glad it was you I woke up to."

She glanced down and spotted the elaborate gold band on Harlow's left hand. Desminda gasped, her eyes lifting to Harlow, then to Evara. "I knew it!" she crowed.

Evara laughed. "Harlow took some convincing."

"I can only imagine," Desminda said.

Harlow rolled her eyes and rose, holding a hand out to Desminda to help her up.

The queen swayed, and Harlow wrapped an arm around her waist to steady her. Evara offered her a canteen that Desminda gratefully accepted, dragging long pulls of water as she drank.

When she was ready, they walked the borders of the new queendom, marveling at the natural wonderland Desminda had created.

And when they were through and back at the spot where Desminda had lain caged for so long, Desminda sighed and sank back to the ground. "I am a queen without subjects," she murmured.

"Not for long," Harlow assured her. "Everyone who passed by this place expressed a desire to move in as soon as possible."

A familiar tingle of magic brushed over her shoulders, revealing Nova's shadows. They bounced and bobbed around them before disappearing. "Nova will be here soon."

"Good," Desminda said. "I'm going to need help rebuilding and want to talk to her to see if she can lend some extra hands."

Harlow sat down beside Desminda and dug through her

bag, producing a hunk of bread and cheese that she passed over to the newly resurrected queen.

Desminda gratefully accepted.

As they sat in the new kingdom, resurrected from a painful death by a healer queen, Desminda sighed and chewed on her cheese thoughtfully before saying, "I have no idea where I'm going to live."

Laughter, the first in Thornewood's brand new history, rang through the woods, brimming with life and hope.

ABOUT THE AUTHOR

USA Today Bestselling author S.E. Babin is a mom, a wife, and a military veteran. She has a passion for writing books filled with heroines you'd like to sit down and drink too much wine with and heroes who love those kinds of girls.

Sheryl holds a Master of Fine Arts in Popular Fiction and Publishing from Emerson College and spends way too much time hanging out in libraries and bookstores.

ALSO BY S.E. BABIN

<u>Book of Virago</u>

Blade of Hope

Blade of Mercy

The Queen's Blade

Urban Fantasy

<u>Cocktails in Hell</u>

A Twist of Demon

A Shake of Succubus

A Stir of Fairies

A Dash of Vampire

A Touch of Angel

A Whisper of Wolf

A Smidge of Voodoo

A Hint of Hero

<u>Vikings of Virginia</u>

Norse Code

Highway to Hel

Just Being Loki

An Odinary Day

<u>The Goddess Chronicles</u>

Out of Practice Aphrodite

Out of Sorts Aphrodite

Out of Options Aphrodite

Out of Chills Aphrodite

Out of Eggnog Aphrodite

Out of Cake Aphrodite

Out of Sanity Aphrodite

Out of Excuses Aphrodite

Out of Patience Aphrodite

Cozy Mysteries

<u>Psychic Cleaner Cozy Mysteries</u>

Murder by the Brush

Maid for Mayhem

Another One Fights the Dust

An Unfolding Crime

The Grim Sweeper

A Draining Murder

A Sponge of Suspicion

<u>Shelf Indulgence</u>

Booked for Homicide

Foreword Fraud

Copycat Killer

Fictional Fatality

Bookmarked for Crime

Literary Larceny

Bookarazzi Blackmail

Shelfie Sabotage

Book Club Bait & Switch

<u>Magical Soapmaker Mysteries</u>

No Lathering Matter

Lyer, Liar

A Spotless Crime

Paranormal Rom-Coms

<u>The Deadicated Matchmaker</u>

The Nerdy Necromancer

The Jilted Jinn

The Clumsy Clairvoyant

The Vegan Vamp

The Deluded Demi-god

9 781648 399381